THE LEGACY SERIES

SERIES TITLES

Lafferty, Looking for Love
Dennis McFadden

All That It Seems
Jim Landwehr

I Felt My Life With Both My Hands
Jessica Treadway

Hands
Pardeep Toor

This Is How We Speak
Rebecca Reynolds

All Gone Now
Michael Tasker

Your Place in This World
Jake La Botz

Apple & Palm
Patricia Henley

Bodies in Bags
Jamey Gallagher

A Green Glow on the Horizon
Dawn Burns

How We Do Things Here
Matt Cashion

Neon Steel
Jennifer Maritza McCauley

Release of Information
Kali White VanBaale

The Divide
Evan Morgan Williams

Yes, No, I Don't Know
Kathryn Gahl

The Price of Their Toys
John Loonam

The Caged Man
Calvin Mills

A Day Doesn't Go By When I Don't Have Regrets
J. Malcolm Garcia

These Are My People
Steve Fox

We Should Be Somewhere by Now
Stephen Tuttle

Burner and Other Stories
Katrina Denza

The Plan of Chicago
Barry Pearce

Trust Issues
K.P. Davis

Adult Children
Laurence Klavan

Guardians & Saints
Diane Josefowicz

Western Terminus: Stories and A Novella
Michael Keefe

Like Human
Janet Goldberg

The Hopefuls
Elizabeth Oness

Never Stop Exiting
Michael Hopkins

Broken Heart Syndrome
Anne Colwell

The Mexican Messiah: A Novella & Stories
Jay Kauffmann

Close to a Flame
Colleen Alles

American Animism
Jamey Gallagher

Keeping What's Best Left Kept Secret
David Ricchiute

Soaked
Toby LeBlanc

The Path of Totality
Marie Zhuikov

Shocker in Gloomtown
Dan Libman

The Continental Divide
Bob Johnson

The Three Devils and Other Stories
William Luvaas

The Correct Response
Manfred Gabriel

Welcome Back to the World: A Novella & Stories
Rob Davidson

Greyhound Cowboy and Other Stories
Ken Post

Close Call
Kim Suhr

The Waterman
Gary Schanbacher

Signs of the Imminent Apocalypse and Other Stories
Heidi Bell

What We Might Become
Sara Reish Desmond

The Silver State Stories
Michael Darcher

An Instinct for Movement
Michael Mattes

The Machine We Trust
Tim Conrad

Gridlock
Brett Biebel

Salt Folk
Ryan Habermeyer

The Commission of Inquiry
Patrick Nevins

Maximum Speed
Kevin Clouther

Reach Her in This Light
Jane Curtis

The Spirit in My Shoes
John Michael Cummings

The Effects of Urban Renewal on Mid-Century America and Other Crime Stories
Jeff Esterholm

What Makes You Think You're Supposed to Feel Better
Jody Hobbs Hesler

Fugitive Daydreams
Leah McCormack

Hoist House: A Novella & Stories
Jenny Robertson

Finding the Bones: Stories & A Novella
Nikki Kallioy

Self-Defense
Corey Mertes

Where Are Your People From?
James B. De Monte

Sometimes Creek
Steve Fox

The Plagues
Joe Baumann

The Clayfields
Elise Gregory

Kind of Blue
Christopher Chambers

Evangelina Everyday
Dawn Burns

Township
Jamie Lyn Smith

Responsible Adults
Patricia Ann McNair

Great Escapes from Detroit
Joseph O'Malley

Nothing to Lose
Kim Suhr

The Appointed Hour
Susanne Davis

LAFFERTY, LOOKING FOR LOVE

stories

DENNIS McFADDEN

CORNERSTONE PRESS
UNIVERSITY OF WISCONSIN-STEVENS POINT

Cornerstone Press, Stevens Point, Wisconsin 54481
Copyright © 2026 Deirdre Harrington
www.uwsp.edu/cornerstone

Printed in the United States of America.

Library of Congress Control Number: 2026931134
ISBN: 978-1-968148-43-0

All rights reserved.

This is a work of fiction. Names, characters, businesses, places, events, and incidents are either the products of the author's imagination or used in a fictitious manner. Any resemblance to actual persons, living or dead, or actual events is purely coincidental.

Cornerstone Press titles are produced in courses and internships offered by the Department of English at the University of Wisconsin–Stevens Point.

DIRECTOR & PUBLISHER EXECUTIVE EDITORS
Dr. Ross K. Tangedal Jeff Snowbarger, Freesia McKee

EDITORIAL DIRECTOR SENIOR EDITORS
Brett Hill Paige Biever, Ellie Atkinson

PRESS STAFF
Karlie Harpold, Abby Paulsen, Samantha Bjork, Sophie McPherson, Jazmyne Johnson, Madison Schultz, Autumn Vine

A NOTE ON THE TEXT

Dennis McFadden passed away unexpectedly in August 2025, having just completed final corrections to *Lafferty, Looking for Love*. The book has been published as Dennis wanted it, with the support and encouragement of his daughter, Deirdre Harrington. Cornerstone Press is proud to offer up Dennis' final published work in his memory.

ALSO BY DENNIS McFADDEN:

Hart's Grove
Jimtown Road
Old Grimes Is Dead

STORIES

Stayin' Alive / 1

*

The Ring of Kerry / 18

Cannibals in Canoes / 37

The Purloined Pigs / 55

The Three-Sided Penny / 75

A Penny Saved / 95

Lafferty's Ghost / 109

A Very Good Cure / 123

Over the Garden Wall / 143

Savage December / 161

*

The Worthless Turtle / 181

Acknowledgments / 203

"So do not think of helpful whores as aberrational blots;
I could not love you half so well without my practice shots."

—James Stewart Alexander Simmons

Stayin' Alive

When he hit it big at the races, Lafferty resolved to bring his winnings straight home to Peggy. They were in desperate arrears on their Dublin flat, but your man, not one to sit idly by in the face of impending eviction, had seized the chance to win it back in the one race, win it back and then some. The inside word at O'Faolain's was they'd been holding her back for the Irish Oaks, and hadn't the tip come when his circumstance was most dire, like an omen, like a gift from God—particularly when it proved sound, and the horse, M'Lady's Manor, came in at fifty to one. One hundred times fifty, five thousand quid! He could see the look on the face of her now, Peggy's awe at the fistfuls of money, making it all up to her, all the rent money he'd squandered having come back to him thundering down the stretch in a cutthroat gallop, eking out the slenderest of victories over a nag called Ho Ho Ho.

But on the train back to Dublin from the Curragh, a five-thousand-quid bulge in his pocket, didn't other considerations begin to pop their heads up out of their holes. Considerations such as thirst. He was gasping with the thirst—sure a pint or two could do no harm. And such as what class of fella would not think to thank the lot at O'Faolain's that put him on to M'Lady's Manor in the first place, stand them a round or two. And such as wouldn't it be terrific craic to come waltzing home late again to the scorn on the pretty face of Peggy until he pulled his fortune from out of his pocket and showered her with all the lovely banknotes floating down. Then by God, there'd be heels in the air.

Long shadows down Drumcondra, he saw to his dismay the crowd overflowing O'Faolain's, under the black Guinness awning amid flowerpots brimming with posies. He'd forgot: Disco Night at the pub. Your man hated disco. Davey, the manager, thought maybe an American rage would bring a tourist or two from downtown up to North Circular, not to mention new life—new profits—to the old corner bar.

Sure enough weren't the profits pouring in, though Lafferty was hard-pressed to find a Yankee accent in the lot, it seemed mostly the natives raging, the younger crowd, and the irony not lost on Lafferty, not yet out of his twenties himself and looking down at a younger crowd. Elbowed his way politely to the black polished bar, through the lovely layers of smoke and the disco din—*stayin' alive, stayin' alive*. A bit of a beat perhaps, but altogether too nervous and twitchy a music for Lafferty's likes. Any number of jackeens dancing the hustle in the wee dance floor Davey'd created cramming together his tables to the side, including one young twit glittering under the disco light in gold lamé, wishing he was Travolta. Over the mirror behind the bar, a *Disco Night* banner, black letters spray-painted on a white sheet, beneath which stood Davey, smiling and sweating, pushing out the drink, pulling in the dosh. His smile was held in check by a thick mustache, and his hair swept straight back in wavy steel rivulets.

Spotting your man, he drew a stout, hustled down the bar and slid the creamy-topped pint across. "Good day at the course?" he said.

"Grand day at the course," Lafferty said with a nod and wink.

Davey slapped the bar. "I'm after telling you—straight from the horse's mouth."

"Where's the lads? I'll have to stand 'em round."

"Jimmy's here, but I've not seen Alfie or Finny."

Davey hurried away. Lafferty began scanning the crowd for Jimmy, three deep at the bar and a mob beyond. Easy to spot, he'd be, the only goose-necked, goofy boyo in the place, hair parted in the middle, Adam's apple big as a fist. Still daylight outside it was, but dim within, shutters on the windows, the light electric and pulsing, Davey's disco globe rigged on the tin ceiling, dangling there precarious.

Still searching the faces, still no Jimmy, when there, halfway down the bar stood a girl, a pretty girl, staring back at him, bold as a brass button, staring undeniably, unmistakably, straight at your man.

Hair like midnight, skin like cream, she blinked and Lafferty swore he could see from there the lovely flutter of her lashes just as a big fellow leaned up to shout his order and she was lost behind him. The big fellow backed away, and she was gone.

Jimmy and his goofy grin appeared with a backclap and a sweaty arm about Lafferty's shoulders, asking how he'd fared at the course, and your man telling him next round's on me, that's all you need to know, which brought a whoop and a holler out of Jimmy. Shouting over the din, Lafferty asked after the boyos, and Jimmy filled him in: Alfie's new bride had insisted on coming with him tonight, so he'd stayed home instead, and Finny'd been shamed into tea with his new bird's family. Jimmy lamented the lack of loyalty, but thank God for Terrance, steady, reliable Terrance, by God, clapping his arm around Lafferty's shoulders once more and ordering another as your man sneakily peeled another note from the wad in his pocket with a smile. Jimmy was a hard case, a wild man with drink taken, meek as a sheep without. He'd just moved out of his mum's to his own little flat off Clonliffe, his bachelor nest he called it, meagerly furnished with cast-offs and hand-me-downs and derelict items found on the street. And forever trying to find a bird to bring home to the nest, Disco Night at O'Faolain's being among the choicest of opportunities. He'd been dancing, disco dancing, sweating like a stevedore, a condition foreign to him, a clerk by trade at a pet shop. Finally Lafferty could hold it back no longer, the tale bubbling up out of him, M'Lady's Manor and

Ho Ho Ho neck and neck to the finish, Lafferty single-handedly urging her home by the sheer power of his will, though he failed to disclose the specifics of the wager and the subsequent wad in his pocket, long since damp with the sweat from his palm. Except one: fifty to one. Jimmy howling and moaning at his timidity in not sending a wager of his own, and it was then that Lafferty glanced down the bar and saw her again.

The girl with the midnight hair. A bit closer now, a glass in each hand as she backed away a step and hesitated. Staring straight at Lafferty, straight and true, a sigh before turning, still staring, an invitation, then moving on, swallowed up in the crowd.

She was with him now, in his mind, here to stay.

The second time sealed it. Now there was nothing else to it, and he felt the chill crawl up his back in a room that was hot as blazes.

Who was she? What was she? *Why* was she?

Lafferty believed in grace. He was old and wise enough, even though he was not yet at the end of his third decade on the planet, to believe that phases befell every life, be they moments or minutes or hours, periods of time that pass beyond the lucky, the happy, the serendipitous, and reach to embrace the beatific. States of grace, as good a name as any. And any day on which the horse carrying your rent comes in at fifty to one would surely qualify as such a state.

Any day on which a girl with uncommon beauty, a stranger among a hundred faces, reaches out to you, slips into your heart wordlessly, without so much as a touch: What other state but grace?

Another hour before they spoke. The throng grew tighter, louder, hotter, Davey ratcheting up the disco noise, the light pulsing through the smoke so desperately thick. Drink was taken in prodigious proportions. Lafferty standing round after round for him and Jimmy, the goose-necked wonder in high-top sneakers chatting up this bird and that, dancing, not even capable of dreaming, or so Lafferty imagined, of the sort of connection Lafferty had already made with the most beautiful girl in the room, to whom he had yet even to speak. Twice more, glances passed between them from across the crowded room, this glimpse and that before she was lost again. Lafferty biding his time, plotting. Positioned himself strategically with a view of the Ladies, where the corridor was not so crammed, the din not so roaring, where a word might be passed. He thought of Peggy. Hadn't it been a similar glimpse, across a crowded hall at the wedding of a cousin in Sandymount, where herself and he had first connected. But Peggy would keep. Her rent was secure. There was no way under heaven he could deny the spontaneous combustion, the attraction that had materialized out of the ether to the girl with the midnight hair. It would be contrary to the laws of God and nature not to explore the meaning, to leave the revelation it promised unrevealed.

"What's your name?" he said. Not a hint of surprise on her at all when she came out of the Ladies to find him waiting.

"Moira." Up close she was even more lovely. And even bolder, her gaze more intrepid—expectant. He wasn't sure exactly what was expected, but this was no time to falter.

"Terrance." He held out his hand. The warmth of hers rampaged up his arm, filling his chest. "Are you with someone?"

"Only my girlfriends."

"No fella?"

"We've just broke up. I'm after finding out the hard way he's a bit of a mentaller. He can be a scary man."

"You don't say."

"I do." Oblivious to those brushing by them in the narrow passage, to the cacophony of noises and nervous music. At the edge of the shadows where they stood, eyes locked, a glimmer of a pulsing light reflected there in the black depths of her eyes. She said *I do*. "But he's here though. My fella. He's here and he's watching."

"You don't say," he said again, anxious eyes scanning the room. "Is he a big one?"

"Not so much." A first hint of frown. "But he is rather strong. And not quite the full shilling. And mean. Did I mention mean?"

"I don't think so."

"You've the softest, warmest hand I've ever touched."

"Moira," he said, to hear the magic in the word.

Jimmy barged in. Lafferty hadn't seen him sneak up. "Pleased to make your acquaintance," he said. "Come, dance with me, there's no future in that one, he's a married man, Terrance is, a sly and married man—but me, I'm single and free as a wren—Moira, is it? Come dance with me!" And he pulled her toward the wee dance floor, Moira half laughing, half protesting, for it was impossible to deny him, drunken, clumsy Jimmy, hair plastered down and parted on top, Adam's apple bobbing, high-topped sneakers kicking high, or to be entirely angry with the boyo and his goofy antics. Lafferty could only blink in wonder at the sudden, comic, tragic twist of fortune, coitus interruptus of the soul, and he stood there in the shadows, not sure whether to laugh or to cry, not sure what to make of his mate, the back-stabbing traitor, the slapstick sidekick, the faux Travolta, and of the girl, Moira, his reluctant accomplice.

Jimmy twirled and kicked and strutted, struck the disco pose, took Moira for a spin tight in his arms, generally acting the fool. Lafferty wondering what would become of them now, when doesn't another lunatic show up on the dancefloor, not to be outdone, trying to steal the thunder, a new lunatic, fresh lunacy, dancing with a barstool this one was, holding it high over his head, bobbing along to the twitchy beat, barstool in the air, two beats to the right, two to the left, two up the middle, all around the floor in a twisty trail, this way and that, till it was next to Jimmy, where it disappeared from sight. The barstool was gone and Lafferty heard the cries erupt over the din, saw the crowd ripple back and away like the water in the pool when the rock splashes in, saw the barstool again, rising and falling, rising and falling, thump after thump, down onto Jimmy, the fresh lunatic bringing it down on him again and again, beating Jimmy with it, beating him like chopping a log. Then it stopped.

The odd moment of silence it took to take it in. Jimmy laid out on the floor bleeding, the light pulsing, the fresh lunatic standing over him, staring down. Then looking up slowly. Raising his arms in triumph, barstool up along, held effortlessly aloft in a hand, shouting, "Here I am, motherfuckers! Here I am! Who wants a go?"

Davey up kneeling on the bar, coming over, pointing at the madman, shouting, "Stop him! Somebody grab him!"

A few heroes moved forward, but the lunatic swung the stool, keeping them away, swinging it like a flaming torch, keeping the pack at bay, retreating in that manner toward the door, where he shouted again, "That's the way, uh huh, uh huh, I like it!" Flinging the barstool at the heroes, he was gone.

Lafferty rushed to Jimmy, Moira kneeling beside him, feeling for a pulse. Jimmy bleeding, a copious flow of the stuff, his eyelids fluttering, trying to open.

A doctor came out of the crowd. "Keep him still," he said. "Call an ambulance."

A mumble from Jimmy's face, unintelligible.

Tears on Moira's cheeks. "Did I mention mean?" she said.

When they left the hospital, left Jimmy, going their separate ways never entered his mind, nor, it would seem, hers. It was magnetism, a force field impossible to overcome. They strolled, in no hurry, no destination to speak of, up streets under stars dim in the inky sky over Dublin, passing under streetlamps and dark-faced brick buildings. After a while he took her hand and when he did his heart began clambering madly, unreasonably, up his throat, as though he'd never held the hand of a girl before.

"Poor Jimmy," she said.

"You were in love with that lunatic?" he said.

"Sure, he wasn't always the lunatic. Not always." His name was Fergus. A tattoo of a heart and Moira on his shoulder, crazy, mad in love, he worked construction, carried a hod, lifted weights in his cellar, and they were happy till he and his mates discovered the pills, the little red pills that gave you energy enough to drink all night and work the next day, but made you crazy as well. Fergus couldn't quit them despite her pleas and demands and threats, and finally she left. Moved out of their place altogether. "And what about yourself, then?" she said. "I have it on good authority you're a married man."

"Aye. That I am."

When he said nothing more, she said, "What's her name?"

"Peggy," he said. Nothing more.

She asked for nothing more. She squeezed his hand, and on they walked. Past a street called Portland Place and over the Royal Canal. She took his arm in her hands and leaned close on his shoulder. They walked in step. She understood. Kindred minds and spirits. There was not enough love in this world. To put more love into this world could only make it a better place. To put more love into this world could not be a bad thing, in any way whatever.

They arrived at Jimmy's having never discussed a destination. There was no other place. She lived with her girlfriends, he with his wife. He could buy them a room for the night, he supposed—the bundle of bills still stashed in his pocket—but Jimmy's seemed best, a tribute, in a twisted manner, to his fallen comrade. And eminently more economical, for your man was not so gobsmacked as to lose touch with his practical side.

They never switched on a light. In the dark, the desperate furnishings might have been fit for a palace. In the dark, the lumpy mattress was clean as a cloud, and she was the softest of shadows in his arms, the stray light through the open window a sheen and a shimmer on her skin, and the sounds of revelers far off in the Dublin night, the sound of a car horn, the strains of a ballad from a flat across the way. Lafferty dreamed all the rest, all the moistness and deepness and softness and warmth.

The light through the window when he woke was a curious shade paler, and the night was more still, and the first thing he did was to try to hold on. Hold on to the grace, for didn't he feel it slipping away. Asleep in his arms, she curled like a warm kitten. Tried to hold on. His arm numb, his bladder fit to burst, his head throbbing for all the drink taken, and a lump in the mattress poking his rib. An ambulance wailed out in the night. Jimmy. He arose gingerly, not to disturb her, out the door toward the jacks but stubbed a toe and switched on the light. The sight of the threadbare sofa, the tattered rug, the battered crates Jimmy fancied as chairs, spelled an end to the magical spell. Not an aspirin in the bloody jacks. Doused his face under the faucet and drank and drank and drank. Not a clean glass in the bloody kitchen to bring her a sip of water.

Light spilled into the bedroom where she peeked out with one eye from under the tangle of midnight hair. Naked and lovely. Lafferty wearing only his shirt. He crawled onto the bed and gathered her up in his arms.

"I can't believe I'm after doing this," she said in a whisper.

He nuzzled beneath her hair for an ear to nibble. "Are you sorry?"

Her ribs puffed up. "Not any," she said.

"Me neither."

"And what about Peggy?"

Of course there'd be wigs on the green at home, when he tried to explain it to her, where he'd been, another excuse, another lie. He didn't care. He had his winnings at any rate to soothe her savage breast. "Who?"

"I've a feeling it's not the first time she's wondered where you are."

He wished he had an aspirin. "And what about Fergus?"

"Poor Fergus," she said.

"Poor Fergus? Poor Jimmy."

"Aye," she said. "Poor fecking all of us." She rested her head in the pillow.

"What are you going to do about that one? He's a stalker. A madman."

A sigh of resignation. "I'll have to deal with him. Sooner or later."

Something about the *sooner* took your man by the ears. His heart spoke up, his mouth went dry. This lovely, naked girl in his arms, all on her own, and brutality nipping at her heels. He should help. Somehow. But of course he wouldn't. He was not one of the heroes. He'd long since recognized he was not among the hero class, and he'd decided this was not necessarily a bad thing. Whether or not it was a good thing, however, was still in the hands of the jury.

"He'd be laying low by now, yeah. Hiding out. In the long grass."

"Fergus? Not on your nelly. He'd be out scouring the city for me."

A sleepy blink, a distant alarm. "You'll be safe here then, with me."

"Will I indeed?"

"Aye. Of course. Sure, he'd never find us here."

"Never. Just because Jimmy was spouting his address to every girleen who'd listen. Just because a pack of Fergus's mates were there. No, nay, never."

"That's not funny."

"No," she said.

Now that he was properly on edge, it was a perfect time to imagine hearing sinister sounds in the hallway, a creak and a crack, so Lafferty imagined he only imagined hearing them, that he didn't really hear them at all. Nevertheless, he said, "Did you hear that?"

And didn't Moira say yes. And then it sounded again. Closer.

"Yes," she said. "Yes. I did."

Your man sat up, heart jumping. Then came the knock at the door, followed in turn by a rap and a thump and a bang.

"Just a neighbor," he said. "Sure, just a neighbor."

"Moira!" He was in the hallway. Fergus. "Moira? You in there?"

Wouldn't he leave if they made not a sound, Lafferty thought, but Moira was up, into her skirt, coiled, poised on the edge of the bed, and Fergus was shouting he saw the light, he knew she was in there, he was coming in, and the thumping and banging grew loud and vicious, and there was a splintering of wood then, and even before the word *Hide!* was escaped from her lips, Lafferty was out the window and the door crashing open.

Jimmy's was a second-floor flat. Out the window was nothing but air, Lafferty dangling in it, a shocking chill to his nether regions, wishing he'd taken the common precaution of donning his drawers, too late, clinging to the sill with his fingers, looking down in the murky night at the garden a few feet below, a wee patch of gravel and weeds enclosed by a wall. Sounds of commotion from inside the room. Never felt nakeder. Looked for a soft spot. Let go. Landed with a jolt, none too worse for the wear, a scrape, a bruise, a bang to the knee, and he caught his breath looking up at the lighted window, hearing the shouts of two voices, Moira and Fergus, shouts and a thump and a shove and the scraping of something on something else again, and doesn't your man begin to feel sick. Out of fear, he supposed, but he knew it was cowardice too, out of fear and cowardice, but weren't they one and the same—*you're terrible, Terrance*, a familiar refrain—shivering and heaving and his privates exposed, but no time to put too fine a point on it, fear or cowardice, for didn't he realize that all Fergus had to do was stick his head out the bloody window and Bob's your man. Lafferty scurried to the back of the garden, out through the gate in the wall. To find himself in an alley between a warren of back gardens, in the light from the streetlamp on the corner, a light that, without one's trousers, was bright as a mid-day sun. And wasn't it an old drunk staggering up the way.

"*Isn't it grand, boys,*" the old drunk sang in a voice like a rusty old bellows, "*to be bloody well dead—*" Spying your man, he stopped short.

Lafferty stared back in the sudden quiet. No sounds from inside the flat, nothing in the Dublin night air but the shuffle on the cobblestones of the old drunk's shoes coming toward him again. "Grand night for taking the air," says Lafferty.

"Aye," the old one says, coming to a halt across the alley from Lafferty, rearing his head back for a gander. A small man in rumpled trousers, jacket and tie, a bogtrotter's cap on his bony old skull. "And a grand night as well for airin' out the oul sergeant major," says he with a nod toward Lafferty's lower half.

He recommenced his stroll down the alley, Lafferty watching him go. Heard him pick up the song where he'd left off so sudden:

"*Let's not have a sniffle,*

Let's have a bloody good cry,
And always remember the longer you live,
The sooner you bloody well die!"

A cat scampered like a bandit across the alley and into the hedge.

There stood Lafferty. A hand on the wall to hold him up. The air tasted of ashes and smoke and the chill was beginning to set in, goosebumps down his legs. Couldn't stand here and his balls hanging out forever. Back through the gate in the stilly night air, the window up above yellow and staring like a cyclops. He'd have to go back in. Armed! In the wee shed at the back of the garden he found a spade that he gripped and swung a time or two like a hurley. Who was he fooling? Overflowing with trepidation, he heard a whistle. Looking up to see her in the window, he found himself shielding his privates with the blade of the tool out of modesty.

"Romeo, Romeo," Moira said. "Wherefore art thou, Romeo?"

"Right here in the fecking garden," Lafferty said. Was it a giggle she gave in reply? "Where is he?"

"Sure he's gone. You can come back up now."

"I can, yeah?" He was leery. "I've no trousers. Toss 'em down."

She disappeared, returned, trousers fluttering down in a flop. He gathered them, looked up at her in the window. "These aren't mine."

"There's a half dozen pair scattered about."

Lafferty sighed, put them on. And no underpants. Desperately hoping Jimmy'd been wearing his own last time he wore the trousers. Too tight in the waist, too long in the legs, but only temporary, he made his way out the back, around, in through the front, up the stairs. Jimmy's door smashed in. Blood on the floor and Moira on the edge of the bed, fully dressed. Lafferty, leery still, glancing about.

"Where is he?"

"I'm after telling you—he's vamoosed. Skedaddled."

"The blood—did he hurt you?"

"No. Fergus'd never lift a finger to me."

"The blood?"

"I didn't say I didn't lift a finger to him. After what he done to poor Jimmy." Lafferty frowned. "I skulled him with a pot—knock some sense into him. When I went to fetch him a bandage in the jacks he was gone. No bandages there anyways. Not even a bloody aspirin."

Lafferty took off Jimmy's trousers, tossed them in the corner amidst the detritus of dirty trousers, shirts and unidentifiable unmentionables, assorted bits and bobs. Moira sighed, hands clasped between her knees. "No, Terrance. I'm hardly in the mood. I'm just after cracking open the skull of my boyfriend. My ex-boyfriend."

"They were killing me." He picked up the pair off the back of chair. "See? These are mine." He held them out, stood holding them, his privates proudly on display. "How's your mood now?"

Moira gave him a smile, of sorts. "Come here."

He did, waggling as he went. She pinched his arse. "Put 'em on," she said. At that your man's mood underwent a change of its own, decidedly toward the darker.

He sat on the edge of the bed, petulantly, sulking, though at the time he was unsure of the reason why, since it was understandable, her mood, that she wouldn't feel like making love again, given the circumstance, given the blood on the floor of the shabby digs, the scent of violence lingering in the air, maybe given too the recently confirmed cowardice of your man. Or maybe it was the lightness of his trousers.

Maybe his subconscious mind had already detected the subtle change of weight, subtracted it, summed out the loss, and maybe that was what accounted for his shift of mood even before he'd finished putting them on, even before he stood up and reached into the pocket, the pocket that heretofore had been stuffed with his fortune, his bundle of bills, Peggy's rent. And found nothing there but a crumb or two and a bit of lint.

Somewhere south of the Liffey in this never-ending neverland of a night Lafferty found himself wandering, following Moira who strode with purpose past dimly lit squares and alleys and lanes and into a neighborhood where two rows of brick houses stood shoulder to shoulder facing one another across a narrow street. The gap of sky above going dirty orange, a window here and there glinting in the new light across the face of the flats. She stopped before a white door, a wee iron fence, a fuchsia bush trying to hide the bin. A streetlamp down the block made a shadow of her face when she turned to give your man his instructions.

Fergus had to have lifted the boodle. This was what she'd told him, and Lafferty believed her. He had to. Fergus's finding and swiping the swag, not the skulling with the pot, she said, must have accounted for his quick skedaddling, for it was the making-up after the quarrel that he'd always relished. Nothing else would have driven him away. Lafferty believed her because it made sense, because what else could have happened, because not believing her would have left him with only an alternative, and that he couldn't believe.

She told him the plan. Where she'd be, where Fergus would be, where Peggy's rent would be, and when. She told him to count to a thousand, tiptoe inside, retrieve his money and be off. She'd take care of Fergus.

Lafferty lost count somewhere north of sixty.

Under the fuchsia he sat, breathing in the dewy scent in high, ginger breaths, deciding that when the little black cloud sailing in the orange of the predawn sky touched the chimney pot high across the way a thousand would be up. Closed his eyes until then. Walking again with Moira through the silent streets toward this place, Fergus's, where she'd lived with him for a year. Once Lafferty had reached to take her hand, again, like before. But it wasn't like before, lasting only a second or so till the walkway narrowed, and hadn't her hand been dry and cool as the manikins' in Clerys. And her eyes. Her eyes that had captured him from across a smoky pub, eyes he hadn't seen since they'd stared into his in the bed, in the middle of the closest and truest thing a man and a woman can do, joined at the eyes, at the soul, joined there more than anywhere else. And now. Hadn't her eyes absconded entirely.

He opened his own again. The cloud was nearly there. And what if Fergus were to burst through the door, barstool in hand, and commence beating him about the head and shoulders. What if he was waiting just inside the door. Moira in cahoots.

The cloud hit the chimney. Your man trembled up to his feet. In through the door.

There, on the stand beside the keys under the coats hanging from hooks. Exactly where she'd said. The money. Back into his greedy, grateful pocket. Heard a wee snuffle of a sob. He had to scram. He had to turn and leave, there's a good lad, sensible fella. He touched the handle, before letting it go again. He turned. Like the first man on the moon, he stepped further inside. One step and then another. Tip-toe quiet. For didn't he have to see.

Around the corner in the dark of the flat was Fergus, on his knees, his back to Lafferty, naked as the day he came into the world, his face buried in the lap of Moira, quietly crying, shivering softly. Moira on the sofa, stroking his neck, patting his back. Over Fergus's battered head she spied Lafferty, and for a last long stretch of seconds, for a moment of time standing still, they stared into the other's eyes, just as they'd done the very first time through the smoke and the din, the very first time that seemed so far away.

Your man was nothing if not resilient. He'd a gift for putting the unpleasantness behind him, for seeing through to the grander scheme, the overall good, a trait he'd picked up from his oul man, whose grander scheme had included leaving home when Terrance was just a wee lad. Morning glimmering off the Liffey, a new resolve took root in your man. Goodbye to Moira, goodbye to grace, goodbye to all that. A new day dawned.

Though numb in mind and weary in bone, he'd picked up a second wind and breathed in the cool morning air of the city, an aroma of fresh baked bread wafting. Made his way to the taxi rank on O'Connell, climbed into the back of the beige Mercedes waiting there for him, gave the man Peggy's address—his address as well, perhaps—and gave himself in to the luxury. Imagining the wrath of Peggy, then presto, change-o, watching it give way to the squeals of delight when your man pulled the shower of bills from out of his pocket.

The two notes tacked to the padlocked door knocked the second wind right out of him.

Next to the Final Eviction Notice, a note from Peggy:

T— I've gone to stay with mother. Go wherever you might, and good riddance to you. Your stuff's in the dust bin out back. —P

The weariness caught up to him then, overcame him, and he lowered himself to the top step in the stairwell and breathed in the stale air. He stared at the walls of patchy dull paint, heard a fly buzz somewhere overhead. Perhaps it wasn't too late. A penalty could be paid, back rent, a bribe perhaps, whatever it took. His foggy, drifting mind labored to come up with a scheme: Take the money to Peggy. Take the money to Peggy. What else? Not much of a scheme, that. Take the money to Peggy.

Sleep. First sleep. Jimmy's bed was his only choice.

In through the damaged door, over the patch of dried blood. Onto the lumpy bed where the scent of Moira still lingered on the pillow. What scent was it? He couldn't put a name to it—like a lotion of some kind perhaps, or like the scent of cream, if cream had a scent at all. Breathing it in was like a memory, a memory from long ago, from his childhood, the way the scent of peppermint always took him back to the visits to his Auntie Claire before his da had gone away. Beside him the window through which he'd fled was open still, the sounds of birds and the noise of distant Dublin.

He awoke with a start some scant hours later, his mind clear and clean as a babby's conscience, a new and better plan having stole over him as he slept.

A block up and across from O'Faolain's was the shop of a turf accountant, Shaughnessey's, and it was there your man found himself this sweltering afternoon, not unlike the one that had gone before, and he realized, a good omen, that it was nearly twenty-four hours to the minute since he'd placed the bet that won back Peggy's rent in the first place, and he looked over the board for a parlay and, sure enough, wasn't a horse called Grace's Day running in the sixth at a course in Galway. *Grace's Day*. Shouting down at him from atop the board. An omen if ever there was one. At ten to one. Not too bad if one placed it all on the nose. Then forget the rent, by God. Buy the fecking house.

And so he did. Lafferty placed it all on the nose of Grace's Day and he stepped outside onto the grit of the sidewalk and he looked up into the sky and he said, *Okay, then, show me what You got*.

And so He did.

The Ring of Kerry

As a girl one day Eena heard someone make mention of the Ring of Kerry. To her childish mind then, a title so grand could never be given to a thing so ordinary as a route for tourists to traipse; a magnificent name such as that could only be fit for a splendid piece of jewelry, a ring that might grace the finger of a queen. Even after the mundane truth became known to her, there was always a spot set aside in her heart for the *real* Ring of Kerry, the genuine, golden, gem-laden article of fabulous beauty and imponderable worth.

And so the first time she laid eyes on her grandmother's ring, there it was. "You should have seen the thing, Mister," she told Lafferty. They were in the bed of her room above the restaurant, she with the sheet up to her chin to hide the flatness of her chest. She was a stray, a mutt, skinny as a reed, unruly red hair immune to the brush, ears that stuck out like the handles on a jug, and brown eyes so big they could occupy her face entirely. Thin light from the cloudy afternoon squeezed through the blinds of the window, and he could hear the warble of a tin whistle from the Commodore Pub across the street. "The grandest thing I ever seen," she said. "Fine, delicate carvings, little circles and twirls all around it, they might have been etched there by the angels. Lovely emeralds like clusters of green stars, and gold thick and shiny as the icing on a cupcake."

"The Ring of Kerry," said Lafferty. "Old, was it?"

"Ancient. My great-great-grandda discovered the thing one day in the bog when he was gathering turf for his fire. In a rotted old leather packet, as though it had been hid there long ago and somehow forgot."

"Whatever become of it?"

"That's the thing of it, Mister. My grandda buried it with her."

He caught his breath. "In the ground?"

She nodded. "Like the bloody Egyptians. He said how she loved it, her only treasure in the world, and he buried the bloody thing with her in her grave."

"Surely someone would have..."

She shook her head. "He told no one, you see. Folded her hands just so."

"He told you."

"I was a lass on his knee. Forever talking about the Ring of Kerry. And doesn't he let it slip out of himself one day when he was well in his cups."

At that moment, the possibility had already unfurled itself before him. He could persuade her to go away with him, to retrieve the ring from the grave of her granny, and run off together, just the two of them. He could do it, he was certain, easy as persuading a flea to hop, for he was aware of his own powers of persuasion with members of the gentler gender, attributable largely to the sincerity of the dimple on his chin.

But would it be right? He was not keen to use the innocent young thing for his own greedy gain. She was a waitress, or tried to be. After his meal at the Sugarshack Restaurant, the first time in the spring he'd ever laid eyes on her, she'd followed him out into the street. "Wait, Mister," she'd called. Ever since, he'd been Mister. "Wait—you're after leaving your money on the table in there."

"Why, that's yours," Lafferty had said. "That's your tip."

"Tip?" she'd said, her freckles all up in a bunch.

There were other considerations as well. His wife, Peggy, for example. The degree of their estrangement notwithstanding, they were still man and wife, and for all the cause he might have given her, she'd never once betrayed him. Lafferty drew the line at betrayal.

And there was a man, Lafferty had learned, an abusive man by the name of Ray, from Dublin, a criminal of some sort, though the exact nature of his criminality remained a bit of a mystery. What Eena was was on the run from him, which would account for how she'd ended up in Godforsaken Kilduff, in the heart of County Nowhere. Ray was in Portlaoise Prison, she'd told him, and Lafferty, aware of the high-security nature of the place, concluded that he was not your garden-variety shoplifter.

Late in the summer, destiny struck one day when Jelly Roll in the eighth at the Curragh came in at fifty to one. There was no reason on God's green earth he ever should have, and Lafferty never would have given the horse the time of day, but Eena liked the name. She was fond of strawberry jelly. Lafferty's turf accountant, Mickey G, was suspicious and reluctant, his nose bright red with worry, but he forked over the tidy sum, and Lafferty headed off to fetch Eena for a proper celebration. The timing was serendipitous as Peggy was off on her monthly shopping trip to Dublin with her girlfriend Judy, leaving Lafferty free to borrow her little brown Ford, Peggy being reluctant to lend it. She was fiercely possessive of the thing, owing no doubt to the time Lafferty'd borrowed it, unbeknownst to herself, and the unfortunate incident with the innocent donkey. Eena was reluctant to miss her shift at the Sugarshack, displaying what Lafferty considered an unreasonable degree of loyalty toward the pitiful place. "Tell 'em your granny passed away," he said. "You won't be lying at all."

He knew of a place in Naas, not far from Dublin, scarcely more than an hour's drive, a place called the Oyster Tavern, where he'd celebrated a similar stroke of good fortune a number of years before with Peggy. It seemed proper and poetic. Eena wore a pair of high heels and a cocktail dress, the likes of which he'd never seen on her before, the likes of which he was surprised she possessed. She looked like a schoolgirl dressed up for show, and she was giddy as a schoolgirl, forever wanting to peek at the big wad of bills Lafferty had stuck in his pocket, wanting to touch it and smell it, the brown eyes of her filled with the wonder. In possession of a small fortune they were, high on the wings of escape, and her dear old dead granny having played a part—Lafferty allowed the notions to entangle themselves, just as he knew Eena was doing, and sure enough, nearly to Naas, doesn't she come out with it.

"Mister," said she. "If we could think of a way to get the ring up out of my granny's grave, we could go to the Oyster Tavern anytime we pleased."

He'd been waiting the months for her to suggest it.

"And how might we go about that?"

"Why, we'd have to dig it up, I suppose."

Lafferty pulled in the reins on his smile, which was chomping quite fierce at the bit. "But wouldn't that be… I don't know… sacrilegious?"

He glanced away from the road to see her eyebrow go up. "Oh, I don't think so, Mister," said she. "Only a wee desecration is all."

They laughed. She'd come far since the spring, when she'd been incapable of deciphering his humor at all. The deal was all but sealed. All that remained was for Lafferty to decide how best to accommodate the matter of Peggy. Betrayal was not his currency, but there were degrees of betrayal, and accommodations could often be reached, given the right rationale.

The Oyster Tavern was a splendid old stone edifice with a doorway of dark heavy oak and, inside, a grand dining hall with beams on the ceiling, a magnificent stone fireplace at the far end. Crisp white linens, waiters in black jackets, and the finest steaks within a hundred miles of Dublin. Candles on the tabletops, music in the air. They settled in to study the menu, Eena hanging on his every word and wisdom, just as she always did, full of trust, safe in his hands. Lafferty was up to high living when he had to be, and he ordered a rare Merlot, had it opened by the table to let it breathe. He couldn't escape her eyes in the candlelight. He held her hand on top of the tablecloth, where it squirmed like a tiny bird.

When the soup arrived steaming hot, he asked her what she judged the ring to be worth—had her grandda ever mentioned it in passing? In response her hand darted from beneath his own to hide in the shadows of her lap. "Mister," she whispered.

"What is it?"

"Over there. Is it not herself?"

Back over his shoulder he looked. Herself it was indeed. Peggy across the crowd, Peggy and a man, a man upon whom his eyes had never been set, leaving the place together, a couple, laughing, tipsy, her arm about his back as she smooched his cheek, his hand on the full of her fine, round rear.

Lafferty listened to the blood clambering in his ear, the sound of a deal being sealed.

He parted the coarse green curtain, raising up a cloud of dust. Rattigan's Motor Court, an apt appellation. He was accustomed to cheap rooms, some of the happiest moments of his life had been squandered in cheap rooms, and he could only hope this would prove to be another. The hardest part was the waiting. Keeping the girl on an even keel. Keeping himself on one as well, his heart still smarting at the revelation of his wife's perfidy. But Lafferty, ever the optimist, viewed it as motivation, pure and simple. Opportunity beating his door in. Outside the twilight lingered till he thought would it never come to an end.

The little motorway in front led into Ballybeg, on the outskirts of which lay the church of St. Brigid, behind which lay the moss-covered graveyard, within which lay Mrs. Bernadette Moore, the granny of Roseena Brown. They'd driven by so he could see for himself the lay of the land, exactly as she'd described, the isolation of it, isolation adequate enough at any rate, after midnight. Now the trick was getting midnight here. And Lafferty with his bowels raging perilously.

As great and tempting as the reward might be, the cost was steep. There was for one thing the matter of the manual labor necessary to dislodge six feet of good, solid Ballybeg earth; Mrs. Lafferty had not raised her boy to work with his hands, and he'd always found hard labor distasteful. Not to mention the gristly and ghastly nature of communion with a corpse.

"Mister." Eena curled on her side in the bed, blanket pulled up to her chin. Underneath she was naked, quiet and still and lost in her thoughts, every bit the opposite of himself pacing the floor in his boxers. "Maybe it isn't such a good idea at that. Maybe we should call the whole thing off."

Lafferty paused at the window. Giving the twilight another dusty glimpse. The first notion that popped into his mind, he was not proud to admit, was of himself carrying on on his own, without her assistance at all. He knew everything he needed to know, the ring was there waiting like a potato in the ground, and how much assistance could she offer at any rate, wee little thing that she was. He would have to do the heavy lifting. But he overcame his selfish inclination. He was nothing if not a moral man. He looked at her there curled in the bed, the size of an orphan. "In for a penny, in for a pound," he said, crawling into the bed behind her, gathering her up in his arms.

"I'm scared," she said, her heart pounding the cage of her ribs.

"Aren't you after telling me your granny would want you to have it? That she'd give it to you herself if she could? After all your troubles, all you been through, all the torment your man Ray has caused you, look at it as your just deserts."

She was still, a captured kitten.

"Think past today. There's a good girl. Think past the unpleasantness to the rewards that'll follow. Think of us free and easy on our own, living the good life."

She was quiet for a long while, and he hoped the idea was soothing her, though still he could feel the working of her heart. "And what about Peggy, Mister?"

What about Peggy indeed. His face began to burn. "Her just desserts as well," he said.

"How did you end up with the likes of her in the first place?"

"Young and ignorant, I suppose. Seemed at the time like the proper thing to do. She was up the pole, so it was the honorable thing."

"And where's the child then?"

"After all that, she lost it."

Eena never turned. Her ear sticking up through her hair like a cookie there for him to nibble on. "Lost it," said she, "or told you she lost it?'

In the shadows of the hedgerow, Peggy's little brown Ford was invisible from the motorway. He wondered if she'd called the cops to report it stolen. Behind the church of mossy stone, the steeple glimmering in the black of the night with the light of a hidden moon, the graveyard climbed along a sloping hill. Beside it a row of trees all slanted and hunched from the wind through the years, like fingers pointing in from the sea. Lafferty waist-deep in the grave of Mrs. Bernadette Moore, his shirt clinging to his chest with the sweat, stinking of it, his hands on fire from the handle of the spade—Peggy's spade he borrowed from her garden. Eena perched on a neighboring stone, sitting morose and worried, knees clapped together, fiddling with the torch in her hand she never once lit, like the candle on the chest in her room.

"Could you spell me a minute, love?" said Lafferty, wiping the sweat from his face.

She tried, but she was useless as tits on a bull, every other shovelful tipping and falling back into the dirt. The spade was lanky in her hands, and she wielded it as though she was uncertain which end to stick into the ground. Reminded Lafferty of her awkward and clumsy way with a trayful of dishes, or how she was in the bed whenever he tried to teach her a new trick, forever shy and clumsy, ill-equipped for the task at hand. But by God, earnest and eager. When she was embarrassed, or hard at work, or deep in thought, the tips of her ears became red.

He caught his breath, looked up at the sky, gray notions of clouds scudding across it. Down across the slope past the church the village lay dark and quiet, save for the odd barking of a dog. A spot of light here, another there. Lafferty was soon impatient to take the spade from her hands. So close he could nearly taste it, the gold like icing on a cupcake, the sticky star clusters of emeralds. He considered she might be wrong, that maybe her old grandda was a liar—for wasn't it after all too easy? A blow to his dreams to be sure, but he found, nearly to his surprise, the shattering of her dreams his foremost concern. He could imagine her all hollow and sad, imagine her shrinking, drying up, blowing away. And he found the oddest thing happening to his train of thoughts, found it twisting and heading down the side track. For it was this thing, the shattering of her dream, he was bound to deter, for if the worst were to happen he would take her, hold her, find the joy for her, somewhere, somehow. He was nothing if not an optimistic man, and in all his exhilaration, perched here on the verge of joy, Lafferty felt such a love for the girl struggling in the hole he wanted to pick her up and squeeze her. So there it was. The fortune scarcely in his mind at all, the joy the ring would bring her having surpassed the worth in value, and so he took the spade from her hands, helped her up out of the hole, and set about his business. He'd never felt more noble, and the feeling of it brought a shiver to his skin, a tear to his eye.

By the time he was up to his chin in the dirt, nobility was fading fast. Exhaustion was only the half of it. The unholiness of the whole bloody project, the graveyard, the smell of earth and sweat, the girl on the stone, the half-lit sky, the wind twisting through the trees, wasn't it all beginning to play on his mind. Wasn't he beginning to worry there was no one buried at the bottom of this hole at all, that he could dig all the way to Pakistan and come up empty. Wasn't he beginning to feel the panic of being down in the grave, the prospect grabbing him by the throat and squeezing tight that he might never come up out of it again. *My mam always told me I'd end up digging dirt for a living*, he said. But Eena up above never uttered a word of response, causing Lafferty to wonder if he'd really said it aloud, or only thought it, or maybe only dreamt it. And then to wonder if his mam had in truth ever uttered the words, though he was fairly certain she had, as she'd never had a good word to spare him or his da, when indeed his da was home with them at all. For a long time he pictured her there in front of the stove in the dark tenement, the smoke lifting the smell of frying rashers, her back to him, her hand clenched up in a fist on the side of her apron, and the sight of it stayed with him till his shovel knocked on wood.

"Are you there, Mister?"

Lafferty might have grunted. The exhilaration was back, jumbled up with a grand dollop of apprehension, as he cleared off the top of the box. He knelt on the lid, on the lower half, and when he reached up to swing it open, he hesitated. He found he couldn't lift the thing up. There was no physical barrier to him doing so, but he found he couldn't lift the thing up at all.

"Mister?" The whispered word sweet as an onion. Lafferty looked up at the head of her peering down. "What are you waiting for?"

Lafferty stood. "Could you give us a kiss for courage?" She had to lie on the ground to do so, and that was the way they held one another, both perpendicular against the dirt, arms embracing, cheeks touching, tears mingling. He wasn't surprised to find her weeping too, for now the circuit was joined, the electricity coursing through them, locked there together and for good. "Okay then," said he. "Okay."

He looked down at the box beneath his feet. "Will the smell of it be something awful?"

"I shouldn't think so. She's been down there so long."

"Will she be dreadful? All rotted and the like?"

"I shouldn't think so. All dried up by now, I'd suppose."

Nevertheless, he held his breath and closed his eyes and pulled up the top of the lid. Warm air rose up to his face. It was the bravest thing he ever did. It was an inanimate object in the box, he told himself, and he did what he had to do. Finally, he stood, turning his face up again toward Eena, standing up, looking down. "I have it."

"From off her finger?"

"Of course from off her finger. From right where your grandda placed it."

"That one's the fake."

"What fake?"

"That's not the real one. That's the replica, crafted to look like the genuine article."
"You never mentioned a fake."
"The real one's tucked beneath her. Underneath her arse." Lafferty's mind stalled in the processing of the words, as he stared at the black of the dirt, the fake ring clutched in his fist.
"Just grab it, Mister. I'll explain it to you later."
And so he did. He took a deep breath, diving in again. Never let the air out of him till he was standing once more. Dizzy, his mind still spinning. "Got it?" said she. He nods. "Hand it up then," and so he did.
She tilted her head as she took it, sticking it straight in the pocket of her jeans. He drew in a great chestful of air, all the dread leaking out of him, and, reaching up to take her hand, doesn't he glimpse the oddest flash, too feeble for lightning, and doesn't he hear the faintest roar, too weak for thunder, a sight and a sound he could put together only after the fact as the back of the shovel coming barreling gangways toward his face at great velocity, behind which was Eena, the wee girl swinging the thing for all she was worth, like a champion hurler on the pitch.

Was he ever truly out? He was never truly certain, for it seemed as though no time had passed at all till he found himself slumped in the corner of the hole, on the lid of the box, white stars in his head drifting away, slowly letting blackness seep back in. And all the while the sight of Peggy in his mind, standing over him with her frying pan. He crawled up out of the hole, dirt crumbling back in with a rattle on the lid. Felt the lump on the side of his head, hair matted down in the dampness there. Down across the graveyard by the hedgerow, Peggy's car was gone. A light or two down across the village. No sounds at all now, the dog having gone to sleep, or having been murdered, just the whisper of a breeze restless through the trees. Lafferty picked up the shovel, wondered what the bloody thing was doing in his hand, and dropped it into the hole with a clatter.

He didn't head down toward the road. He went up higher instead among the gravestones, resting himself up a ways by a mossy Celtic cross, not far from the hunched-over trees.

There he waited. Not another five minutes gone by till he saw the headlamps. Sure enough, turning into the carpark. Peggy's little Ford, the girl climbing out, Eena. Scrambling up toward the grave of her granny. If indeed it was her granny at all.

"Mister?" she cried. "Mister! Where are you? Jesus, I'm sorry!"

Down the hill, down his nose, Lafferty watched her panicky antics. Lighting the torch, she pointed it down in the hole, the beam bounding up again as if swatted away, and then all about the graveyard in a skelter of bedlam. Far too feeble to reach him. Lafferty watched, breathing in the cool night air.

"Where are you? Mister? Terrance? I don't know whatever come over me."

He watched. Watched the spirit seeping out of her. Saw the torch beam droop and falter, then fail altogether. Watched the shadow of her trailing away back down across the graveyard to the car. He considered showing himself, confronting her, but in the end he couldn't do it. In the end he couldn't be certain the passenger seat of the car was empty.

So he watched. She climbed into the car and drove away, tail lamps disappearing down the road. When they were gone, when the sound of the engine had trailed off altogether in the still night air, not until then did he unclench his fist, no easy feat, so cramped was it from the work and the will. He held the thing up. Beheld it there. Even in the black of the night it gleamed against the sky, the genuine article, the real glimmering thing, the actual Ring of Kerry.

Mrs. Lafferty had not raised her son to work with his hands. He'd always found manual labor distasteful, and so it was with travel by foot. So it came to pass an hour or two later, maybe more, when the eastern sky was beginning to give in to gray, and the car came up the motorway, Lafferty changed his plan and stuck out his thumb.

For a long while the magic of the ring on his finger had sustained him, the heft and history and beauty and gold lifting him above his weariness, and he'd vowed to trek on till morning, get as far away as he could on foot, then find shelter, rest, then plan out the rest of his life. He'd have put the ring in his pocket in the first place, only there were holes there, bloody holes his bloody wife could never be bloody bothered to sew, so he'd slipped it on his pinky instead, where it fit snug as a rubber. But the weariness at last overcame him, that and the ache of his head, and after first determining that the car in question bore no resemblance to the little brown Ford of his erstwhile wife, Lafferty stuck out his thumb.

It was a big, black car, gleaming of polish and riches, that came to a stop on the side of the road. Lafferty hustled up, climbing in. A man was behind the wheel, a man all dressed to the nines with his vest buttoned up, a man with a faceful of smiling teeth, his hair pulled back in a ponytail and gleaming as bright as the car. "Lonely night for thumbing," he said.

"It is," said Lafferty.

"Where to?"

He was totally unprepared for the question. "Which way are you heading?"

The driver had to smile again, leaning up to the wheel. "West."

"West it is then," Lafferty said, pointing like a cowpoke. "West across the island."

There came a loud metallic click, the sound of the doors being locked, and Lafferty felt a jolt. The driver wasn't driving. He nodded toward Lafferty's lap, where his hand lay. "Lovely ring you're wearing."

The first thing he was was surprised. The last thing he supposed was the thing could be seen in the dark. He was about to respond with the first inanity that popped into his head, *nothing special*, when he looked at the lap of the driver, where a gun was quietly glinting beneath the face of smiling teeth.

"You'd be Ray then," he said.

Ray smiled even broader. "And you'd be Mister Lafferty." He nodded again toward the ring. "Hand it over."

"I can't get it off."

"What do you mean you can't get it off?"

"I mean it won't come off."

The gun twitched up with impatience. "Give it a yank then."

"I'm after giving it a yank. I'm after giving it a yank and a tug and a jerk and a pull. The bloody thing won't budge."

"Try spitting on it."

"I'm after spitting on it too—do you think I'm a bloody eejit?"

"Try it again with the spit. Only wipe it off good before you hand it over."

To no avail again. Lafferty nearly pulling off the skin.

"Stick it over here." Lafferty did, and Ray grabbed and yanked, yanking the finger nearly out of the socket, the shoulder nearly out of its own. Nor did twisting, prying, cajoling and cursing do any good at all. Ray sat back and slapped the wheel, twisting his head to glare out the window at the sky growing bright. "You're spoiling my morning, Mister Lafferty."

"Get some butter," Lafferty suggested. "Butter always works."

"Mister Lafferty," said Ray, leaning over calm and peaceful. "I have no butter. Do you see any butter? Do you think I'm carrying butter in my fucking pocket?"—the volume gradually increasing, as was the redness of his face—"Do you think there's butter in the glove box? There is no bloody butter! No butter on my person, in the car, lying out by the road, no butter within miles of this god-forsaken shithole! There is no fucking butter!"

"I should have known butter," said Lafferty. Why, he didn't know.

Nor did Ray. He glared a moment, then started the car with a roar, turned, heading back toward Ballybeg. He settled into silence for a while, though it was a fierce silence to be sure, the ferocity of which was exhibited by his reckless driving, the likes of which would have caused Lafferty to fear for his life, had that fear not already been in place.

Finally, he slowed to a civil speed. "Mister Lafferty. Reach into the glove box there. A celebration, a wee drop to the recovery of the ring."

Lafferty, leery, did as he was told. It was a bottle of Powers, clear and gold.

"Well?" said your man, glancing askance at the faltering Lafferty. "Not thirsty?"

"Awfully early," said Lafferty.

"Give it over," Ray said. Lafferty handed him the bottle, and he took a gurgling draught, handing it back to Lafferty. "There. No poison. Now drink."

Lafferty shrugged. "To the Ring of Kerry," he said, tipping it up.

Ray looked at him, puzzled by the mention of the tourist trap. "Take another," he said, and so Lafferty did. "There's a lad," Ray said, smiling now. He'd the face of a child, Lafferty noticed, the face of a child of the streets. Dangerous to be sure, but innocent as well, with a certain capacity for compassion. They drove for a while in time to the gurgles and swallows, Ray seemingly pensive, peering out through the windscreen at the windy little road. Nearly back to Ballybeg, he spoke. "Do you like puzzles, Mister Lafferty?"

Lafferty, puzzled, neither nodded nor spoke.

"Have another," Ray said, "and I'll tell you a puzzle. Eena—our mutual friend—calls me up in Dublin, what, not three hours ago, and isn't she crying, full of grief and misery to tell me what's happened, how Mister Lafferty has absconded with our ring. And what do you suppose is the story she tells me?" Looking Lafferty's way again, drawing a blank again. "No guess in you then at all? Not very keen at the puzzles, are you?

"Why, she'd wanted to surprise me. To fetch the ring back to me all on her own, to atone for all the harm she done me back then." Glancing again at Lafferty. "You'd be unaware of the harm, then? How she cost me four bloody years of my life?" And so Ray told him. How Eena, five years before, had brung the ring to his attention in the first place, a legend from her village, Ballybeg. And how she botched a simple, stealthy snatch-and-switch, knocking over a trayful of dirty saucers and such, after the snatch but before the switch, alerting the family who apprehended your man beating feet down the lane. Eena escaping under cover of the ruckus. And Ray with the replica still on him—which they took of course for the real McCoy, Eena having stashed that article under the old lady's arse before fleeing. And how her clumsiness cost him four years in Portlaoise—from which he'd been sprung but a few days before.

"So here's the puzzle then. Am I to believe she was going to fetch the ring back to me? Or was she planning to make off with the bloody thing all along, go off on her own, and myself left in the proverbial lurch? What am I to believe, Mister Lafferty? Do you yourself believe little Eena Brown to be capable of treachery and betrayal? For I understand you've got to know her well since the day you left her the stinking little two punt tip."

Lafferty was stung, though he kept it to himself.

"But the thing of it is, Mister Lafferty," said he, "the thing of it is, she could well be telling me the truth. That's the nature of her. That's Eena. She might well have been planning to bring me a get-out-of-jail present. Or she might have been planning to fuck me. With Eena, you just never know."

Lafferty didn't know, couldn't even think about sorting the thing out in his mind. Ray nodded. "Take another drink," he said, and Lafferty did, thankful for small blessings.

Pulling in at Rattigan's, everything was gray, everything from the sky right down to the pavement beneath his feet when he stepped from the car. Something moved in the window—Eena peeping through the ratty green curtain. Peggy's car nowhere to be seen, and only one other car in the carpark, several doors down, Lafferty concluding the owner of a rusty yellow Fiat with a dent in the fender would not possess the formidability to come to his aid at all.

Eena rushing to Ray where she buried her face in his shoulder left Lafferty more stricken than ever. Wounded and hollow, and light-headed from the whiskey, not to mention the thump on the head. Shot through with fear and sorrow. Though how much of the burying of her face was out of love for your man, how much out of not wanting to look Lafferty in the eye? Ray gently stroked the nape of her neck under the rowdy red hair.

"Mister Lafferty," said Ray, pointing the gun toward the bed. "Sit."

Lafferty did. Ray handed the gun to Eena, who held it in both of her hands like a foreign object, like a spade or a trayful of dishes. Ray took off his jacket, hanging it neatly on the rack. He unbuttoned his vest, removing it as well, hanging it beside the jacket. From the pocket of his trousers, he withdrew an object that Lafferty at first couldn't identify. When he placed it by the car keys on the rickety table, he saw it was a knife. A long knife. A long, shiny knife, and this before the blade was ever out of it. Ray removed his trousers, lined up the creases, hung them neatly over a hanger. Unbuttoned his shirt, hung it by the rest of his clothes, then stood there in his boxers and undershirt, Lafferty noticing the round pucker of a scar above his knee.

Eena looked at him as well, puzzled as well.

"The ring won't come free of his finger, love," said Ray. "I have to perform surgery, and I don't fancy ruining a good suit of clothes with the blood."

"Butter," Lafferty said.

"Butter works," said Eena.

Ray stamped his foot on the threadbare rug. "There is no butter!"

"There's always butter somewhere," said Lafferty, his mouth dry as a cobweb.

Ray took the gun. "Into the bathroom," he said, taking Lafferty by the collar. "Eena, love, bring the knife. Gather up the towels."

Lafferty naturally resisted. Ray naturally pressed the gun to his cheek. "Mister Lafferty. I'm not a heartless man. I'm after allowing you your anesthesia—here, have another." He handed Lafferty the bottle of Powers from the nightstand. "Now I intend to cut the pinky from your hand to take possession of the ring that's rightfully mine. I paid four years of my life for it. I intend to cut it off you and leave you alive, without a pinky, which, in your line of work as I understand it, will not be much of a hindrance. However, if I must, I will cut the finger from a dead man. It would, in fact, be a far easier trick."

The bathroom was small, a sink with a little glass shelf and smeared mirror above it, a standing shower stall and the toilet with the lid up.

"Would you like to sit then, Mister Lafferty? You might be needing to."

Lafferty shook his head. His voice had deserted him.

"You wouldn't have an apron in your bag, would you, love?" said Ray, looking down at his undershirt.

Eena bit her lip and shook her head, the tips of her ears going red.

"Pity," said Ray. "Hold his hand there, love, tight to the side of the sink."

"Wait," said Eena. "Let me try."

"You'd like to carve?"

"Let me try to get it off. I used to be able to get the things off my own finger when they were stuck."

Ray nodded.

She came to Lafferty, her brown eyes big and close. She took his hand in both her own, raising it up to her face, taking his pinky into her mouth.

"Easy, love," said Ray. "You're getting me all up."

She didn't hear him… Lafferty watched her eyes that never left his own, feeling his pinky in her mouth so warm and moist it nearly stopped him trembling. Nearly. He watched her lips at their work, lips he'd never seen so skillful before, watched her cheeks suck in, felt her tongue laboring every bit as hard, the ears of her going redder and redder, his pinky wanting to disappear down her throat. He felt the ring loosen. Felt it loosen then come free, sliding quickly away down his finger, too fast, away from his finger and into her throat, too deep, into her throat where it caught.

She drew away quickly, coughing, choking. Ray clapped her on the back, hard, once, twice, a third time, and the ring came shooting up out of her, lifting through the air, arching straight toward the toilet where it landed with a neat little splash. Settling down to the bottom, lying there gleaming in all its golden splendor, beneath the foul water on the stained and dirty porcelain.

The three of them stared at the thing. "Get it," said Ray.

"You get it," Eena said.

"I'm not putting my hand in that," Ray said. "Mister Lafferty, you do it."

Reaching over, Lafferty flushed the toilet.

The ring disappeared, sucked down a different throat. Lafferty looked at Ray. Eena stepped back. Ray trembled, the tremble going to quaking proportions, red all over with the boiling blood, and he sputtered unintelligible syllables, and the gun in his hand came up, pointing at Lafferty, his finger on the trigger twitching. Lafferty felt his knees buckle and go under, and he was falling toward the floor.

"No!" said Eena, stepping in to knock it away, but doesn't the bloody thing discharge with a bang that shook the shower curtain. Lafferty, concussed by the sound and the shock, took a moment to divine what was happening, for it was the oddest dance they were doing, Ray and Eena, clutched together there swaying, Ray's little-boy face over her shoulder all white and grim and pulled back tight, and the head of Eena flopping loose and lolling.

And the red splash of blood coming down.

"God!" said Ray. "God, help me—Lafferty! Help me! Get something!"

Lafferty reached up handing him a cheap scrap of a towel Ray pressed to her chest. He lowered her to the floor, her eyelids fluttering, looking up from one of them to the other. "Get help," Ray said. "Hurry—get help!"

Lafferty arose, riding his rubbery legs.

Eena, surprise lingering on her face, stared up past Ray, straight into the eyes of Lafferty. "*Hurry*," said Ray. "Get help."

Snatching the car keys from the rickety table, Lafferty galloped out the door, pulling it shut behind him. The carpark was empty, no one out from the office, nor from the room near the Fiat, no one roused by the gunshot, no one wondering as to the mortal goings-on in the room at the end of the court. The morning was sleepy, motionless, as if he'd stepped into a painting, a still-life, a landscape, all the trees arranged alongside the road, the house across the way with the tidy blue shutters, the clean gleaming glass of the petrol station next door, the letters on the sign so bold and red. The Audi started up in a fine, smooth purr, hitting on all cylinders, unlike his mind, for hadn't he been sleepless the whole of the night, engaged in the most desperate of physical labor, thumped about the head, his finger nearly cut off him, his very life in mortal jeopardy. He squealed away out of the carpark, heading west, west across the island, the countryside sweeping by, the rock walls and hedgerows, the tumbled-down cottages, leaving it all behind him, the cold awful touch of the dead woman, the porcelain white face of Ray, the blast of the gun and the blood.

But even as he crested the hill and flew toward the next, the eyes stayed with him, the lying eyes of Eena, full of hope and truth at last, going bigger and browner as the color leeched from her face. The eyes stayed with him, and the ring, the dreadful, awful, never-ending ring.

Cannibals in Canoes

That he was even in the Oyster Tavern at that particular time was only happenstance. Returning to Kilduff, he'd remembered the place off N7 in Naas at the last minute and stopped on a whim, hoping to salvage a bit of craic after a disappointing trip to Dublin. It was a grand place, the Oyster Tavern, a splendid old stone edifice with a doorway of dark heavy oak, and, inside, a magnificent dining hall with beams on the ceiling, a massive stone fireplace, crisp white linens, waiters in black jackets. The prices of course were dear as well.

In Lafferty's mind, dear prices and opulence were forever entwined with warm comfort. And didn't your man feel deserving of comfort.

He headed to the lounge, and there sat a young woman alone.

He glanced up to the dark gleaming beams of the ceiling, beyond which might lay heaven. Warm comfort? Pretty, but not too pretty, her pug-nosed face was a bit oriental in aspect, and she was underdressed, as was he in his jersey and jeans, the only two underdressed patrons in the whole of the place. Soul mates immediately sprang to his mind. She wore a green billed cap, backwards, sprays of dark yellow hair peeking out from the hole above the strap over her forehead. Her expression was neutral, close to pleasant, wary, the look of a woman who could stare down the devil.

She was at a low round table in a corner of the lounge, waiting. For whom? For what?

Love? Lafferty liked to think of himself as an incurable romantic. His wife, Peggy, among others, liked to think of him as something else—as a womanizing, good-for-nothing, indolent bastard for example, a view she'd expressed many times over, ever since she'd become immune to his charms not all that long into their marriage of nine years. Or maybe ten. He'd lost count.

He ordered a pint of plain, watching his pennies, and tried to stare at the woman in the corner of the lounge without staring, keeping watch in a non-threatening way, alert to any signals she might send, open to reception. Once or twice she made eye contact, but in a neutral, unreadable manner, neither welcoming nor warning, and so Lafferty was biding his time, you can't hurry love, when a man walked in, hesitated halfway to her table, and said the word to her, "Fiona?" And didn't she respond, "Oliver?"

Leaving Lafferty a bit stymied. She'd not looked as though she were waiting for a man. For a man she apparently didn't know. She did not appear to be the blind date sort. The man, Oliver, crossed to her table. The words they spoke now couldn't reach Lafferty in the hubbub of the soft music overhead, the quiet chatter and clatter of the drinkers and diners.

Oliver did not sit. Fiona stood instead. The conversation was not a long one, inaudible words growing heated. Soon wasn't his finger poking into her chest, and wasn't her hand just as quick to slap it away again. The slap, unlike the words, could be heard across the lounge, resoundingly, and everyone turned to watch, the barkeeper, the patrons all across the room, one and all. Fierce and red was the look on the face of her, as well as that on the face of Oliver when he turned and strode away, a face where, Lafferty perceived, mean, fierce looks were at home.

The dust settled. Fiona sat, poked a finger in her drink and stirred, the flush slowly leaving her face, all the spectators turning away. All but Lafferty. Mightn't now be a fine time to ride to the rescue? Or would it be too soon, too intrusive? When, at what precise moment, might too intrusive slip over the line into a fine time for comfort?

He glanced at the ornate clock high on the wall above the bar for a clue, but when he looked again, Fiona was standing, slinging her bag over her shoulder. She walked with seven-league strides toward the door, passing close by Lafferty at the bar with only the briefest of glances at your man, his smile, the charming dimple in his chin unnoticed, a glance with no apparent discernible meaning. Where he nonetheless attempted to discern meaning.

Perhaps the moment for comfort had not yet arrived. But perhaps it might before she reached her motorcar. Ever the optimist. Ever in need of comfort, particularly now, after his journey home to his old haunts, Dublin, had found none of his old mates about, no craic to be had, no gentle members of the opposite gender, no welcome, and him dreading the return to Kilduff and Peggy's sour homecoming. And spotting Fiona there how his heart had soared, taking it as an omen, only to come crashing down again, dashed upon the rocks. On the wide stone stoop before the doorway of dark heavy oak, he saw her walking across the well-lighted carpark, her stride still determined, though diminished by now to perhaps three- or four-league, with no backward glance. To see if your man might have followed. Lafferty wilting.

The dark van came up quickly behind her. Rocking to a halt, a man—it looked for all the world to be Oliver—jumped out, seizing Fiona, wrestling her toward the door that had opened in the side of the van like a dark, hungry mouth. Lafferty saw himself running to the rescue, shouting, waving his arms, attracting attention, straight into the teeth of undoubtedly deadly retaliation. Instead, he stepped behind the pillar, hidden. Fiona's cries could be heard, though not the sound of her fists slamming on the man, on the side of the van, before she was maneuvered into it, before it sped away.

On knees that were wobbly, hollow to the core, he walked toward the spot in the carpark where the abduction had taken place. Why, he wasn't sure. He stood there looking around at all the parked cars and lampposts, not sure what he could possibly be looking for. The van would be well away down the road by now. Down some road. He would call the Gardaí. Of course. He would hasten back inside, call the authorities.

The squawk of a car door opening. He saw no one until a child emerged from between two cars. She was slight, a blink and he might miss her, with light hair in the lamp light like cotton candy, like wisps of yellow air. She looked one way then the other, up the row and down, glancing at Lafferty, dismissing him just as quickly. She walked across the lane and stooped to pick up the green hat that had fallen from Fiona's head, the hat he'd failed to notice. The little girl's eyes, big and white, settled then on Lafferty.

"Mister," she said, the hat drooping forlornly from her tiny fist, nearly touching the black pavement. "Why did those men take my mum?"

Against his better judgment. What did that even mean? Every time the phrase came into play, the arm-wrestling commenced. His better judgment and his instinct were always at odds. Was better judgment better than instinct? Not in Lafferty's book. But he couldn't be sure, as he'd no real basis for comparison; whenever the situation arose, he invariably sided with instinct.

Better judgment told him to run to Fiona's rescue. Instinct told him nay. If he'd listened to his better judgment, he might well be banjaxed by now.

Thus your man found himself, against his better judgment, fleeing the scene of the crime with the little refugee. Someone else had seen and called, and the sounds of distant sirens were growing closer, more urgent. The instant the little girl heard them, she dropped the hat and ran.

Lafferty chased. Catching her, he scooped her up, her tiny fists battering at him, tiny feet kicking. "Where are you going? Stay here!"

"Let me go! Get *away* from me!"

"They're coming to find your mum!"

"No! Noooooo!" A mighty squall escaped her.

"Okay, okay—shhhh. Okay. There now. There, there." A little banshee in his arms, fierce as her mother, but frightened, frail, heavy as a sip of water. "They're coming to *help*," he tried to explain.

The fearful big eyes boring into his would have none of it. The great muster of a frown didn't believe it. "Noooooo! They took away my *daddy*!" she said. As Lafferty tried to process the rude accusation, she poked a sticky finger into the dimple in the middle of his chin. "You!" she said. "*You* help me find my mum! Pleeeeeease? Pretty please!"

There was more. But even as he was bargaining and cajoling, even as she was insisting and pleading, and kicking, didn't his instinct barge in and shoulder better judgment aside.

Your man was never much one for red tape in the best of times. He'd always been, however, susceptible to the inveiglements of a pretty girl.

He'd always been a sucker too for the tinkle of a little girl's giggle—perhaps even a little boy's on the odd occasion—one of the most magical sounds in the world. He could no more imagine a giggle coming out of this one than an egg coming out of a cow. She was all business.

"What's your name?" He was driving down the street she pointed out, the way she said her mum had come. She ignored the question. She was kneeling, giving him her back, face to the passenger window, the bill of the green hat Lafferty'd plucked from the pavement nearly to her waist. Watching for her mum.

"If you don't tell me your name, I'll have to call you Stinky. Would you have me calling you Stinky?"

She turned, casting a cold glance over her shoulder. "My name is Gracie."

"There. Good. That's better. Mine's Terrance."

"So what?"

"No, So-What's my brother's name. People confuse us all the time. Is that Terrence Lafferty there, they say, or is that his brother, So-What?"

She turned again, another disdainful glance.

"Brilliant," he said. "Where do you live?"

"We have to find my *mum*."

"First we have to find where you live." Your man was not a detective, nor did he intend to become one. Truth be known, what he wanted to find, more than Gracie's mum, was a way out of this bollocks that was beginning to feel like a sucking bog hole. "Maybe your mum left some yoke laying about that might point us where to look." Or to tell the guards where to look, he didn't say aloud. Nor did he utter the next word: *anonymously*. "Who else lives with you and your mum? Does anyone else live with yous?"

He thought he saw her stiffen and bristle. "No."

He found Gracie's kip eventually by way of hints and clues she provided, streets and turns sworn to and recanted, as well as advice solicited at a petrol station or two, an adventure in navigation. The place was on a quiet lane heading north out of Naas, near the outskirts of town—he knew, having traveled beyond the border and doubled back. Though the adjacent row of cottages was neat and trim and well kept, Gracie's place showed signs of decrepitude, its once-white walls shaded and fading to black, the pebble-dashed wall in front gouged and scarred, a thousand pebbles having fled for higher ground.

The lights were on. Gracie was out of the car before Lafferty switched it off, racing to the door. "Mum!" he heard her cry as he followed. "Mummy!"

No answer, of course. Gracie stood just inside the door, surveying the shambles: beer bottles of green and brown on the table and floor and on the threadbare sofa, some spilt and stinking, crisps and pretzels bags about the room in crumpled disarray, crumbs scattered like confetti. She yelled, "Mickey!" She stomped her foot. "Wait'll my mummy sees this mess you made!"

The mention of her mummy took her by surprise, and she burst into sobs.

Mickey? He watched the bouncing wee shoulders, the little girl sobbing into her hands like the queen of the opera, and thought, *Mickey?* He moved to scoop her up, unsure of her reaction, ready to withstand fists and feet. She was not an easy one to comfort.

To his surprise she didn't resist, hanging limp and warm against him, her arms about his neck, her wet face buried in his shoulder. He made his way to the sofa, bent to swipe away a layer of crumbs, sat with the girl on his lap, sobs subsiding. "There, there," he said once or twice, "We'll find your mum," patting her gently, biding his time—chomping at the bit—until he thought the time was safe to change the subject. "Who's Mickey?" he said.

She was an exhausted little girl. Her head never moved from his shoulder. "My mum's boyfriend. He's a maggot."

"I thought you said nobody lived with yous, yeah?"

She lifted her head to look into his eyes, the anger gone. "He doesn't *live* with us," she said in a tutorial tone, "he *stays* with us."

"Oh. I see. Where do you suppose he is now?"

A ripple of a shrug. She rested her head once again on his shoulder, her body becoming even more limp than before. Soon he felt the bottom give way, Gracie giving in to sleep. A wee facsimile of a snore.

He was knackered as well. He thought it best not to give in, not in this precarious situation. He thought it best to plan how the devil he was going to wriggle his way out of it—for both him and the girl. Fiona as well, he supposed, although that bit seemed more formidable. Quite possibly undoable. Oddly, the formidability, and the corresponding unlikelihood of success, didn't concern him greatly. He hadn't ridden to her rescue in the first place, so the precedent was already there. He wondered, foggily—sleep was making inroads—if he might feel differently had she been a wee bit more receptive to his signals in the lounge of the Oyster Tavern.

When the phone rang it blasted him from a deep, dead sleep. Gracie was still atop him, breathing heavily, undisturbed by the bell. He put her on the sofa, hurriedly found the phone on a rickety stand near the telly, answered it before the fourth ring.

The man's voice said, "Mickey?"

"No," Lafferty said. "Oliver?"

"Who the feck is this?"

"Never mind who this is. What do you want?"

"We have Fiona. We want Mickey. Mickey owes us something. Where is he?"

"He's not here. We don't know where he is—and yous ought to be ashamed, leaving a wee little girl all alone in a carpark, miles from home, snatching her mum away from her."

Oliver hesitated. "Her mum left her alone in the carpark first." In the background, Lafferty heard Fiona's voice, urgent, angry, frightened.

"That's no excuse—God knows what might have happened to her. Ignorant. Ignorant." Your man felt confident enough, scolding violent men from over the phone.

"Sticks and stones may break my bones," Oliver said, leaving Lafferty without an appropriate rejoinder. After a bit of the silence, Oliver sighed. "Right then, the girl's grand now, and her mum's unharmed as well—for now. Mickey's her man. This we know because Mickey works for us. A tidy sum of money he was responsible for is unaccounted for. That money belongs to us. We want it back. We'll have it back. The sooner we talk to Mickey, the sooner this whole bollocks can be put to rights."

"Brilliant," Lafferty said. "I told you, we haven't a baldy notion where your man's got off to. Maybe he's done a runner."

"Not likely. Not without his oul doll. Your man doesn't know which hand to wipe his arse with unless Fiona's there to tell him. He'll turn up. Tell him to stay tuned."

After Oliver hung up, the adrenaline quit Lafferty more quickly than he could have imagined, leaving him in no condition to think the thing through or formulate a scheme of any sort. He needed sleep. Gracie was still on the sofa, a patch of drool spreading out from her mouth in a shadow the shape of a teddy bear. He picked her up, found her bed, tucked her in. He went back to the sofa and reclined, pondering the irony of an undeliverable ransom note. *Return to Sender* came to his mind from out of nowhere, *address unknown*, as crooned by the King.

Not more than an hour later, wasn't he awoken again, this time by a crash and a clatter, the lamp on the table nearest the door having been knocked to the floor by an intruder, shattering to bits. The intruder was a man with gaping eyes, a short, wiry man whose head was utterly bald, bony and gleaming, his wide eyes filled with blood as he seemed to teeter in an oddly lopsided gait toward your man. The intent, the blood in the eyes, would normally have prompted Lafferty to flee posthaste, had they not been veiled by a nearly impenetrable glaze. The intruder was peloothered beyond recall, also accounting for his curious gait, consisting of one menacing step toward Lafferty—and Gracie, who'd stolen from her bed as he slept and was cuddled up to him on the sofa—followed by another step sideways and two to the rear. Lafferty and Gracie watched with something like awe. The man stammered and growled and shouted a thoroughly garbled, unintelligible phrase or two before marshalling a semblance of coherence: "What're you? Some kind of bloody kiddy-fiddler? Get away from that wain!" Gathering all the resources at his disposal, he attempted another mighty lunge forward, meant to culminate with his hands about Lafferty's throat, when he stepped on a beer bottle and tumbled hard to the floor. There, he lifted his head once, twice, then gave up the ghost, his lips puttering into silence.

"That there's Mickey," Gracie whispered.

How much time had passed? Your man would be hard-pressed to tell. There was no clock on the premises, none that had made itself known to him. It was dark—he'd turned out the one remaining lamp, the one that had survived Mickey's drunken, stumbling rampage—although soon he could see well enough in what faint light seeped into the place from the lamppost down the lane, or from the pearly black sky, or from the energy generated by the burning of the dread that buzzed through his conscious mind and seemed to permeate the little shambles of a cottage. He'd tucked the girl back into her bed. Somehow, she'd slipped into his pocket and made herself his, at least for the here and now, and while your man was something of an expert in the giving and taking of comfort and love— his *raison d'être*, he liked to think—this was of another class altogether, far more simple, and altogether more complicated.

And altogether foreign to him. He could barely make her out there on her bed among the stuffed and threadbare bears and rabbits and mice and such. Mickey he'd let lie in his drunken heap, unable to bring himself to even cover the scut with a respectable blanket.

It was quiet, perfectly still—dead. Unnaturally silent—why was there no barking of a dog from down the lane, no humming of a fridge, no stirrings of critters behind the walls? He could almost hear the silence. Why, for that matter, was he here? What was he waiting for?

Nothing good. Nothing good was in store, that was a dead cert.

In Kilduff, some miles away in the midlands, Peggy would be home by now from her shopping trip, home and stewing, fuming over the whereabouts of her motorcar, her little brown Ford, her car that, ever since the unfortunate incident with the poor donkey, she'd been reluctant to lend him—or, truth be known, she'd resolutely refused to let him touch. Her car that she needed to transport her to work in the morning, to her nursing post at St. Christopher's. Even though his reason had turned out in the end to be the soundest imaginable—the rescue of the little girl—it was a reason that would never make a dent, would never gain an ounce of purchase with her because of all the other reasons, or lack thereof, that had gone before.

Perhaps if he showed her.

Perhaps if he brought proof. Maybe if he brought the little girl, brought Gracie home with him. Peggy was forever wanting a child of her own.

Out of the question, of course. A fleeting fantasy. When it had blown over, when the thought had distilled, this was the essence that remained: Why *was* he here? What he needed to do was vacate the premises pronto, vamoose, do a runner, get the hell out before Oliver showed up with God-only-knew what other class and manner of menace—he needed to flee, something he'd always been good at.

But could he leave the girl behind?

Surely she'd be grand. What harm could befall a wee innocent creature such as that? Sure no one could lift a finger to her, not even the most desperate of desperados.

He heard her cry out then, as if the very thought of abandoning her had raised the alarm in her head. He tiptoed into her wee room, where the curtain on the window—a paler bit of the dark—had been frilly at one time, maybe white, but now what remained of the lace was tattered and scant. She cried out again, a gibberish of fear and anguish, another cry for help. "Gracie—Gracie, pet, what is it?" He touched the skinny bone of her shoulder.

"Cannibals," she said, as if she were perfectly awake, awaiting the question.

"Pardon? Cannibals?"

"Yeah—cannibals! Cannibals are coming to eat me!"

He tried to see her face in the dark. Was she even awake? "Why the devil would a cannibal want to eat *you*? Sure there's more pickings on a fence post."

"I do so have pickings!"

"Where would you ever come up with a notion such as that? There's no cannibals in Ireland. Sure, there's no cannibals anywhere near here. They're all over in Africa or New Guinness or some such place."

"They have canoes! They showed 'em on the telly. They eat people and they have canoes, and they can go over water—it showed 'em paddling canoes over big, wide water."

"But you got me here," he said, somehow reluctantly, somehow fearful of what felt like commitment. "You're safe with me here. I'll watch over you."

A small hand out of nowhere grasped his wrist, hot and shocking. "How'll you stop 'em from eating me?" she said.

He had to think up a good lie. "I'll slip 'em a Mickey," he said.

At last; there it was: the little girl giggle, musical, magical, so singular in the dark and quiet of this night. Soon it faded off again and she said nothing else, nor did he, and soon her breathing was even again, deep and peaceful. As if she'd never been awake. If indeed she had been.

How much time had passed? He couldn't know, but it couldn't have been long since the little girl's nightmare. He was back in the lounge, sitting upright and uneasy at the end of the crumb-covered sofa, and still no inkling of sleep had entered his mind. There was no room for it there, as the mounting dread left little room for anything else, save Gracie's nightmare. It was not as quiet as before. Mickey's state of unconsciousness had grown more restless and noisy with gasps and moans and yips of fear. Lafferty went to the window. Nary a cannibal in sight. Was the sky a bit brighter? The sound of a motorcar began as a thought, a possibility, then came true in his mind, creeping into his ears. An early shift man leaving for work?

Maybe. The sound of the car seemed to come closer. Maybe not.

The dread upon which he'd been sitting the whole night through suddenly hatched. If Mickey had stolen money from them, enough to cause them to resort to such drastic tactics, why would they give him a warning, simply ask him to stay put, to sit and wait?

What did they plan to do when?

He guessed Fiona would have told them about Mickey's drunken habits. And that they would wait until they were sure he was home, then come calling. But when might they judge the best time to be? When did they plan to do what?

Quickly back into Gracie's room. It was a shade or two brighter. Now he could make out her sleeping face. Had he come to say goodbye to her then? Or had he come to lift her in his arms again, to take her in Peggy's little brown Ford and head for parts unknown? He stared at the face, a smudge on her cheek, peaceful and serene in the knowledge that Lafferty was there protecting her, keeping the cannibals at bay.

From the lounge came the sounds of Mickey stirring: an undecipherable exclamation, the sharp, muted slap of an unsteady footstep, the moan of pain coursing through a hungover brain. More footsteps, ragged and uneven.

Lafferty followed them out through the lounge to the wee kitchen. He heard the faucet squeak, water splashing down. He could make out Mickey bent over the sink, water running full tilt over his head, into his cupped hands where he copiously gulped. Oblivious to Lafferty and the rest of the living world. When he stepped up close behind him and uttered Mickey's name, didn't your man jump as if he'd been goosed by a rogue billy goat.

"Ah Jesus," he said, hand splayed over his chest, eyes wide in his bony skull that gleamed even in the dim light. "Who the feck are you? What are you doing here?"

"You don't remember meeting me a couple of hours ago?"

"Sure, I never laid eyes on you."

"Do you remember Gracie? The little girl?"

"Gracie—of *course* I bloody well remember Gracie." His face underwent a metamorphosis, from angry and defiant to confused, doubtful and panicked in four easy steps. "Where is she? Where's Gracie?"

"Where do you suppose?"

"At her granny's. That's where she's usually at when her mum's out traipsing about."

"Gracie's tucked up safe and snug in her own bed. But her mum's not out traipsing about." Lafferty needed to unburden himself, deliver Oliver's message, be done with it, be free of it. He decided Mickey was sober enough by now, or at least close enough to sober. He started from the beginning, with Fiona's abduction in the Oyster Tavern carpark at the hands of this Oliver fellow and person or persons unknown, the abduction that Lafferty had witnessed only by happenstance. Then Gracie emerging, alone and abandoned. And the phone call from Oliver upon their return, as well as his message: that Mickey had stolen money from them, and Fiona was their bargaining chip. "They told me to tell you to stay put," Lafferty added. "They'll be in touch."

Mickey said nothing. They'd come back out to the lounge, Mickey slumped on the sofa, heedless of crumbs or posture, Lafferty's words having battered him into a heap. Lafferty sat on the cheap chair with the scuffed wooden arms; between them, the wee table buried in debris. It was still mostly dark, one lamp still smashed, the other still off, though out through the window the patch of sky above the trees had turned the color of mustard. "So what did you steal?" Lafferty said.

"I swear to Christ," Mickey said. "I stole nothing. What'll I do?"

"Why would your man think you did? What become of it?"

Mickey sighed and dragged his open palm down the length of his bony face. "Fiona," he said. "It had to be her took it. It's the only thing makes any sense at all. Though I can't believe she'd do me that way."

"And what was it she took?" He was having trouble imagining Mickey, entirely unformidable, playing any role of consequence in any self-respecting criminal conspiracy.

"Ten thousand quid," Mickey said. "A small bit, actually. But sure don't they keep track of every bloody penny. You'd think it was their own bloody money."

"Well, whose bloody money is it?"

Mickey looked surprised. "Why, the cause's. The republican movement's."

Didn't the hairs on the back of Lafferty's neck stand up and take notice at that. The republican movement: the IRA. Mickey went on. Lafferty recalled bits from the news. The IRA had pulled off a multi-million pound heist from the Northern Bank of Belfast a couple of months before, setting off a political and criminal brouhaha that had yet to die down—and which Lafferty, as apolitical as the next man, had managed to soundly ignore. The IRA was adept at money laundering. In addition to the pubs and clubs they owned, they also sent scores of volunteers—such as Mickey—to carparks all across Ulster to filter the cash, a laborious process, putting small notes through payment machines to receive legitimate change. "I'd finished the job," Mickey said. "Took me bloody hours. When it was finally done, I stashed the dosh all neat and tidy in my camo rucksack ready to deliver back to 'em. But when I went to retrieve it, wasn't the bloody thing gone. Nowhere to be seen."

"Where'd you leave it? On the kitchen table?"

"No, not on the bloody kitchen table! I hid it. I hid it good and proper."

"Where? Are you sure you looked in the right place?"

Mickey didn't answer right away. A sigh, or a snort, or both. "I can't remember."

"You can't remember."

"It was either under the bed, or under the bag of dirty shirts on the closet floor. Or in the cabinet under the sink there, behind the toilet paper."

Lafferty only shook his head, causing Mickey to take umbrage. "Well, I couldn't bloody well bring the thing down to Lanigan's with me and stand a bloody round with it, now could I?"

"No," Lafferty said. "Of course you couldn't."

"I looked everywhere."

"Maybe it's the camo," offered Lafferty. "Maybe you looked right at and didn't see it." If he got it, Mickey failed to appreciate the humor. After a bit, Lafferty said, "And she's the sort to throw you under the bus, Fiona is? She'd steal it, then tell Oliver and his crew it was you?"

"No," Mickey said, puffing his chest out to defend her, then deflating again just as quickly. "I wouldn't have thought so. But it must be so. It's the only thing makes any sense. No one would break into this dump off the street thinking they'd find so much as a farthing."

Lafferty could identify. He'd only just been imagining Peggy reporting her stolen car to the coppers, describing the suspect in detail, the dimple in the middle of his chin where at one time long ago she used to touch with her finger when she kissed him. He was feeling restless as well, and the fear was creeping in. It was a familiar feeling only more intense, the alarm sounding, like the feeling he'd often had before when the mister was due home any minute, and he'd yet to find his trousers. He was about to explain to Mickey how it would be for the best that he remove the little girl from the premises—not to mention himself, which he didn't intend to mention. "Listen," he said.

"Did you hear something?" Mickey said, sitting up straight on the edge of the sofa.

"No, no," Lafferty said. "I just been thinking—it might be a good idea for me to take Gracie away somewhere—take her off to her granny's, maybe. Get her out of the way here while you settle things with Oliver and Fiona and them."

Mickey's eyes flailed about in a panic. "Leave me alone here?"

"Sure, I got nothing at all to do with it. Nor the little girl either, that's for sure."

"No, but—" He grasped his knees, as if to keep them from bucking.

"I suppose you could always do a runner yourself."

"And leave Fiona in their clutches? You don't know them boyos. I couldn't do that. I couldn't leave her alone to fend for herself against the likes of them."

Lafferty left him sitting stiff on the sofa, a new sheen gleaming in the dim light off the bony skull and hollow face of him. In her room, he found Gracie still sound asleep, more deeply than she had been before, the way only a child can surrender to sleep, limp and boneless. When he lifted her, wrapped her in her blankie, and took what he guessed might be her favorite teddy, she scarcely stirred, murmuring, drooling into his shoulder. He patted her back in gentle strokes, soothing her. He stood for a moment or two, holding her as he looked out the window. The sky definitely brighter. A flicker of breeze in the trees across the lane. Silent. No sound of approaching car. He moved as quietly as he could. It took him no more than a couple of minutes, but when he walked back out through the lounge, wasn't Mickey slumped again back against the sofa, asleep. Or, more properly, passed out. Lafferty studied his face for a moment or two, deciding it seemed to be more or less at peace as well, concluding that bold Mickey had decided he had nothing to fear from the cannibals.

Through the quiet streets of Naas—in the car he coaxed consciousness enough out of Gracie to show him the way—yellow lights were coming on in kitchen windows and a streak of pink and gray was unveiling itself in the eastern sky. Lafferty drove the purloined little brown Ford as though in a daze. He knocked long and loud on granny's door, and when she finally answered—a rotund little woman with laugh wrinkles at the corners of her eyes and mouth—he was quick to assuage her concerns, to erase the look of panic on her face at seeing her sleeping granddaughter clinging to the neck of a stranger. Assuaging the fears of women he'd only just met was one thing he excelled at. The smile, the dimple, still worked.

Gertie—her name was Gertrude Flowers, though before the front door was shut again wasn't she insisting he call her Gertie—showed him the way to Gracie's room, and he followed, carrying the girl, tucking her into her bed, where the stuffed animals were much newer, more colorful and plentiful. She rolled over, her back to the annoying, jabbering adults, and plumped her head firmly into her pillow, determined to sleep as long as she pleased. Gertie commented that Lafferty seemed utterly knackered as well, and he had to admit the truth in it. Again, the adrenaline that had sustained him through most of the night and across the town had evaporated. He was in no condition to undertake the drive back to Kilduff, not yet, and when Gertie offered him the sofa in the parlor, off the kitchen, out of the way, he readily, greedily accepted.

He was asleep in an instant, though he remained so for not very long. He was awakened by a wee finger poking at his cheek and the dimple in his chin, lifting his eyelid to see what was in there. "Terrance," the small voice said. "Terrance, are you awake?"

He blinked his eyes, sticky with sleep. "I am now, yeah."

"Do you want to play store?"

"Store?" Big eyes staring into his. Little hand clutching a fistful of money.

Lafferty sat up, wide awake. His head jerked a nod.

Taking his hand, she scampered ahead of him back to her room. He stopped at the doorway to take it in. The camo rucksack half out and half under the bed, piles and piles of banknotes stacked all about in gaudy array. Gracie smiled. "Okay," she said. "Buy something."

He raced across town, if the little brown Ford could ever be accused of racing, wondering was he too late. He parked in the lane by the gouged, pebble-dashed wall. The cottage seemed the same as before, no sign that anyone had come or gone.

He walked across the yard as if on thin ice. He tapped gently on the front door, then opened it and stepped in, stopping after only a step or two. It was the raw scent stopped him first. Like the inside of a butcher's shop. Then his eyes adjusted to the dark and he saw Mickey there, on the floor before the sofa, and Fiona as well, close beside him. In the gloom the blood looked like shadows. He hurried outside but didn't make it to the little brown Ford before he had to vomit. He fell to one knee to do so, and he felt, oddly, as though he were praying.

The bitter taste remained in his mouth even after he found his way back to N7 and was heading toward Kilduff. He thought of Peggy, Peggy throwing up. Back in the days when they were still friends, a pub crawl invariably ended with her sick to her stomach. Not him. Never. He never threw up. It occurred to him he should tell Peggy about what had happened, how he'd had to vomit. It might buy him a bit of goodwill. A bit of peace. He'd a gift of gab after all. He could couch the cause in words that mitigated the horror, in words she could accept, in words that made it clear it might never have happened at all, and that, even if it did, it happened in another world and another time and had nothing at all to do with the pair of them and the lives they were living. And all would be forgiven.

The Purloined Pigs

When he was three or four his mam told him there was no such a thing as Santy Claus, nor Father Christmas, nor any of them. She told him Santy Claus was invented in the Dark Ages by Oliver Cromwell solely for the purpose of keeping the Paddies simple and deluded. His da disagreed, saying there was no way a Brit could ever be so clever, but his mam was nothing if not firm in her convictions, and the one time his da brought home a Christmas tree—a spindly wee orphan of a tree at that—didn't his mam come in and pitch the thing straight through the window, tinsel, ribbons and all. A brilliant enough event in its own right, made all the more so by the fact that they were living at the time in the third-floor tenement on Rutland Place, the tree narrowly missing oul man McGonagall as it crashed to the cracked and dirty pavement down below. Up until now, that had been Lafferty's most memorable Christmas.

Up until now. The snow falling on Blue Bucket Lane, a rare and fabulous thing, was only the beginning. *Miraculous* mightn't have been overstating the case, not so much for being the first snow to fall on the village of Kilduff in any number of years, and not so much for happening on the very eve of Christmas, but for the nature of the transformation, Blue Bucket Lane going from a squalid stretch of brown mud, dead grass and bland cottages into a wonderland of glitter and grace. Lafferty stood for a time in the doorway, watching the plump flakes float down dark and white through the lamplight, gathering on the berm of the lane and the dirty yards, clinging to the clusters of branches and limbs.

Miraculous too, the snowfall, for its timing. Had it come two nights earlier, it would have found your man shivering sleepless and homeless under his sodden old newspapers at the base of the Kilduff Cross on the green across from his turf accountant's shop. Having finally been tossed out of her house for all and good by his wife, Peggy, the locks on the doors changed, the Gardaí forewarned and watching. The last straw—his extended visit to tend to the needs of the widow Reagan—having finally broken the back of the camel in question. So it was easy for Lafferty to look out now at the new snow, spotless as the soul of a baby, and imagine a fresh beginning. He was no spring chicken anymore, Lafferty wasn't, turning the corner at forty before you knew it. Time to settle down, grow up. Time to try to make a go of it with Peggy. Hadn't they once upon a time been crazy mad with the lust and the love for one another, two decades ago to be sure, but wasn't that a feeling that might be recaptured, and wasn't the snow falling so white and fresh a sign that slates could be wiped clean, that leafs could be turned, that lives could start over again.

Peggy came up to him in the doorway. "Move your arse, Terrance, or I'll be after tossing it right back out in the snow again. My guests'll be here any minute."

"Yes, my love," said Lafferty.

"'*Love*' my arse," said she.

"Oh, I do," said he, "I do," and Peggy had to smile, at last. Having long ago grown immune to his charms and inveiglements, it had been a while since she'd smiled at his clever *bon mot*, and he took the smile to be confirmation that the sign of the snowfall was true, that clean slates and turning leafs and fresh beginnings were all possible in God's sweet world.

"The toilet needs scrubbing," said Peggy, the smile run away from her face.

She was giving her Christmas party. She'd invited her friends and co-workers from St. Christopher's where she was a nurse.

In addition to a pack of promises concerning the nature of his future behavior, which included gainful employment, it was the party in fact that helped him worm his way back. Not just the labor of the preparation, mind you, for appearances beyond polish and shine were important, the appearance in particular of a happy couple graciously, *charmingly* (this is where Terrance came in) entertaining their guests on a Christmas Eve. She cooked, he cleaned. And cleaned and washed and dusted and swept and mopped and scrubbed and polished, one chore after another, eager and uncomplaining, at least within her earshot. His mam hadn't raised her son for physical labor, much less physical labor befitting a scullery maid, but a night or two in the cold and barren roads of Kilduff could fine-tune a man's attitude, and nor had his mam raised a fool. Lafferty looked at the condition as temporary. He figured after the new leaf was turned, after the relationship was reestablished, then the labor would naturally sort itself out by appropriate role and gender, and the old order would eventually reemerge. All he had to do was keep his nose clean and his tool sharp. And though he doubted the old order would go so far as a move back to Dublin, who knew? He'd never wanted to leave the city in the first place, to move to a God-forsaken village the likes of Kilduff, out in the heart of County Nowhere. When she'd told him she wanted to leave, to quit the city, to start anew in a small cottage in a little village, where perhaps she and Terrance could start over as well, without all the gambling and drinking and unsavory sorts to lead him astray, and maybe even have the child she'd been hoping to have, he'd told her by God he was staying. He was a Dublin boy through and through, born and bred. But once again, the want of a roof over his head put the spoil to his best-laid plans, forcing a reconciliation, a reluctant move to the country. That particular reconciliation, like all those that followed, had faltered, and so Lafferty hoped—sincerely this time, perhaps—that this one might somehow fare better.

It was in the very spirit of that reconciliation in fact that Lafferty went to the bother of procuring a gift, a Christmas gift, for the first time he could remember, maybe for the first time ever. In the thrift shop by Connor's News Agent, he found a porcelain pigs figurine, forking over the last two bob to his name, two bob he'd worked hard to attain, a coin or two at a time here and there, beneath the cushions of Peggy's sofa, in a little ceramic box in the corner of her dresser, scattered in the junk drawer of her kitchen cabinet. For didn't herself collect pigs. If there was any irony in her penchant, Lafferty never looked for it. She had porcelain, pewter, stuffed and plush, pigs of all sizes, shapes and colors, on this shelf or that, this room or that, kitchen, bedroom and parlor. The figurine he'd spotted amidst the junk in the thrift shop stood out head and shoulders above the other pigs, and he suspected it might be what Peggy might call adorable: six inches high, white in color with only a blush of pink, a mama pig and baby pig standing up on their hind legs, clutching one another as if in fear, looking up with four large and wondering eyes at the world at large. It came in a box that Lafferty wrapped in pretty paper he found in Peggy's desk and stashed the thing on the top shelf of the closet in the bedroom behind a shoebox and well out of sight to surprise her with come Christmas morning. He couldn't wait to see the look on her face.

Guests began arriving, smiles as white as the snow they were shaking from their shoulders. Time and again, Lafferty showed his own teeth, as well as the jolly dimple in the middle of his own chin. They were nurses mostly, of either or indeterminate gender, with significant others and spouses, a receptionist or two and technician as well. Some he remembered from this gathering or that, some he didn't, though he'd have been hard-pressed to put a name even to those he did. He saw to it that all were hailed and well met, that a drink was in every hand, including his own to be sure, nibbles within easy reach, taking their coats to brush off the snow and pile on the bed in the bedroom. The tree was lit up and sparkling, the music loud and choirful, the gas flame in the stove sputtering blue and red and yellow, a fine approximation of a Yule log. The chatter was loud as well, bouts of laughter frequent and earnest. An hour in, it was apparent the thing was going right as the mail, and when Lafferty looked at his wife talking up a big fellow with gold in his teeth and his wife who was skinny and pale, Peggy all smiles and ease, he figured the roof over his head was secure, at least for the immediate future.

A woman named Cassidy came, a woman known by all as Cassie. When Peggy introduced him he said pleased, and Cassie said she'd met him before, did he not remember, and Lafferty had to admit he did not. At the Commodore Pub, said she, the day they gathered to bring in the summer. If drink was taken, Lafferty explained, that might account for his failing to remember a face so pretty as hers, at which point Peggy interjected that with Terrance there was always drink taken, which might account for his failing to remember where he lived a great deal of the time. She'd a pretty face indeed, Cassie did, nose regal and thin, brown eyes hiding a quiet panic, her eyebrows, sandy and fine like her hair, set straight in a line beneath a forehead with an eternal crease of incomprehension. She appeared entirely unable to quite put a name to whatever it was she was watching. When Peggy told him from the corner of her mouth a bit later that Cassie, plump, lonely and neglected, had "problems," that her husband had left her, and Peggy had invited her mostly from pity, Lafferty took in the desperate and thirsty look of the woman and saw her for what she was: a mortal temptress God had placed on the path to his reconciliation. The flesh of her body, near as Lafferty could judge beneath her loose-fitting dress and sweater, seemed at the crossroads of aging, still firm enough to be enticing, ample and relaxed enough to be inviting.

He caught himself holding his breath. He neither meant nor intended to be judging the flesh of another woman. He meant to spurn temptation. He looked at his wife. Pretty, prettier, dark hair in thick waves and ringlets, fine fistfuls of flesh evident beneath the close-fitting clothes. She was the woman for him. Amen and case closed.

For a time, Lafferty chatted up a fellow with the ugliest wife he could find. His name was Conboy, beanpole tall and lanky with a small face and square jaw, hair balding back across the crown of his head. He paused before every laugh to make sure, Lafferty guessed, that he got it. His wife, Angelica, was a frightful scramble of straight hair, chicklet teeth and a wee nose buried by the heft of her glasses, but Lafferty loved her wit. When the topic turned to the lamentable earthquake in Turkey and the countless hundreds dead, didn't she say, "Ah, sure, they probably all had it coming," and Lafferty hoped he could grow up someday to appreciate a woman such as that. Passing through the parlor he exchanged cowboy quick-draws with a big heavy fellow by the name of Quinn with tight curly hair and a roadmap of red veins and splotches on his cheeks, the big fellow clutching his chest like it was shot full of hot lead, and in the kitchen he fell in with Browne, a grave and studious man, the prominent gray hair of his eyebrows threatening to conquer his face altogether. Browne was espousing to his wife, Ginger, and a cluster of others his conviction that there was no such thing as the present, that the present didn't exist, that the word itself should be stricken from the dictionaries of the world. Someone said what about now? Right now, when they're all standing about, weren't they in the present, and Browne said certainly not, it's in the past by the time the word leaves your lips. Someone said *now* quicker but Browne insisted it still existed only in memory, nowhere else, and for a time they stood about shouting *now* quicker and quicker, trying in vain to snatch the present and keep it from becoming the past. Lafferty saw Cassie standing at the fringe, feigning interest, trying to hide the confusion on her brow. She was standing directly beneath the overhead light of the kitchen, which lent her fine, sandy hair a metallic and reflective quality that Lafferty could have taken for a halo, if he'd been so inclined.

When the time came for party pieces they congregated around the tree, great flakes of snow still licking at the window from the darkness outside. Ginger Browne went first, encouraged by the crowd who'd heard her first-rate voice before, giving a grand rendition of *O Holy Night*, hitting the high notes with gusto. Song after song followed, three nurses in a fine bit of diddlyie, Lafferty concluding they must practice in the ward when they ought to be healing people, and a little man named Enright offering a quavering version of *Wild Mountain Thyme*, making the most of a voice that was mournful and thin. *Will you go, lassie, go*, sang every voice in the room, except for that of a dark fellow by the name of Adams who'd been sulking behind his close-cropped beard since the moment he arrived on the outs with his wife. When it came time for Lafferty's own piece, he demurred, glancing at Peggy who knew that his usual was a rousing rebel song, *The Boys of the Old Brigade*, far from a favorite of hers, and he'd not had enough drink taken at any rate, wasn't in the mood, too busy being the host, too busy minding his P's and Q's—a redundant effort on his part, as Peggy was minding them too. When they urged and insisted, Lafferty stepped to the middle of the room, cleared his throat and recited:

"Eggs and bacon, eggs and bacon,
If you think I'm going to sing it,
You're sadly mistaken."

The rhyme was well received and Lafferty was off the hook, and he opened himself another bottle of stout, and looked at the clock on the mantle. Another piece or two ensued, till it petered out over a sad effort by Mr. and Mrs. Quinn, who stumbled through a Bavarian folk song they picked up on German holiday. Lafferty noticed his own cheeks had got sore from smiling. A sad state of affairs. In an evening at the Pig & Whistle with his mates, didn't his smile last twice as long, and didn't his cheeks never grow weary of it. There were different qualities of smiles, those that came easy and those that did not, those that took place, say, for instance, at your wife's Christmas party with a passel of partiers you hardly knew, and with the keen eye of your wife forever watching for the smile to be sure it was there and sincere, and which required all the more toil to maintain. Cassie was one of the first to leave, fetching her coat from the bedroom and carrying it with her out into the snow, pausing only to say a few words to Peggy passing by. Lafferty thought she'd have slunk out undetected if she'd been able, and he was relieved to see her depart, taking with her the fleshy temptation, seeing it as the first step toward an empty house, which was to say toward an empty bedroom in which he and his wife, Peggy-o, could at last consummate their reconciliation. For wasn't your man growing all the more randy with each passing stout, each passing hour, the longer he'd looked upon the temptation, having been celibate now for so many days. Five at least, going on six.

But weren't his hopes to be dashed. For after the last guest had finally straggled out into the snowfall, after your man had made a conscientious and conspicuous effort to tidy up the desperate litter of bottles and ashes and saucers and such while herself only sat in the quiet and rested, didn't she go into the bedroom then all alone. And tell him through the closed and locked door that he'd earned his way back into her home, but not yet back to her bed.

There was always the pigs. His ace in the hole was the pigs up his sleeve. Lafferty, disgruntled and randy and lonely, stood for a time with his simmering blood in the dark of the living room looking out through the window at the flurries still chasing one another around the lamppost. The ground was covered and glistening, the tree limbs gleaming as well. Two nights ago being warm and dry and sheltered from the snow would have been plenty enough, but now it seemed scant consolation. You always want more than whatever you have, a truth he was born with. He considered for a time tapping on her door again and telling her of the pigs, of the gift he had for her that couldn't wait till morning for her to open. See what else it might open. But in the end he did not. Best not to press the issue, best not to hurry the woman. In the end he decided to wait. He was certain she'd adore the pigs once she'd laid her eyes on them, and the morning would come soon enough. Love in the morning was a favorite of his. In the end he was content to take the little wool blanket from the shelf in the hallway and wrap himself up on the sofa safe from the snow and the cold, listening to the warm hum of the flame in the stove, savoring as he fell asleep the pleasant anticipation of delayed gratification.

As soon as he heard her next morning with the kettle he was up and into the bedroom, and straight to the closet shelf. But there was nothing there but empty. He reached deeper. Still nothing. He knocked aside the shoebox, the other boxes and what-nots and bric-a-brac, searching with increasing anxiety for the gaily wrapped parcel of pigs. He looked on the floor of the closet, in the rest of the room, on the shelves with the other pigs, everywhere there were pigs, to see if she'd discovered the thing and placed it on display. It was nowhere to be found. The pigs were missing entirely.

In the kitchen she stood, in her purple robe, her hair sideways to Sunday from sleeping. He in his rumpled trousers said, "Did you find it? Did you open it?"

"Find what?" says she. "Open what?"

"I'm after buying you a gift, which I hid in the closet. It's not there now."

The look on her face said not again, Terrance. The lips on her face said nothing.

"I bought you a bloody gift—it's gone. It's missing. It's not *there* now."

"Terrance—"

"I amn't lying!"

She couldn't look at him. She turned to her cup saying nothing. Lafferty's heart was hammering. He *wasn't* lying. Not *this* time. Peggy stood at the kitchen counter, her head with a sad little shake, not looking toward your man in the doorway. Outside through the window the morning was blazing, a brilliant sun rising on new fallen snow. Lafferty let his fist unclench, his blood settle down, his thoughts travel back. There was the time he'd given her the squashed box of chocolates. Another time the empty ring box, and once before that the roses that were spotted and wilted too soon, and there'd been other assorted gifts down the years, all ruined or flawed—all ruses of one sort or another, all attributable to imaginary thieves or cheaters, all engaged in imaginary plots to beat down the good intentions of your man.

But *this* time he wasn't lying, not at all. Except in the eyes of his Peggy-o.

Peggy went off to work, St. Christopher's being open as ever, Christmas day or not. Lafferty sat at the table while she fixed herself another cup of tea and toast, never offering any to him. If you get hungry, help yourself, she said as she was leaving, which was something at least, he supposed. She showered and dressed behind closed doors, and as she was leaving she told him to finish picking up from the party, if he didn't mind, not bothering to hear if he minded. He stood at the window and watched her drive off in her little brown Ford, watched the warm sun turning the snow to slush. Blue Bucket Lane shiny, wet and black.

He looked around at the leftover litter, then back again out through the window. The leftover litter could wait. He hadn't given up hope, not yet, for the idea of the pigs and the role they might play was still very much in his mind. He hadn't given up on his pigs.

He showered and dressed. Made himself a cup of tea, took a biscuit from the tin, brushed his teeth like a good lad. Glanced out again at the sun going higher, the snow going slushier. Never once taking much notice of the shower or clothes or tea or biscuit, the toothbrush or sunshine or slush. Lost in thought was he, of pigs and reconciliations. He rummaged through Peggy's desk till he found her address book, and sure enough there was the one he was seeking. Peggy was nothing if not an organized woman. Putting on his jacket, he walked down the lane into the heart of Kilduff, squinting against the brightness from under the bill of his cap. He made his way past the Pig and Whistle, so regrettably closed, past the green which was still mostly white, where stood the Kilduff Cross, his erstwhile home. A pack of brats on the green, noisy and busy, building snowmen, throwing snowballs, all in a frenzy, racing the sun. One he recognized by his crimson cheeks as the Gallagher lad, nephew of one of his mates, and when he flung a snowball at your man, Lafferty caught it on the fly, returning the thing with a good deal more velocity, and, sure enough, not another was flung his direction. At the corner by Connor's, closed up too, he stopped and waited. That was where the bus stopped as well, and soon it appeared down the road.

Three stops and a half hour later, one town over, he disembarked, walking up a slushy street of squat trees and close-packed flats, checking the numbers on the doorways. When he found the one he was looking for, 36, he climbed the small stoop and gave a good rap, and the woman named Cassidy came to the door, still dressed in her bathrobe and slippers.

"Terrance Lafferty?" she said.

"In the flesh," says your man.

"I never thought I'd see your puss again." The confusion on her brow at its deepest.

"In the flesh," he repeated. "May I come in? We need to talk."

"We do? I'm not really dressed."

"If it'll put you at ease, I'm willing to undress as well."

A flash of red shot through her face. The confusion, though, entirely gone.

What was it truly that brought him to Cassie's? The suspicion ignited by her reputed "problems," along with the fact that she'd fetched her own coat from the bedroom, all on her own, and ventured out into the night and the snow falling down and the bloody thing over her arm? Not wearing it on her at all?

Or was it the fleshy temptation? The gratification too long delayed?

It was a fine distinction, not worth the time to consider. For didn't she step aside. And didn't your man step into the void.

In the grand scheme of things over the length of his life, Lafferty had accomplished nothing. He lived and loved the best he knew how, according to his own set of rules, perfecting the art of getting by, and so he'd never climbed a high mountain, nor built a great bridge, nor won any prize in a race. Nevertheless, he knew how it felt. He believed every life was touched by moments of grace, moments when all things come together in harmony, and the soul rises up in the gooseflesh to take a peek for itself, and this was what Lafferty felt as he stepped inside the neat and dim little room, seeing immediately his pigs on the mantle shelf, feeling the closeness of this woman, this Cassie, who stood sharing his space, sensing a kinship both ancient and new. He looked about the room, goosebumps letting up. Not a stick was out of place. The curtain hung down in pale wavy pleats, a yellow hue from the sun beating off the boards of the house next door. A clean, soft carpet of dark and light circles, a trim sofa beneath the window with plush crimson cushions, a doily of lace square in the middle of the coffee table, the chairs and the lamps and tables just so. And the mantle with the candles—the candles and pigs.

"Lovely," said he, and took a deep breath.

"What is?" she said. Then, "Are them tears? Are you crying?"

"Aye." He wiped at his cheek. "Tears of joy."

"Joy? Aren't you the strange one though."

"The joy of reconciliation." Crossing to the mantle, he looked at the pigs, the mama and baby clutched there together, returning his gaze with their wide fearful eyes. He seized the figurine, held it high, then clutched it to his tweeded bosom. "Reunited once again with my wee piggy darlings."

How the face of her blossomed in shock and surprise, a dozen replies scrambling helter skelter in her eyes. Not a one found its way to her mouth. "Why'd you take 'em?" said he.

She finally spoke. "I didn't know they were yours."

"Rubbish. You took 'em off my closet shelf."

"*Peggy's* closet shelf. I thought it was something she'd purchased for you. She's ever after saying what a pig you are. That's why she collects 'em, she tells everyone. She calls 'em her bevy of Terrances."

Though stung, Lafferty nevertheless soldiered on. "Why in bloody hell would you be after taking 'em from *any*body?"

She sighed looking down at the floor, at the dark and light circles underfoot. "That's what we're trying to find out," says she. "That's what I'm seeing the shrink for."

A flaming kleptomaniac. A new one on Lafferty. He'd known plenty of light-fingered chaps in his day, had indeed himself been known to borrow the occasional item that didn't belong to him in the strictest legal sense, but only out of necessity, when no other option was available, and only when the item in question was something which was well and truly needed at the time of its procurement. The idea of stealing on impulse, of taking something utterly useless just because it was there for the taking was something he sat on the sofa beside your woman as the whole story poured out of her and tried to wrap his head around. She'd been arrested. A convict she was, indeed, indeed. Six months of weekends in the hoosegow after her fourth arrest for shoplifting, and the reason she was seeing the shrink was because it was a court-ordered condition of her probation. Wasn't her thieving the reason her husband, an accountant with a hairy back and smudged eyeglasses, had left her in the first place.

"Is he doing you no good at all then, the shrink?" Your man leaned back on the soft sofa cushions, the yellow-hued curtain just over his shoulder. Cassie leaned up on the edge of the thing, her knees this close to touching his own as she wrung her hands, wrung the story out of her. Her bathrobe was soft and pink, of a stuff he thought was called chenille, and it kept falling loose with the wringing. He wondered was she wearing anything underneath, a distraction he found annoying as he tried to listen with sympathy and compassion.

"Well," she said with a dab to her eye from a ragged scrap of tissue, "I amn't stealing as often. Your pigs was the first in a fortnight. Nearly." At that she lifted her face up to look at a far corner of the ceiling, as if trying to put a name to something.

"That's a bit of progress, sure it is."

She looked down again with a sigh, avoiding his eyes just the same. She laid a small hand by his knee. "He believes it's all the fault of my mother."

"Sure your mother was nowhere near my house."

"Because my mother never gave me a gift, says he—she was a farming lass, dirt poor and hard as rock she was, and the giving of gifts on a birthday, or even on a Christmas, was something they never fell into. My shrink says it's because she never gave me a gift, never gave me nothing, not love enough after all, is why I steal things to this very day—still trying to get my mother's attention, says he, still trying to get her to love me."

At this didn't Cassie look up at your man, the incomprehension on her brow replaced by an utter and painful understanding. "Terrance, I can't remember the woman touching me at all after the day I turned ten."

What was your man to do? Had he any choice then but to touch her? Even kleptos need love, he concluded. A little hug, he decided, only that and nothing more. A wee bit of comfort then.

He awoke in mortal discomfort, the sun on the other side of the house pouring in through the bedroom window. His elbow was aching, his arm was asleep, his ankle was itching like blazes, and Cassie asleep in the bed on the crook of his arm, her breathing trying to rise up to a snore. He'd dozed a bit himself, the session of love having been that vigorous and wholehearted. His skin all over—face and neck and arms and chest, his nether parts all down below—was flaky and crusted, the result of the drying up of all the lovely, salty fluids in which they'd been so bathed. Your man was not prone to regrets, nor could he ever imagine, philosophically, regretting the making of love in any form or manner, yet wasn't a good deal of the discomfort he felt in his body infecting his thinking as well. Wondering the effect this tryst of fate might have on his reconciliation with Peggy. And sure wouldn't she be home by now from work, wondering where the hell he was. What time was it? The clock on the stand was on Cassie's side, facing an inch the wrong way, and no way your man could see it without moving. The sun pouring in was heating the room. On the little chair by the dresser sat the great, fat teddy bear, whose name she said was Eldridge when she moved him from off of her bed. And placed him where now he sat, staring at Lafferty with hard button eyes, the sun on his lower left foot. Just behind the closet door then, he noticed it there, for the first time, the end of the briefcase poking out.

When she came awake a few minutes later rubbing her nose, a bit of drool had pooled on his arm, and she wiped it away, then from her chin, embarrassed. She looked into his eyes, inches away, and for a moment he thought the confusion would run away with her face entirely, as if the memory of who he was was gone. As well as that of who she was. He watched the pieces fall together, a few of them anyway, behind her eyes as she blinked. "What time is it?" she said.

"You're after reading my mind," says he.

She sat up and looked at the clock. "Half four."

"I'd best be heading home," he said. "Peggy'll be back by now."

"Where was she?"

"Work," he said, as though the question was a silly one. "You should know."

"Peggy wasn't working today. I make out the holiday shifts myself."

Lafferty borrowed her confusion, put it on his own brow. "She told me…"

Cassie smiled, her wagging finger coming up to the dimple of his chin. "Don't tell me you thought himself was the only one stepping out for his wee adventures." But her finger quit wagging at the look on his face, the eyes of her growing tender. "I'm sorry, Terrance, I just assumed… Everybody knows. We thought it was an open marriage kind of a thing, yours and Peggy's."

He sat up on the edge of the bed, his back to her. "Of course I know." Of course he did. Hadn't he seen her once with another man, or thought he had. But the restaurant where he thought he had was dim and smoky and he'd not got a clean look, and never made a word of mention about it, for hadn't he himself been there at the time with another woman who was not Peggy. And hadn't he convinced himself in all the days since that of course it hadn't been her. And wasn't the biggest, thickest, most self-centered eejit that ever breathed air sitting right here and now inside his own skin. "Of course I know," he repeated. "What class of bloody eejit do you take me for?"

Cassie behind him said nothing. She touched his back in a kind of tickle where a small birthmark the shape of a tear was reputed to live. "I hope you knew," said she. "You better bloody well have knew. Terrance, I amn't the kind of woman to sleep with somebody else's husband, not unless I thought it was…you know…"

He turned. She was leaning up against the pillows, clutching the sheet to her chest in earnest, the ache across her face. "Of course," he said. He showed her his teeth. "You'll steal the odd pig now and then from a woman, but never the same woman's man."

Cassie smiled too, a smile of a faltering sort. "Yes," she said, "that's it."

He touched her cheek and he kissed it. Then he stood up to dress. Passing by Eldridge toward his clothes in a heap, he noticed the briefcase again peeking out from the closet. "What's this?" says he, grasping it by the handle, hoisting it up.

Cassie sighed and slumped back down in the sheets, rolling away from him. She buried her face in the pillow, the words coming out of it muffled and low. "That's the only other thing. That and your pigs was the only two things this past fortnight."

He turned it, taking in the look of it. Sturdy, brown leather scuffed and worn, brass snaps and locks and corners. "Where'd you steal it from?"

She came up for air. "From the back of the ambulance. I was walking by on my way out of work. Sitting there offering itself to me, it was."

"Ambulance?"

"They brought in two men, a car wreck. Desperate shape they were in, skulls cracked open, blood everywhere, this close to dead. I don't know if they made it or not."

Lafferty looked it over more closely. "What's in it?"

"I have no bloody clue, Terrance. It's locked."

"Heavy," he said, giving the thing a heft or two. Cassie sat up and started to dress, bra first, then underpants. Not your man. He sat back down naked on the bed, placing the briefcase across his knees. "Don't you wonder what's inside?"

"Aye," says she, dropping the dress down over her head. A plain thing it was, with green dots. "But I hate to break it open. Ruin the bloody thing."

"Probably nothing but papers inside."

"Maybe magazines, I was thinking. Maybe books."

"Have you a paper clip?"

She fetched one and stood watching him pick the lock. When he lifted the lid, the sight turned them both into stone, except for the quick blinking of four bulging eyes. For wasn't the thing filled to the brim with bright Euro banknotes, high denomination notes at that, all purple and yellow and green, from side to side, corner to corner, top to bottom. Reaching up over the rim. "My God," she gasped when finally she could.

Lafferty thought his heart was going to attack. "What the bloody hell…" was all he could manage. He slammed the lid shut.

"Open it back up!" says she.

"Did anybody see you take it?"

She thought for a moment. "I don't know. I never looked around. Sure I never do."

"Suffering ducks and the price of turnips."

"Terrance, I don't care for that kind of language. Open it up again."

He did. The money was still there. "What the bloody hell are you going to do?"

She sat down beside him on the edge of the bed. They both touched the banknotes, his right hand, her left, caressing, lingering. "I'll have to get it back somehow. I certainly can't keep it. I'm not a bloody thief."

He looked at her. "You know what I mean," she said. "Not a thief like this. I'll have to get it back somehow to its rightful owner. Somehow without getting collared again."

"Your rightful owner might be hard to find," says your man. "The men carrying this around are not likely to be rightful owners. Nobody rightfully carries around a hundred thousand quid in cash." They caressed a bit longer. "Someone'll be looking for it. Someone'll be looking hard, very hard."

"How'll I get it back to 'em? Do you suppose they'd miss just a few of them bills?"

"Yes, they would, and I don't know. But you better be about it quick."

Her hand dug down, riffling up through the bills. "I've an idea," she said. The tone of her made him look up from the swag for the first time since he'd opened the case. He saw the face of a naughty girl, Cassie, no confusion on her brow whatsoever. "Let's pour it all out on the bed," says she, "and we can do it right on top of it like the king and queen of Siam. We can say we come into money."

Lafferty sighed a worried, sweaty sigh, which may have been accompanied by a nervous giggle. Not a bad idea, he supposed, but not one he could wholeheartedly endorse. "I don't think you appreciate the gravity of the situation here."

"I do," she said. "Of course I do. But what's another hour? And, I might point out, Terrance, your oul fella there is plumping out at the very idea."

He couldn't deny it. The danger, the decadence, the pure raw power of possessing, even for a bit, a bald fortune such as this were a strong aphrodisiac, not to mention the suggestion itself coming from the mouth of the woman. Nevertheless, your man was reluctant to dump out the money and all the unholy jumble, wondering how they'd ever pack it back together by neat denomination and stacked so tidy, but he was just this close to overcoming his qualms when the first knock sounded at the door in front. Followed by another more urgent.

Lafferty froze, but Cassie says, "Just my neighbor for a happy Christmas or some such," and leans down for quick peck, saying, "I'll be back in shake. Dump it all out on the bed," but he didn't. Instead, he shut the case, wondering how she could know the knock of her neighbor, doubting she could, a doubt soon confirmed when the next knock was a crash, the front door shattering in, followed by voices, the deep, angry voices of men. In his naked panic he snatched the first garment at hand, her pink bathrobe, shoving the briefcase aside with his foot, heading for the door in back. Donning the robe, slipping outside in the slush hard and cold of the yard, the sun hidden low, the protests of Cassie in the living room growing louder, the gruff and mean voices of men, then the sound of a fist thumping flesh.

The sound made him sick, stopped him short. He could run back to the rescue. No. There was more than one man, there were two or three men, they would be men who fought, mean men, not men who only loved for a living, him and Cassie would just be beaten or killed, or worse. Lafferty's thoughts raging a blind frenzy. Help. Getting help was the only thing. Police, no matter, anyone, anything. A neighbor. A phone. He ran to the door of the house that was closest, his robe flying open, his naked feet unaware of the cold and the wet. He pounded but nobody answered, the door was locked when he jiggled the knob. Wrapping the robe tight, he went to the next door, and the one after that, door after door, but nobody answered at any, though there were curtains moving, faces peeping. No one would answer a door, no one would listen to the pleas of a man in a pink chenille robe up to his elbows and knees and open in front, shouting and pounding and running wildly from this door to that.

There were three men, tattoos and earrings. Crouching in the slush behind a juniper bush he watched them leave Cassie's place. Carrying the briefcase, casing the road. When they'd driven away in a silver Peugeot, he waited, the curtains of the neighbors moving and shimmering still, and when he'd waited long enough he made his way back to her door. Through the shattered thing on its hinges he stepped. Cassie on the bedroom floor. Her face red meat, pulp, swollen and split, her fine, sandy hair all matted and red, dress gathered up by her waist, her nakedness there on display. Blood all about. He felt for a pulse. She was breathing. Sirens in the distance. He pulled down her dress to cover her decent, then dressed in a hurry—another art he'd perfected—returned quickly to the mantle, and was gone again out through the back, from garden to garden behind the flats, slipping off like a thief in the twilight to wait for his bus.

"*Oh my God. They're absolutely adorable.* Terrance—" She looked at him standing there as though seeing him for the first time. "I can't believe you actually bought me a gift. You actually bought *any*one a gift. I'm impressed. It tells me something, Terrance."

"What does it tell you?"

She stood. She'd been sitting at the kitchen table with a solitary cup of tea when he'd come in and presented the parcel without a word, watching her open it. Now she came up to your man, put her arms around him. "I'll show you what it tells me," says she. Lafferty sniffed, trying to catch a whiff of the other man.

In her bedroom they took off their clothes. Peggy was leaner, younger than Cassie. Lafferty looked for signs of the other man. Over inch after inch of his wife's naked body, he looked closely for signs of the other man so as to block from his mind the image of Cassie the last time he saw her. He climbed into bed beside Peggy. When she began to kiss and grope he took her chin, gave her a peck, said let's go slow, and when he did that, she looked at him again with the same awe the pigs had inspired, wondering who on the face of God's sweet earth was this man in the bed beside her, this new man, mature and tender. She reached to the stand for the figurine, holding it there for them both to admire. "They are *so* adorable. I just *love* them."

Lafferty looking in vain for something adorable. What he saw was two helpless pigs clutching one another in fear, four eyes filled to the brim with mortal terror.

The Three-Sided Penny

Old Foley was the first to discover the thing, followed by your man Terrance Lafferty. Foley brought it into Cleery's public house to show it off one evening, a year or two gone by now. He was a farmer, Foley was, a poor excuse for a farmer, a man who couldn't afford the price of a belt so he kept his trousers up with a piece of rope. Nor could he sustain himself on his own wee patch of potatoes, possessing little more than an old donkey named Isadora which was fit only for glue and a fierce and malicious old bull called Cromwell. So he worked at odd jobs, Foley did, one of which was cutting turf on the MacGregor estate for his lordship. Standing at the bottom of the bog cutting his last sod of turf this particular day he looks down and there it lay, there beside his slean like it just fell from God's own pocket, this little piece of metal in the shape of a triangle. From God's pocket to Foley's own, and not a word was spoken.

A coin it was. An old coin. Foley called it a penny although there was no hint of a denomination on the thing at all. Only a picture of a man's head, a man wearing a crown, the words *Johannes Rex* beneath. On the other side, a cross of some sort.

The nature of the metal fell into dispute. "Sure it's gold," Foley said, "pure."

"Fool's gold then if it's in your pocket," says Gallagher, a regular. "It's copper. You can tell it when you smell it."

"Balls," Cleery says, "it's brass. They made everything out of brass back in them days." Cleery, your publican, was a man in the wrong line of work. He'd a wayward black mass of curls on his head going gray here and there at the edges, and lively, black eyes that were guarded. His tight smile was seldom seen, and never a how-do-you-do except to a paying customer with cash on the bar. A mysterious limp that seemed to come and go.

Lafferty himself didn't venture an opinion on the nature of the metal. He preferred watching men paint themselves into their own corners, then pointing out their predicament for them.

"What'll you give me for it?" says Foley to Cleery.

"A kick in the arse," replies Cleery. "A worthless piece of shite. And so's your penny."

That wasn't the last heard of the penny, however. A month ago doesn't Foley show up again with the thing. A dismal April evening it was, rendering the ambiance in Cleery's pub even more gloomy than normal – in the best of times the only illumination comes from whatever God or the village of Kilduff might send in through the one wide window in the front, that and the old string of Christmas lights nailed up on the beam over the bar and one bright lamp by the cash register. So it took a while for the great wide smile of Foley's face to come to light. A niece is after ringing him up from Dublin, he informs the congregation at Cleery's, telling him she's seen a coin identical to his penny up on eBay, the bid rising up like a rocket.

"Over a hundred thousand quid," says Foley. "An archeological treasure!"

"You're codding me!" says Cleery, old Foley commencing a jig. He carried his treasure to the bar, Cleery clearing a space and providing a cut of fine white linen to display it on, and everyone in the place tripping over one another to get a glimpse. "Johannes Rex," says Foley, as proud as if he'd deciphered the Rosetta Stone, "is Greek for King John." Word spreads, as word is wont to do, and it wasn't long before every soul in the village of Kilduff as well as a good number from without, was packed into the place to have a look. You'd have thought the Pope was in town, a joyous celebration, everyone toasting Foley's good fortune. Foley, of course, never reached into his own pocket. This is the ironic nature of wealth. For forty years your man comes in every evening friendless and ragged and stinking of muck with scarcely the price of a pint and no one to stand him the next. But as soon as he's rich, by God, he can't spend a bob of his own.

Foley was not averse to entitlement, however, figuring after sixty-odd years of hardship he'd earned it. Notwithstanding that his good fortune was in fact purloined from another man's property, a fact duly grumbled about by certain malcontents among the clientele, Foley felt entirely obliged to accommodate the largess of each and every citizen willing to spring for a pint or a whiskey. He was by nature a cautious man and as the stout kept flowing he buttoned his fortune securely in his pocket, wrapped up in the clean white linen.

Next morning when he awoke however, in the straw of his own shanty, beside his own donkey Isadora, and no idea how he got there, his fortune was nowhere to be found, for wasn't his pocket as empty as his heart.

The hue and cry was raised and the Gardaí set about the investigation. But if you were to number every person in the pub that night among your suspects, the number would come up to hundreds, and travelers had been seen in the village as well. Travelers are thieves and grifters, and though no one could swear any were actually seen within the confines of the pub, no one could swear they were not. Their caravans were long since departed. Suspicion naturally fell too upon Terrance Lafferty, misperceived by many as a ne'er-do-well with no visible means of support, the intricacies of the dog and pony tracks being incomprehensible to most men. They looked long and hard at John Cleery too, the publican, a man of cloudy disposition and dubious northern heritage whose affability was only for purchase and whose only redeeming virtue was the beauty of his wife, Mary. And Pat Gallagher, an old sot with a complexion like that of a boiled lobster, a man who drove the length and breadth of the island selling his pots and pans and any number of opportunities to consort with big-city hoodlums. Francis Byrnes as well, a bald and bitter man, a barber who stood on his feet the whole day through gritting his teeth in jealousy over the heads of hair he was cutting. But then not a one of the regular clientele was above suspicion, for merely frequenting a place such as Cleery's was grounds enough to cast shadows on the character of any man.

In the end, they blamed the travelers and closed the book. Old Foley gave in to despair. Friendless before, he was now all but shunned, seen as possessing enough bad luck to rub off on anyone misfortunate enough to give him the time of day. Only Lafferty stood him a pint or two when he could afford it, the Murphy's not the Guinness. One night Foley shows up dressed to the nines, in his tweed jacket, threadbare but clean, and a fine woolen tie. His best trousers held up by his rope. When asked the occasion he smiled and stood a round. Says he, "I'm after closing a deal," and he'd say no more on it, despite all the prompting and cajoling, the speculating rampant that he'd found his three-sided penny, in a different pocket from where he'd thought he'd stashed it, the old fool, or hidden elsewhere where he'd forgot in his state that night, or that indeed he'd discovered another. But wasn't he found next day in his shanty, beside his own donkey Isadora, Cromwell the killer bull suspiciously frisky in the field beyond. He was hanging from the rafter by his rope, Foley was, his trousers dangling loose about his feet.

And then it was Lafferty's turn. A couple of weeks after the end of old Seamus Foley, R.I.P., here's your man on a fine May evening, the evening's getting a grand stretch into summer, lying innocent and expended in bed, snug as a babe in the arms of the missus, halfway from dreaming. The birds were singing outside the window and a soft breeze was stirring the pretty curtain. Lafferty felt blessed. He should have suspected all along, from everything his thirty-eight years on the planet had taught him, that it was a ruse. An ambush. His da always told him when you feel as though you haven't a care in the world, look long and hard till you find one.

THE THREE-SIDED PENNY • 79

It started with the tears of the missus.

Now the missus in question, let's be clear from the start, was not his own. His own was called Peggy, though Lafferty sometimes called her Peggy-o, a charm she'd long since grown immune to. They had for the most part gone their separate ways, Lafferty and Peggy, Lafferty's separate way being toward Mary Cleery, the publican's wife, a deeply depressed woman long neglected and abused and entirely susceptible to the charms so egregiously spurned by Peggy-o. Mary was unaware of her own great beauty. So ignorant of it in fact that when it was repeatedly pointed out to her, she repeatedly accused the pointer of being a liar. This she did so often and so convincingly that Lafferty wondered sometimes if indeed he mightn't be lying, if indeed he might be the only man in existence able to see the angel in the woman, her fragile white skin you could see nearly through, her wispy black hair with a mind of its own, the beautiful sculpture of her ears she considered too big, her eyes so deep and green and fretful. The last of seven kids, she'd been born unwanted, married unwanted and no one in her life, up till Lafferty, ever wanted her. For when it came to wanting, Lafferty was your man.

When he heard the quiet sniffle, he says, "For God's sake. Are you crying?"

"I certainly am not," says Mary, even as a second sniffle betrayed her.

Lafferty held her close. "What is it? You're not worrying again over John, are you?" The beauty of loving a publican's wife, as Lafferty had frequently pointed out, was the regularity of his schedule, the certitude. The man was as good as chained to his bar, particularly during happy hour, the busiest time of the day, particularly a man such as John Cleery and his natural dread of missing so much as a penny that might come across it. Cleery's happy hours had grown to become even happier for Lafferty.

"Always," said Mary, squeezing his arm. "He'd kill me if ever he found out. Only I was thinking of old Foley just now."

"Foley? Jesus."

"Such a sad lonely ending. The poor man." In truth, Lafferty hadn't been all that mournful and in truth, the thought of the smell of the man, the stink of the muck, coming into this bed caused Lafferty to wrinkle his nose. Seeing it now through Mary's eyes, he felt bad for the old sot, though at the same time he suspected Mary was feeling as sad for herself as she was for Foley. Three of her own sisters had died young, and Mary was herself possessed of a mortal dread, scared to death of dying. Making her live for the day and ignore all the nonsense about meeting her maker had been one of Lafferty's long-term projects.

"Sad to be sure," Lafferty said. "But look at the life he was having. No joy in his days whatsoever. God bless him, but old Foley's probably a happier man dead." He wasn't sure if it was the right thing to say, but he was taken aback nonetheless by her reaction, how she stiffened and how he could feel her blood going cold. "I only—"

"Shhh!"

"What?"

"Terrance?" A scream of a whisper. "Did you lock the door?"

Perhaps the five most dreaded words in the language, particularly when you hadn't. "Mary?" came the call of John Cleery from his own living room not six steps away from the bedroom door and Lafferty hadn't the time to feel his own blood go cold before he was under the bed. The door comes open. Lafferty reaches for his trousers, shirt and shoes piled in a heap by the bed and pulls them under, thankful he hadn't had the decency to hang them up proper. "Mary?" says Cleery. "What are you doing in bed?"

"What are you doing at home?"

"I came home to get you in bed. Sure it's a sign from God. I'm after trying one of them wee blue pills only my timing was off and I can't mind my business. I'm walking around behind the bloody bar knocking over bottles and glasses with the front of my bloody pants."

"John—why on earth—?"

"To surprise you, love. To rekindle your fondness for the carnal."

"But I have an awful headache. That's why I'm in the bed."

"Take an aspirin then and spread your legs."

"No. Not now. My head's pounding with the pain."

"I have to hurry. I left Gallagher behind the bar who's undoubtedly robbing me blind."

"No, John. I said not now. I said I can't." The words a plea, not a demand.

"I amn't asking, love," says Cleery in a fine, gentle voice.

Mary resisted and Cleery insisted, his pants falling to the floor with a clatter, so loaded were the pockets with change and keys and such, so heavy the belt. The bed sank appallingly near to Lafferty's ear and it was oddly silent for the longest moment as he imagined the sound of torque, like the twisting of flesh, and then came Mary's sob and the bed commencing to move. A helpless rage consumed Lafferty, along with a frightful, claustrophobic dread of the bed crashing down to crush him, and his heart pounding to escape from his chest and he squeezed his eyes shut through the sweat and the tears and the sounds of Mary crying and Cleery grunting and the springs a-squeal and when he opened his eyes back up again he noticed the staples. He focused on them to block out the rest. The staples that held up the undercover of the springs had been removed in one corner, replaced by shiny new tacks. The handiwork was recent. The undercover itself was a stretch of opaque material through which he could barely make out the springs working, and even before he could form a speculation in his mind as to why the staples had been removed and replaced by tacks he saw the thing peeking out over the edge of one of the crossways slats near the corner, working closer with the movement of the bed, what appeared to be, the more he gazed upon it, an object of some sort all wrapped up in white linen. A three-sided object at that.

He didn't move from under the bed for the longest time after Cleery was gone, nor did Mary move from above it. They lay together there the two of them, inches and light years apart, never more together yet never more distant. Never a sound from neither. When the light had faded enough so their faces couldn't be seen, when the long shadows crawled across the bedroom floor, Lafferty crawled out among them and stood up and put on his clothes. Mary curled away in a tangle of covers. She could not have seen him reaching out but just at the instant he might have touched her, she uttered the one word, "Go."

And so go he did, as quiet as he could, as though if he could leave quiet enough it might be as though he'd never been there that day, out the back and through the little garden hidden from the neighbors, through his hole in the hedgerow and down the lane, his heart heavy with the weight of the sorrow, his pocket heavy with the weight of the three-sided penny.

Every afternoon at the holy hour Mary would bring Cleery his supper in the pub. This was the circumstance when Lafferty first laid his eyes upon her, Mary laboring with a heaping trayful of steaming eggs and rashers and tea and toast. When she looked over the tray and into Lafferty's face at the bar it was the unexpected intimacy of the look—at once sheepish and timid and hopeful and longing—that marked the sadness of the occasion four years later when Lafferty crawled out from under the bed and Mary was unable to look at him at all.

He never forgot that first glimpse. He'd followed his wife Peggy to Kilduff, not out of love of course, for the blush was long since gone from that rose, but for want of a roof over his head. He hadn't intended moving to the country at all. When she'd told him she wanted to leave the city, start anew, in a small cottage in a little village with a lower-paying nursing job at the local hospital, where perhaps she and Terrance could start anew as well, without all the gambling and drinking and unsavory sorts, and maybe even have the child she'd been longing to have, he told her he was staying in Dublin, by God. A vow he kept steadfastly until the first month's rent came due on the flat and he found himself embarrassingly short on cash and inconveniently out on the street. All on account of a nag called

DeValera's Chance, a nag presumably still running to this day and Lafferty swore he'd never bet on another republican.

Immediately following that first glimpse, Lafferty reached across the bar and snatched the tea towel from the tray, quickly and secretly stuffing the thing under his shirt. After that first look into his eyes she'd been scared, warned away by Cleery's sudden glance, and she'd never looked again in Lafferty's direction. Lafferty left by the front door as Mary was leaving by the rear. Caught up to her in the lane. "Excuse me missus," says he. "You're after dropping your towel back in there."

He held it toward her and she took it but Lafferty wouldn't let go. His fingers found hers in the folds. "I am?" says she, her face going red to white and back again, her eyes taking his in at length this time, leisurely, this time drinking their fill. It was the boldest she'd ever been or ever could be.

"Is it not your towel then?

"No. It isn't my towel."

"Of course it is. I seen it fall from this very tray."

"It is not my towel," said Mary. "In truth it belongs to my husband."

Years on, Lafferty was to look back on the happenings of that day, the day God handed him the three-sided penny, and, in his darker moments, wonder if he ever truly climbed out from beneath that bed. Some men might view cowering there where the one true love of your life was under assault against her will by a mindless brute of a man as shameful or cowardly. But the fact that the man in question was her legal husband carried a lot of weight in the mind of Lafferty. As did the fact that the man was a mass of muscle with a mean disposition. Lafferty had come to realize that had they been dogs instead of men when first they met, Cleery would have growled and bared his teeth at the first sniff and chased him away in a fury. But your man Lafferty was nothing if not resilient and was blessed with the gift of an optimistic nature. He had, in his thirty-eight years on the planet, done any number of things them less in the know might misinterpret as shameful, but he was always up to seeing through to the truer motive, the grander picture, the overall good. And so it was that day. Lafferty harbored dreams of wealth and escape, of him and Mary transported away, to America perhaps, or Canada, living the life of ease and plenty they both so richly deserved.

But those dreams were in a far harbor, with a sea of stormy details that first needed settling. Foremost was the immediate dread of what John Cleery would do when he discovered his ill-gotten gains were gone. For who could he blame but his Mary?

Lafferty went early to the pub next evening where Cleery greeted him with little more than a grunt and a nod. And though he seldom greeted him with more, wasn't it a bit ruder this night. And though in fact he seldom smiled at all, wasn't he a bit more dour. And though he was in fine shape, a man who'd done amateur boxing, a man once feared on the hurling pitch, wasn't he a bit more fearsome and primal in his physical demeanor. And though he never allowed an empty jar to linger on the top of his bar, didn't Byrnes have to call out three times for a refill, and didn't Cleery then yank the handle back with such a force it nearly came off in his hand. And didn't he look at Lafferty more frequent and sideways than ever he did before. After the place was filled with men and smoke and noise, Lafferty excused himself to step out and place his customary nightly bet with his imaginary bookmaker and sneaked up the lane, through his hole in the hedgerow and through the garden to tap on Mary's back door, and didn't the door never open. Wasn't it oddly locked. Weren't the lights all out and the house quiet as a churchyard.

Back at the pub an argument raged over the latest cease-fire to the north, Byrnes taking the military position that the whole thing was nothing more than a tactic by the 'RA, Gallagher insisting the motive was political and pure, a first step toward lasting peace, and your man Gerry Adams up for the Nobel. A third position being advanced by Cathal McGuire was that economics was the cause, the realization in London that the Celtic Tiger was leaving them to eat their dust. Cleery loved to foster arguments at his bar, as they were invariably fueled by stout, and he particularly encouraged three-sided disputes such as this one—not only encouraged them but jumped in himself to ensure their longevity—but in this particular engagement, Cleery was no more than a bystander. When he saw Lafferty return, he motioned him down to his end of the bar. "You're looking at a troubled man, Terrance," says he.

"You don't seem yourself tonight," allowed Lafferty.

"It's Mary." Cleery used the pause, and his black, guarded eyes, to study Lafferty's face. "She's after stealing from me, stealing something of rare and precious value."

"Your Mary? No."

"*My* Mary?"

"Mary," said Lafferty, "Mary Cleery, your wife. That is the Mary in question, is it not?"

Cleery nodded. "Little, innocent, light-fingered Mary."

"Can't picture it. Sure she could never steal nothing from nobody. Not Mary. Mary?" With a powerful effort, Lafferty made himself shut the hell up.

Cleery looked at the floor. Gave a rude swipe with his bar rag between himself and Lafferty, though there was nothing there, nothing that needed wiping away at all. "Stick around then, Terrance" says he. "I've something to show you, something you'll be anxious to see."

In the times before he convinced her that her own house was the safest refuge in the world for them to be, that he, Terrance Lafferty, could be an invisible man when the situation demanded, that no one would see him coming or going, but that everyone in the village might see them out and about, before then Lafferty and Mary used to meet wherever and whenever they could. In fine weather sometimes they met at the tumbled down ruins of a cottage up a lonely boreen overlooking a sweep of fields owned by MacGregor where the yellow of the gorse and the purple of the heather waved and nodded in the breezes. Sometimes they would walk and sometimes only nestle in the shelter of what was left of the thatch.

And afterwards hold one another and linger, sometimes talking, sometimes not, as though they had all the time in the world. "Let's go away," says Lafferty one day.

"The man's a dreamer," was all Mary said.

Clouds scudded across the sky, blocking the sun then freeing it, God flipping his light switch on and off. Down the valley when the light came on they spotted a man on a horse, May sunshine blinking off his fine, polished saddle. MacGregor, lord of the manor, out prancing about, appreciating his property, relishing his riches. Lafferty moved to put on his pants.

"What's to hold us here?"

"And what are we to live on Terrance? Bread-winning's not your strong suit."

"My good looks?"

Mary laughed. She touched his good looks, running her fingers in his curly brown locks with a gentle tug, then down his narrow chin to pinch the dimple. "John," she said. "John is what's to hold us here."

"He'd hire another cook."

"He'd hunt us down."

"He'd give it up sooner or later."

"You don't know the man. What's his stays his, and he considers me his. He'd let me go only over his own dead body."

"So we'll murder the bastard then."

Lafferty smiled his killer smile to reassure Mary he was joking, for he knew she held a soft spot in her heart for her husband, the gruffness of his shortcomings notwithstanding. She'd told Lafferty how John had saved her, taking her on as his live-in housekeeper and cook after her mam was dead and gone, her da old and tired and anxious to be rid of her. And how he'd married her then, after two years of watching her bend over the stove and the hearth and the fastidious makings of the bed, when finally he gave in to the urges. Urges, she admitted under cross-examination by Lafferty, she'd done nothing to discourage.

And so what does Mary do next but smile in return, a new kind of smile unfamiliar to Lafferty, a tight-lipped kind of smile dancing all the way up to her eyes. "And how would we do the murder then?" says she.

No sooner had he said he had something to show him than Cleery was called away down the bar to fill a brace of jars, leaving Lafferty with his boiling blood, his mind empty of everything but dread. *So soon, so soon!* He thought he'd have had more time, a day or two at the least. Though the urge to flee was scrambling for supremacy within him, he could only sit and watch the man at the end of the bar, watch him glance his way with solid regularity, as a welter of thoughts lashed at his mind, thoughts as to what Cleery might have done to Mary, thoughts as to what he was planning to do to him. When Cleery looked again, Lafferty's own gaze faltered, down to the rough-grained surface of the bar and the ashtray sitting there. It was made of hard black plastic in the shape of a triangle, like the eternal trinity, and Lafferty wrinkled his nose at the stink of burnt ashes and stale butts and at the memory of Sister Richard and her stout leather belt.

Cleery closed the pub up early. He doused the lamp by the cash register and pulled the plug on the string of lights above the bar, leaving it to dangle down like a hangman's rope. "Are ye right then, Terrance, are ye right?" he said with a grim smile and a clap of his hands as though they were two chums embarking on a pub crawl. *Right and ready*, the usual reply, Lafferty hadn't the slightest inclination to utter, and he soon found himself in a brittle state in Cleery's old yellow Peugeot clattering down the road in the general direction, he knew, of Foley's decrepit old place. Fighting the urge to take flight with every rising breath, sitting with all the composure he could muster in the passenger seat, watching the hedgerows and hillocks pass by in the long, lingering twilight.

Five minutes passed in silence till they were well up the countryside. Cleery said, "Do you recall, Terrance, your reply when I told you that my Mary was after stealing something from me, something of rare and precious value?"

Lafferty looked at him blankly.

Cleery said, "I told everyone the same bloody thing, everyone in the whole fucking place, one at a time. Do you know what they all said to me, Terrance? To a man, every one? They all said what the fuck did you ever possess of rare and precious value? Everyone, to a man. Everyone but you."

"Every man has his treasures." It sounded feeble coming out.

"What you said was Mary. Mary could never do this. Mary could never do that. So to my way of thinking then Terrance, you were the only man on the face of the earth who knew I had something in my possession of rare and precious value. And, I'm after learning, the only man on the face of the earth in a position to steal it from me."

"Where's Mary?"

Lafferty could see the flash of Cleery's glance even through the shadows of the thickening evening. He saw him relax perceptibly and shrug. "Mary. There's more to Mary than meets the eye, you know. Has she never told you about her sisters dying young and her mam and all that? Has she never told you about them?"

Lafferty nodded, not a noble nod. "She has."

"I don't believe she's after telling you the whole bloody story then, Terrance. How they died by their own hands, one at a time, years between, and all the rest."

"What have you done to her?"

Then Lafferty saw the oddest thing: the flash of Cleery's glance seemed to be running down his cheek. "What has who done to her, Terrance?" says he. "What has *who* done to her?"

Once upon a time Lafferty met her in the carpark of the Starry Plough, a ramshackle pub on a crossroads a few miles up from the village. Rode his bike through a spitting rain to meet her there. When he climbed into the car the heavens parted and the rain came down in buckets and they were able to play all their games there in the car seat with no fear of any passersby passing by. Afterwards they lingered, watching the rain pound the bonnet of the car, Cleery's old yellow Peugeot. "We could drown him," says Mary.

The woman was susceptible to the power of suggestion. Once before a roaring fire she suggested they could roast him. How to dispose of her husband had become their own private parlor game, which Lafferty encouraged for it seemed to amuse her, to put her to rights when she was feeling down. A harmless enough outlet for a powerless person was how Lafferty viewed it. "Electrocute him," said Lafferty. "Hand him the toaster as he's standing out in the rain."

Mary laughed and again they fell to silence, the rain showing no signs of giving it up, Lafferty's mind remaining on the topic of Cleery. He was always with them. They were never alone, it was always the three of them, and Lafferty could only appreciate the fine irony of God's scheme, how a man who only sold him his drink, like a thousand men before, could end up such a force in his life, unbeknownst even to himself. "We could set him up as a tout and have him shot," Mary said.

The north was far away. "Are they still doing that sort of thing nowadays?"

"They'll forever be doing that sort of thing."

Mary had mentioned Cleery's shadowy Belfast history before, something he'd never utter a word on, though once or twice she'd overheard a call and once she'd seen a letter. He'd told Mary the cause of his limp was arthritis, though there was a baffling scar that made her come to suspect a kneecapping. He told the boyos at the pub it was an old hurling injury.

Though now, sitting beside your man in the old Peugeot, Lafferty remembered watching him this very evening walking up and down behind his bar, prowling this way and that the entire evening, and no hint of a limp whatsoever.

Cleery pulled into Foley's, between the little cottage with the door ajar, windows smashed and splintered to the blackness within, and the shanty, where Foley'd kept his donkey and cart and such. Cleery nodded toward the shanty. "In there," he said.

She was sitting on the three-legged stool off which Foley'd hanged himself, her hands and ankles bound, loosely tethered to the stall. Her face was battered, dried blood flaked about her lips. Lafferty couldn't see into her bruised and swollen eyes as he untied her. Not a word did she utter.

Cleery stood in the doorway behind them, his old hurley stick having materialized in his hands. "The beauty of Foley's desolation," he said in a fine, gentle voice. "Nobody can hear the wailing or the crying or the calling out."

Lafferty held Mary's face in his hands, but she couldn't look up. She wouldn't look up. "My God, Mary. What has he done to you? What have I done?"

"No worse a thumping than my old man gave me on a regular basis," said Cleery. "Love taps, he used to call 'em." Lafferty heard the tap of the stick on the palm of the hand. "Now then, Terrance. The time has come to settle the penny."

Lafferty stood turning from Mary and in the same instant, in the same breath and motion, he gave in to his urges and ran. Running he was good at. Cleery swung the stick but came up empty, so fast and agile was Lafferty by him, the swoosh of the troubled air filling his ear for an instant before he was out the door. Cleery close on his heels in the near dark till Lafferty vaulted the fence to the field, bringing the chase to an uneasy halt.

"I can't believe you'd leave her here with me like this, Terrance. Have you no shame? I'll beat her brains out, I will. I'll finish the job."

"Then what?" called Lafferty. "Then you'd have no penny and nothing on me."

"And where'll you go to? Sure, I'll hunt you down and you know it."

There came a slobber and a snort and Lafferty could almost feel the hot breath. The hot breath of Cromwell the bull. Lafferty froze in his tracks near the fence. On the other side, Cleery came closer, smiling. With Foley's death they'd sold his old donkey Isadora for glue, but Cromwell, too fierce and mean and ferocious to handle, they'd left to his own devices. Lafferty looked over his shoulder, gingerly. Cromwell not twenty paces away.

"I'd say my stick looks more gentle than them horns," Cleery offered.

Foley had been a poor excuse for a farmer. The fence was poorly constructed, a single waist-high rail laid atop your standing crossways pieces where Lafferty put his hand. Cromwell pawed, snorted and charged and Lafferty lifted the rail as easy as lifting a pint and dropped it to the ground as Cleery, maybe ten paces beyond, watched, the puzzled expression overcoming his face still clear in the gathering gloom. Cromwell burst through, exultant in his freedom, enraged at the audacity of the big man with the big stick and the big voice, charging past the invisible Lafferty, closer and closer to the heels of the screaming Cleery who was running now, running off in a peculiar lop-sided gait, his limp having returned with a purpose. Cromwell thrust and raised his massive head, his left horn seemingly goosing your man Cleery who responded with an appropriate yodel of a wail as he was lifted high in the air and sent flying.

Scarcely on the ground again, Cromwell was at him with the right horn, inserting it into the groin of your man, flinging him up in the air again high. He landed with a dull thump. Cromwell was on him again and again, tossing him about like a child's doll, undressing him, shredding his shirt and trousers, thumping at him, jabbing him over and over. Finally, when Cleery was still, Cromwell snorted again and pawed, prancing off all in his glory, blood dripping on his horns, with never so much as a glance toward Lafferty. Nor toward Mary, standing against the doorway to the shanty, watching the life bleed out of her husband. Neither Mary nor Lafferty approached him, even as the moaning commenced. Lafferty could smell the blood of the man and the sweat of the bull. He went and held her and they stared at Cleery, little more now than a hump on the earth in the darkness, as the moans went weaker and lower and fewer.

"Jesus Christ I'm killed," says Cleery, gentle and soft. Right as rain he was.

How does it feel, watching a man being killed? For Lafferty, it was a great gushing eruption of relief and he was nearly giddy with the joy of it. He might have thought there'd be some compunction hidden somewhere within it, a bit of remorse, but he couldn't find a shred of the stuff anywhere. Though the joy was held in check by his worry over Mary, by his guilt over causing her pain. He wanted to hold her as long as he could till the hurt all went away.

For a time he did. Standing there, trying his best to surround her, his lips resting in her hair. Finally, she stirred. "I'll drive," was all she said.

Still, she hadn't looked at him, and look at him she didn't, her eyes following the light across the countryside back toward the village. Finally, she reached out for his hand. "God."

They crept into Mary's house in the darkness. In the loo he washed her wounds and dressed them and as he cared for her injured face, finally her eyes came around. The depth was back, but at the bottom all he saw was fear. "God, Terrance," she said. "What'll we do?"

Lafferty shrugged, trying to contain his mounting elation. His guilt was fast diminishing, as he was beginning to see through to the greater good, the grander scheme of things once more. "They'll find him, a horrible accident, and they'll hunt down the bull with the blood on his horns and they'll shoot him. I'll leave Peggy, delighting her no end to be rid of me. That'll leave us, the two of us, together. We'll go away, to America maybe. To anywhere we like. We'll buy a house, a wee place in the country. We'll live like kings, we will."

Now at last a light, a spark in her eyes Lafferty read as joy trying to ignite. "You have the penny then?"

"Aye. Right here in my pocket."

"Your *pocket*? You're joking me."

"Not at all."

He fished the thing out, unwrapped it, and they examined it sitting there on the white cloth in the palm of his hand. Staring at it so as to confirm it was real. "The genuine article," says Lafferty. "Sure look at the craftsmanship." In truth he could see nothing special about the craftsmanship, but knowledge of the preciousness of the antiquity lent it plenty. King John seemed to be smiling a little knowing smile and all the three sides sparkling.

In the bedroom, he placed the penny atop the dresser, on the white cloth, on display, where they could look over at it in the dim light and feel the comfort of it as they fell asleep together. Fell asleep, together, in the bed, for the night, and nothing at all to hide from. Nothing at all to chase them. He held her for all he was worth, cuddling her back, his hand over the heart in her chest to feel it growing calm.

After a while Lafferty says, "We could gore him to death with a mad, raging bull."

It was quiet for a second, till Mary giggled. Then they laughed. Only a chuckle at first, but the joke sank deeper and they laughed harder, and the harder they laughed, the more they fed off one another, till they had to roll apart and sit up and clasp their knees to laugh. And then he heard the sobs and looked and saw her laughing and weeping all at once, at the same time, mixed together like smoke and air, the puzzling likes of which he'd never before witnessed, tears and peals of glee.

When they were spent Mary leaned over to kiss him, though she winced a bit from the split of her lip and Lafferty wiped the tears from her cheeks and Mary smiled and the cuddling commenced anew. Off they drifted toward sleep, Lafferty holding Mary safe and sound in the confines of his own arms and himself feeling blessed. He never considered a ruse. Never entertained the possibility of an ambush. Nowhere to be found were the words of his da—when you feel as though you haven't a care in the world, look long and hard till you find one.

When he woke up with the first light wasn't the bed as empty as his heart? Wasn't the dresser top as bare and desolate?

Lafferty waited, hoping she'd hid the penny for safety and stepped up the street to Connor's for a box of milk and a loaf of bread for their breakfast. He waited and waited till he knew he was waiting for nothing and then he waited some more.

Finally, he slipped out the back through the garden and the hedgerow and up the lane to Peggy's to fetch his bike. Peggy would be at work. He peddled past Byrnes' Barber Shop without looking in, ignoring the hails and calls of the neighbors, paying no mind to crimson Gallagher waving by the darkened window of Cleery's public house. On and on he peddled through the countryside toward Foley's.

Not knowing which he feared more, that he would find her or that he would not. He hoped in the end, as he climbed the final hillock toward Foley's, that he wouldn't, that he'd never lay his eyes on her again, that she'd taken the penny and sold it and run away for good, to somewhere where she might be happy, but as he came over the hill he saw the yellow Peugeot parked just where Cleery had parked it the night before. And he found her there, where he knew he would, in the shanty, the three-legged stool tipped over beneath her feet.

He sat on the ground outside the door, leaning against the wall, his back to his Mary. Staring at the heap that was the mortal remains of Cleery just beyond the car, trying to pretend he couldn't hear the sound of the flies buzzing there, buzzing too behind the door. The sun was in his eyes, so he closed them and listened to the heat on his face. Saw the steam rising up from her morning cup of tea, saw her bringing it to her face to sip, the way her eyes closed, the way her lips kissed the rim so soft.

Lafferty resolved not to search for the penny. The least he could do. It would be an insult to Mary, to her memory, a blaspheme, a sacrilege. And wasn't it inconsequential after all in light of the love and the loss, the life and the death, wasn't it nothing but a spit in the ocean. Wasn't it a source of evil. He held firm for the longest time.

But then he began to see through to the higher plan, the grander good, the overall scheme of things, and he searched and searched, but to no avail. Of course, wasn't the bloody thing never to be seen again at all, not in this lifetime.

A Penny Saved

The dead cat didn't help. The dead cat couldn't be a good sign. Lafferty ran over the poor creature in the rain driving Cleery's rattletrap of a car back into the village from the tumbled-down ruins of the cottage where he and Mary used to go to play their games.

It was the last place he'd gone to search for the penny. He'd looked everywhere and come up empty, come up to the realization that the penny was not to be found. He was making his way back over all the bumps and ruts and holes in the little lane when the sky opened up and the bottom fell out. And then the flash of something moving quick followed by the thump that was bigger than all the others in the legion of thumps.

He got out of the car in the lashing rain. It was loud, the thrum and rumble of it causing a turmoil in his ears, slapping the wee leaves in the hedgerow senseless, taking great leaps and bounds off the bonnet of the car. He was soaked in an instant, the raindrops like cruel little blows. Behind the car in the mud lay the cat, dead indeed. Ran right out the bloody hell in front of him.

A suicide maybe? Another?

He stood there looking down at the thing. Couldn't bring himself to look away. Why would a man stand in the pouring rain looking down at a dead cat? The cat put him in mind of something. Of someone. The scrawny, balding, mangy fur, the bulging, hollow eyes.

Tommy Hogan was who.

Sure, the likeness was uncanny. Wasn't Hogan every bit as skinny and scrawny and bald and hollow-eyed. He'd known him since they were wee gurriers growing up in Dublin, best mates till Lafferty's discovery of the charms of the feminine gender had pried them apart. And why would he think of him now, standing there in the lashing rain looking down at the dead cat, the likeness notwithstanding. To be sure, he must have laid his eyes on plenty of scrawny, mangy, bug-eyed cats in years gone by and never thought a thing of it, never thought of the oul bowsie Hogan at all. A nostalgia thing?

Or something more? An omen of some sort?

Back into the car dripping. What had brought him to this moment, sitting sopping wet in a dead man's car, obsessing like a lunatic over the fate of an ancient penny?

It was months ago he'd followed his erstwhile wife, Peggy, to the little village of Kilduff, deep in the heart of County Nowhere, for want of keeping her roof over his head. There, he'd begun to frequent Cleery's pub; Cleery was a gruff one, a hard one, a man of mysterious history and a scar and a limp to prove it. There it was too he'd fallen for Cleery's neglected and abused wife, Mary, a shy, clumsy angel of a woman possessing a fragile-skinned beauty that Lafferty often felt he was the only one could see.

On an evening not two months back doesn't an old farmer named Foley, a regular, come strolling into Cleery's to change the world. He'd unearthed an ancient, three-sided coin while out digging turf—an archeological treasure, it turned out to be, worth a hundred thousand quid, maybe more. The long and the short of it: Cleery stole the three-sided penny—no hint of a denomination on the thing at all, and so Foley called it a penny—and didn't your man Lafferty, interrupted in a moment of intimacy with Mary, steal it back again.

But Cleery, nobody's fool, sussed it out.

The confrontation took place at Foley's derelict farm, only a week or two after Foley, the old scut, had taken his own life in despair over losing the penny. Cleery had thought to hold

Mary under threat of abuse to force Lafferty to hand the penny over, but Lafferty turned the tables in a happenstance of rare serendipity, freeing Foley's malicious old bull, Cromwell, who promptly dispatched Cleery at the end of his bloody horns.

Weren't he and Mary free as wild sparrows then, free to do as they pleased, and the wealth of the penny to lift them, ease them over the trauma of the violent, albeit just, decease of her husband. But alas. Didn't the happy ending turn sideways.

When Lafferty woke next morning with the first light the bed beside him was empty as his heart. Mary was gone. And the three-sided penny gone with her. Lafferty waited, hoping she'd hid the penny for safe-keeping and stepped out to Connor's for a box of milk and a loaf of bread for their breakfast. He waited and waited till he knew he was waiting in vain and then he waited still. Finally slipped out the back to fetch his bike. Peddled through the village, ignoring the hails and calls of the neighbors, peddling on and on through the countryside toward Foley's.

His heart dipped as he came over the hill to see Mary's own bike by the yellow Peugeot where Cleery had parked it the night before.

And he found her there, where he knew he would, in the shanty where old Foley had hanged himself, Foley's three-legged stool tipped over beneath her feet.

He sat on the ground outside the door, leaning against the wall, his back to his Mary, trying to pretend he couldn't hear the sound of the flies buzzing behind the door. The sun was in his eyes, so he closed them and soaked in the heat on his face. Saw the steam rising up from her morning cup of tea, saw her bringing it to her face to sip, the way her eyes closed, the way her lips kissed the rim so soft.

He resolved not to search for the penny. The least he could do. It would be an insult to Mary, to her memory; had she not disposed of the penny as best she saw fit? Her last will and testament. And wasn't it inconsequential after all in light of the love and the loss, the life and the death, wasn't it nothing but a spit in the ocean?

He held firm for maybe an hour.

Then he began to see through to the higher plan, the grander good, the enormous worth of the penny, and he searched and he searched and he searched. But nothing was all he found.

Up to his room above Cleery's pub he traipsed, leaving puddles up the narrow stairway, up to the room he'd had to let when Peggy had tossed him out on his ear yet again. Wouldn't the neighbors and the regulars already be wondering where the bloody hell was Cleery, why wasn't the bloody place open. And his wife Mary gone as well, as soon they'd discover. And Cleery's car, of course, his rusty old yellow Peugeot nowhere to be seen—for Lafferty'd parked the thing hidden in a gully behind the hedges out at the edge of the village.

It was only midday, but the darkest of days. He didn't turn on the little lamp by the bed, though he did raise up the torn and dirty shade. Rain hammering at the window. There was a wee wooden chair beside the chipped chest of drawers—them and the bed and the little stand beside it took up nearly the whole of the room—and he sat in the gloom and shadows to drip dry.

He'd made the bed before he'd left, and he could not bring himself to muss it up. Nor to get it wet. He'd made the bloody thing yesterday (as he never had before), tucked the threadbare blue blanket about it neatly, smoothed it out, patted down and fluffed up the pillow invitingly under the headboard. All for Mary. All in the chance he might lure her up.

She'd hinted often she'd love to see the wee room where he passed the minutes of his life without her. But that had never happened, and now it never would, and now the bed had taken on the hushed wonder of a shrine, as if it would somehow be an insult to the memory of her to wallow about on it, to leave it sullied. So the wee chair would have to do. He stared at the bed, then at the rattling smear of the rain on the window, then back to the peaceful bed. Brought to his mind the softness of a coffin awaiting the corpse.

What now? Walking away was not an option. Since his early noble notions, he'd come to realize that no force in the known world could bring him to give up on an archeological treasure of inestimable worth. But where else could he search? His mind was a raging blank. He'd looked everywhere he could think of that Mary might think of.

He gave in to a shiver. Damp and clammy clothing turning cold, clinging over him like dead skin. And to think he'd thought, with the penny in hand, his troubles were behind him, all of his and Mary's troubles behind them.

He was at a bloody dead end in his cold, dead skin. What he needed was something to stir the pot. He needed a bloody pint. He needed warmth and noise, a chinwag, a bit of craic. He needed a sounding board, fresh eyes and ears, an oul mate. The dead cat came to mind.

He headed out to the Pig & Whistle on the outskirts of the village—Cleery's, his own local, having removed itself from consideration—to call his oul mate, Tommy Hogan.

By the time Hogan arrived, the Pig & Whistle was thick with smoke and people and loud music from the ancient juke box at the back of the bar spewing American country tunes. He saw more than one of Cleery's erstwhile patrons at the bar, pretending he didn't.

Hogan arrived. Lafferty watched him pause, bewildered, in the doorway—bewildered was how he remembered him best—as he looked about the room trying to spot Lafferty. When spot him he did, a look of bald joy came over his face, and Lafferty couldn't recall the last time he'd caused joy in any beholder; sure, Peggy's was long since dead, and Mary'd been always afraid of the joy. Afraid it might turn on her and attack.

He made his way over, Hogan did, five years older, but still skinny and scrawny and balding with only wandering wisps of hair, too flimsy to have even earned a color. And his big wide pools of eyes the color of stones in the rain, full of wonder—not the marveling, would-you-ever-look-at-that kind of wonder, but the what-the-hell-just-happened kind of wonder.

After the hugs and backslaps, Hogan says, "Jesus, Terrance, I can't believe you're standing here. The middle of nowhere—do you remember? The middle of nowhere you said you'd never step foot in if your bollocks depended on it."

"I'm nothing if not flexible, Tommy. Green acres is the place for me."

"And how's Peggy?"

"Don't ask."

Hogan needed no further encouragement to not ask. "Can we get a bloody drink around here?" he said. "My poor stomach thinks my throat has been cut."

Pints of stout, black and foamy and scarcely touched before Hogan got to the point—to lure him from the city out to Kilduff, over an hour away, Lafferty'd had to bait the hook well. "So tell me more," Hogan said, "about this missing penny yoke."

Lafferty told him more. Told him about Cleery the publican and Mary his wife. He had to fairly shout it, such was the clamor and clatter of the merriment about them, two old farmers having produced tin whistles, another a bodhrán, and a room full of singers joining in, and the session well underway, ragged and lively—there was no fear in Lafferty's heart of the wrong ears overhearing.

He told Hogan about the three-sided penny. He told him about the worth of it. Told him about the well-deserved murder of Cleery by the mad bull Cromwell, and about the tragic ending of poor Mary. And the tragic vanishing of the penny.

Hogan's eyebrows hoisted themselves high up his brow early into Lafferty's story, and they never came down again. "By God, green acres *is* the place to be," says he.

Hogan ordered fresh pints. The news of the penny would take some time to digest. They chatted amid the clamor of the crowded pub, for after all, wasn't there five years of non-penny news to catch up on, the antics of Hogan's beleaguered wife Bridie, his job selling pots and pans up and down the east coast of Ireland, and wasn't there an entire roster of memories from their school days in Dublin to revisit. But didn't every venture into the years past always lead roundabout back to the penny. And what could be done. For Lafferty was far from finished when it came to lamenting the penny, and talking about the penny, and wondering where on God's green earth the penny could be.

But there was only so much could be said about the bloody thing. Hogan asked him had he searched here, had he searched there, and Lafferty said yes to here, yes to there, yes to every bloody where. Would it do any good to go back and search it all over again? Sure, couldn't he have missed it first time through in all the fuss and hurry, the deaths so fresh, the mind so gobsmacked, such a wee thing it was after all. Maybe, allowed Lafferty, though the time was short. How much of a grace period they might still have, he couldn't be certain. Sure, maybe Cleery and Mary had already been found out at Foley's decrepit place.

Hogan said, "We should look up the brother superior—what was his name, Brother Francis, Brother Joseph, I lost track of 'em by now—we should have him do the search. Sure, he'd ferret out the bloody thing in a hurry, wouldn't he?"

Lafferty knew the memory Hogan was referring to. "The time Kevin nicked the medallion from the new boy," he said, "sure, they turned the whole school inside out, looking for it. Brother Joseph, Brother Francis, Brother Needledick, whatever the feck his name was, at the head of the pack."

"Hah! Do you remember the snout on the man, a yard long it was, and the bristles of a pig sticking out of it." The pair slapping at the bar, laughing.

"Like a bloody root-hog he was. Sniffing out truffles and medallions."

"But by God, they never found it." Hogan laughed.

"No, by God, they didn't."

Hogan wiped away a tear. "Same with your fecking penny, no doubt. That bloody thing'll probably never be found either, sure it won't."

Lafferty frowned and sniffed at a sudden thought. "Do you remember why they never found the bloody medallion, yeah?"

"Aye, I do indeed," Hogan said. "I nearly choked in my hole laughing at the sight of Kevin choking, swallowing that bloody wee thing. With the brothers closing in on him like a pack of wild dingoes."

This was the moment their dazed and bleary eyes locked in horrible revelation.

The bloody thing would just have to stay lost. If Mary'd swallowed it, if indeed she'd hidden it inside her, it might just as well be buried on the far side of the moon under the Great Wall of China in the heart of a raging volcano seven leagues under the sea. If she'd swallowed it, that would be rock solid, lead pipe cinch confirmation of her last wish, that she indeed wanted it never to be found. Wanted to take it with her.

On the other hand, wasn't that at odds with what he'd been led to believe all his years on the planet: You can't take it with you.

At any rate, the price was too high, the blasphemy too big, the desecration of her.

At any rate, there was no way he could do what would have to be done, even with all the justification in the whole bloody world. There was no way he could take a knife to her, a woman he'd loved. A woman who, he thought, had loved him back as well. A woman who, if it wasn't for the bad luck in her sad little life, would have had none of the stuff at all.

It was settled then.

When the Pig & Whistle finally shuttered, Lafferty took Hogan back to Cleery's. Not to his room above the pub, a place altogether too dry and too close for comfort, but in through the back of the bar using Mary's spare key that he'd borrowed from Mary, though Mary and Cleery never knew of the borrowing. There they drank and talked the night away in the dimness, not lighting a single light, relying on the little that the village of Kilduff sent in through the front window.

What were the odds she'd been so desperate as to swallow the penny?

What if she hadn't hidden the bloody thing at all?

What if it had only fallen out of her pocket? Somewhere. But where?

Finally, nearly dawn, they fell into restless slumber.

When they got to old Foley's place next day to search anew, they were too late. The night before, as they were whiling away the hours at the Pig & Whistle, hadn't Cromwell the mad, murderous bull come strolling down the main street of Kilduff, lord of the manor, poking his fierce and horny head into whatever doorway he deemed needed poking into, wreaking havoc on the normally calm custom and commerce of the village. The origin of the beast having soon been ascertained, Cromwell was shot and the guards dispatched out to Foley's.

News of a scale this grand would take days to simmer down. Lafferty and Hogan sat at the corner of the crowded bar in the Pig & Whistle that evening trying to be invisible, as the smoke rose up and the rumble and jangle raged around them.

Kilduff's own Romeo and Juliet was all the talk: Mary, having witnessed the love of her life—Cleery—being gored to death by a rampaging bull of horrific proportions, gored to death no doubt in the act of laying down his own life in defense of his damsel, was tragically moved to do her own self in, at the end of a rope. From the very same rafter of the very same shanty where, only recently, another tragic ending had taken place, oul Foley's own.

Why were they at Foley's in the first place, Cleery and Mary?

The penny didn't pass without mention. The three-sided penny was well and widely known. Had Cleery gone there, taken his missus with him, thinking they might turn it up? Was it his searching and rooting about that had driven the mad bull to exact his fierce and deadly revenge?

"Where would she be waked, do you suppose?" Hogan wondered.

"Why? What difference would it make? Why would we care? If she swallowed it, she swallowed it, end of story."

"I was only thinking you might want to pay your respects."

"Oh, aye," said Lafferty. "To be sure."

Across the room, beneath a plastic Powers clock in the cloud of neon smoke, a red-headed lad and a black-haired girl in striped pants and puffy shirts were handing out flowers, yellow posies of some class or other (Lafferty never knew which posies were which) to whoever in the place might fancy one. In memoriam, Lafferty supposed. He raised his hand, and the girl spotted him. Made her way through the milling throng, her handful of posies thrust out before her like the prow of a ship.

"Would you like a flower?" She was a pretty girl, though her eyebrows were thick as a hedge.

"I'd love one, Love."

"Isn't it awful, then. Did you know 'em well at all?"

"Aye. Well, her I did. Where is it she's being waked at?"

"What I heard is she's no family they know of. They're trying to find a next of kin." Then she looked at him sideways. "Are you kin to her? Do you know her kin?"

"No, no, not at all. Do you know where she's keeping the night?"

"I would think at Rossa's, if the cops have done with her. It's the only mortuary about."

"I would think."

"Would you like a flower?" she said, sticking one under Hogan's nose.

"It's Bird's-foot is what it is," Hogan said.

"What is?" Lafferty said.

"The flower," said Hogan. "Bird's-foot-trefoil, to be exact. Common."

"Jesus, Tommy. What are you doing knowing that?"

The girl said, "She's part of the flower now, Mary is. She's no longer in her body, her body is only an empty vessel, a shell that she's shed, and now she's part of everything that's glorious and beautiful in the world. The flowers and the sunshine and rainbows. She's all the colors of the rainbow."

"I couldn't dispute it," Lafferty said.

"That's a tall order," said Hogan.

The girl's smile faltered for only a moment, and she withdrew the flower that Hogan hadn't touched. "Peace," she said.

"Of what?" said Hogan, confounded.

"Thanks for the posy, Love," Lafferty said as the girl shied away.

"Bird's-foot," corrected Hogan.

"Are you going in with me, or are you going to wait out here?" Lafferty said. They were in Hogan's Austin, in a row of cars parked for the night in front of the greengrocer and newsagent's shops, both long since shuttered for the night.

Across the street at the corner of the little lane sat Rossa's Funeral Home, a plain, decent-sized house, puffed up by a grand cornice along the roofline in front. A plum tree in the yard. Lafferty'd never have known the kind of tree it was, but Hogan had kindly pointed it out for him. Rossa had turned out the lights, locked up the door and walked away down the lane an hour ago, an hour after last call at the Pig & Whistle. The front seat of the wee Austin was getting smaller.

"So, you're going in, then? You made up your mind then have you?"

"I don't know," said Lafferty.

"Then what are you asking me for?"

"I was asking in case I do decide to go in are you coming with me or you going to wait out here in the bloody car?"

"I'll cross that bridge when I get to it," Hogan said. Reaching into the sack in the backseat, he pulled out two more bottles of stout. "Here. For courage."

"It's not courage I need."

"Then what is it you do need, Terrance?"

What was it he needed indeed? He needed to know it was right. He was not a devout man, not a spiritual man, he seldom made Mass of a Sunday, but he needed to know it was not a mortal sin. He needed justification. A clear conscience. He needed to know how it was at all possible in this world for a man to take a sharp instrument in his own hand, the same hand that had caressed and comforted the same woman, a woman he'd loved, and insert that sharp instrument into the body of her. And then to stick in his hand and grope all about.

All right then, he needed fecking courage. "I don't know what I need."

"You couldn't take the knife to her. Sure you couldn't anyway."

"Could you?"

"Me?" Lafferty felt Hogan's wide and beggaring eyes wheel around on him in the dim light from the streetlamp. "Where would a question like that even come from?"

Good question. He remembered watching the heels of his mate fleeing the scene, himself not two steps behind, to avoid battle whenever any scuffles, tussles or kerfuffles had threatened to break out and upset the harmony of their youthful existence. He remembered Hogan nearly fainting at the sight of blood from the gash on the noggin of the lad who'd fallen off the monkey bars at the playground. Lafferty looked over at his mate, who was staring bug-eyed at Rossa's again, as if the building itself might break loose of its foundation and try to tip-toe off.

At the end of the day, no—he couldn't picture Hogan wielding the knife.

Could he picture himself?

Hogan looked over. Lafferty could almost see the light bulb light up over his head. "Maybe it's only just under her tongue," says he. "I wonder did they look there."

Lafferty said nothing, staring at Rossa's. Wagged his head.

He told Hogan to wait in the car. He wanted no one there to witness his failure of courage if he was unable to bring himself to do it, nor did he want any witness if he could, any witness at all to the mortal desecration. He told himself Mary would understand, that if he could talk to her, he could talk sense into her, persuade her it was for the grander good. He told himself she'd only just been out of her head with the shock and the grief and the depression. Told himself what a fine tombstone, bollocks, a monument, a bloody fecking mausoleum, he would buy for her grave so she'd never be forgot.

He felt calm enough passing under the plum tree in the faint reaches of the streetlamp, dew licking his brogans. On the streets of Dublin he'd learned invisibility. Other skills he'd picked up there as well, and the soft tinkling of breaking glass scarcely made a dent on the night, and the wee glow from the skull-and-bones nightlight—Rossa's savage sense of humor, he supposed—in the hallway was plenty enough to skulk by, to the stairs, down to the cellar mostly by touch alone, the steps groaning mournfully, where another soft light of a blue hue on the wall showed the empty coffins, lids yawning open and hungry. Two lumpy gurneys covered with sheets. He lifted the sheet over the lesser lumps. On a nearby counter Rossa's instruments lay gleaming and grinning.

She's no longer in her body. Her body is an empty vessel. A shell she's shed. No longer in her body, only an empty vessel, a shell she's shed. No longer in her body an empty vessel a shell. A hundred thousand quid. Empty vessel, a shell she's shed. A hundred thousand quid. A shell… a hundred thousand…a shell…a hundred thousand quid…

A different man came out of Rossa's than the man who'd walked in before. A space man in a space suit walking across the dark side of the moon, he made his way slowly across the lawn, beneath the pear tree, across the lane, up to Hogan's car. He leaned against the door of the Austin for the longest time, head hung down. Hogan stared up at him with the question in the wide pools of his eyes. Lafferty only shook his head.

"Pity," says Hogan.

Lafferty slumped into the car. "The awfulest thing," was his only murmur.

They headed up to his room above Cleery's pub, Lafferty quiet as a spider. He pulled the shade before turning on the wee lamp on the stand by the bed, scarcely light enough to fill the little room. He sat roughly on the side of the bed, the bed he'd made up for Mary, her shrine, not caring now in the least if he despoiled it.

Hogan sat on the tipsy chair by the chipped chest of drawers to wait. He hadn't a baldy notion what he was waiting for.

She'd wanted to see his room, Mary had, but had never got to, and Lafferty, now, a different man than before, clenched at the edge of the bed, his blood beginning to stir and rise again, volcano-like. Hogan sitting patient, a patient waiting for the bad diagnosis.

"Feck her," Lafferty said.

"What?" said Hogan. "Who? Mary?"

"The bitch."

"Bitch? I thought you were sweet on her. All this yabbering about love. I thought you could barely stand to…to, you know, do what you did. Do what you had to do."

"That was then. To think I loved the bitch. Well, there's no way she could have loved me, or she'd never have stole the thing from me. From us. It was my penny, I had it in my possession,

I offered it to her, to share it with her, bollocks, to share a life with her, and what does she do? She steals the fecking thing. She takes it. I don't give a fecking toss what state of mind she was in, there's no bloody excuse. I'm *glad* I took the fecking knife to her."

Hogan, the bug eyes of him desperate to help. "Did you look under her tongue?"

Lafferty stamped his foot and gave out with an animal howl, and picked up the pillow to hurl at his mate. There, tucked tidily under the pillow, lay an object all wrapped in white linen.

A three-sided object at that.

Lafferty's Ghost

In the bed of another woman was by no means unfamiliar ground for your man, but this time there was a twist. This time, he could reasonably argue, it was in the interest of the missus, not merely his own (not that herself would be much persuaded). This time, in the service of their marriage, he'd proved beyond a doubt that their counselor could not be trusted, the same counselor she'd demanded that he accompany her to see if he harbored any hope at all of keeping her roof above his head. He'd demonstrated conclusively that all the rubbish their counselor had been spouting about trust, communication, sharing, that indeed her *Ten Golden Rules for a Great Marriage,* were nothing but a load of fluff and dander. By Lafferty's way of reasoning, any marriage counselor worth her salt must be honest, trustworthy, and above reproach, attributes he defined to include being above the temptations of the flesh, particularly when the flesh in question is hanging from the bones of one of her very own clients. And so, he'd put her to the test. And so, she'd failed utterly, the proof beside him here in her bed. Of course, how to frame the proof for Peggy, the missus, without jeopardizing his roof or his life and limb was the challenge with which he was now faced, even in the warm throes of post-coital bliss, those of himself and the counselor in question, Katherine Flanagan, LPC, IACP.

"I suppose I'll regret this," she said, though something in her tone suggested to Lafferty amusement more than regret.

Lafferty said, "I get that a lot," and, sure enough, she laughed. A handsome lady she was, a lady who, unlike most of them Lafferty had known, seemed to become less exposed and vulnerable the more naked she became. She was plenty naked now. She'd a polished smile like that of a shark, and eyebrows painted like breaking waves. The short part, like a scar at the front of her slippery black hair, showed a root or two of indeterminate color.

"Don't be so hard on yourself," she said. "That's my job."

"And I've noticed, Mrs. Flanagan, you're bloody good at your job."

"Please. Katie."

"Katie? I'd have thought Katherine."

"Katherine, Kathy, Kate, Katie-bar-the-door. Take your pick. I *love* the variety."

"I think Katherine the Great, given the grandeur of your position."

"And which position did you find most grand?"

Lafferty considered. "The one hanging by your heels from the trapeze, I think."

"Sure, the blood rushing to your head enhances the sensuality."

"*Keep Romance Alive*. Is that not one of your ten golden rules?"

"It is. And now you've had your lesson, you and Peggy can find your own trapeze, and I'll claim another victory in the war against the disintegration of the traditional marriage as we know it."

Lafferty ran a finger down her ribs like a keyboard. "What's this?" He'd encountered a scar scarcely visible to the naked eye, a gouge on her side in the shape of a crescent.

"That," she said. "That's my emergency smile. I take it with me wherever I go."

"How did it happen?"

"This skinny fella was asking me too many questions one day, and I had to bump him off."

A moment of musing on Lafferty's part. "And how did that result in a scar?"

"Who said it did?" She smiled, eyes simmering.

"I see. We'll just settle for emergency smile. A scar by any other name. Curiosity is overrated at any rate."

"There's a good lad," she said, rewarding your man with a squeeze and a snuggle, though he found the bones of her a bit sharper now than they had been before. Lafferty allowed his God-given tendency to retreat in the face of confrontation, of any class of unpleasantness, to shut his gob for him, though a bit of the curiosity lingered still. The mysterious Katherine Flanagan, whatever else she was, was evidently good at her job all right, her propensity for the odd lapse in judgment notwithstanding. For that, he had to allow her a bit of leeway, he supposed, given the nature of his own charms, compounded by the dimple in the middle of his own chin. Her success was apparent in the opulence of the place, the breadth and depth of the bed, the silkiness of the sheets, the shine of mahogany everywhere, the grand sweep of crimson drapery covering the wall of windows overlooking the village of Kilduff down below. The office in the front of the house was furnished in teak and brass and warm, soothing hues. And the bathroom, when he'd gone there earlier, had been like nothing he'd ever encountered before. He'd been almost reluctant, in fact, to defile the place by doing his business there.

It was back to the bathroom his daydreams took him when the woman slipped into a dreamy quiet and he thought he heard a wee snore. For didn't he have to pee again. And he thought about Peggy, his own wife and her niggardly ways, particularly with the hot water, which she seemed to think required the burning of banknotes to heat. And he imagined luxuriating in steamy water and bubbles in the sunken tub of the blue-tiled room just beyond the polished doorknob there across the poshness of carpet. Decadent and delicious to be sure, the perfect complement to a day such as this.

As Katie dozed, he slipped away for his pee, the bed so fine and firm there was never a squeak to betray him, the carpet soaking up his footsteps like a sandy beach. And doesn't your man himself succumb to temptations of the flesh, though of a different class altogether, soon finding himself in the tub, up to his chin in hot water. Snug as a fist in a mitten. The flow of the warm water burbling in his ear, the piquant scent of the bubbles tickling his nose, he allowed himself to surrender to the comfort, having earned it, having performed so admirably in the service of his wife and their marriage, and on the other hand, so splendidly in the service of Katherine Flanagan, LPC, IACP, a widow with needs and wants of her own. Whose other hand, after a while, he heard on the knob of the door, whose footstep on the blue of the tiles, in perfect harmony with his dream of a balmy beach in the south of Spain, a dark-skinned girl in a white kimono, and a pitcher of green margaritas. Warm washcloth soothing his eyes, he showed her the dimple in his chin, which he lifted for a smile. "Come join me, love, the water's grand."

But Katie only shuffled her feet.

"Plenty of room in here for a pair," he said, his invitation enhanced and made all the more sincere by the stirring of his nether part, the blood flowing again, the buoyancy of the lovely hot water lifting him up, the thoughts of her nearby accessibility making him randy as a pup.

But Katie made no reply.

Removing the cloth, Lafferty opened his eyes. To lay them on two of the ugliest men he'd ever seen, standing there gaping down at him as though he were a two-headed donkey in the circus. Though it wasn't the pure ugliness that first caught his eye, to be sure, it was the gun in the fist of the first one, the cluster of yellow daffodils in that of the other.

No stranger to tight spots, Lafferty had indeed found himself naked in tight spots before, although tight spots such as those had generally been occasioned by a jealous lover, never before by two calm and ugly men. And seldom before had weaponry been involved, except for the once near Ballyjamesduff, the weapon in question having been a sailing cookie jar (the jealous lover in question having been of the female persuasion), a far cry indeed from a nine-millimeter pistol.

They brought him to the lounge, where he stood naked, dripping onto the carpet. The nakedness was the worst of it, and no place to hide, his heart wanting to jump from his throat. The man with the daffodils was the older and fatter of the pair, with lips and ears as thick as your thumb, his jacket brown and stained and two sizes too tight. "Where's the woman?" said he.

"What woman?" Lafferty said.

"What woman says he," said the fat man.

"The woman whose name is on the fucking sign out in front of the fucking house," the other man said. He was skinny and pink and jumpy, twitching the gun as he spoke. The black eyes of him never rested on any one object too long, and his checkered jacket was yellow and baggy and blue.

"Did you look in the bed?" Lafferty said.

"Did we look in the bed says he," said the fat man.

"Of course, we looked in the fucking bed," said the skinny man.

Lafferty said, "She was there when I slipped in for my tub."

"She was there when he slipped in for his tub says he," said the fat man.

"Listen," said Lafferty, "could you quit repeating everything I say?"

"Could I quit repeating everything he says says he," said the fat man.

"Well, it is bloody fucking annoying," the skinny man said.

"That's your problem," said the fat man. "No appreciation of irony whatsoever. Everything's black and white to you."

"We got a job to do and last I looked irony wasn't in the job description."

"That's your problem, right there," said the fat man, the tips of his ears turning red. "No appreciation of irony whatsoever."

"Can I put on my clothes?" Lafferty said.

"Fuck no," said the skinny man.

"The nakeder you are," the fat man explained, "the less likely are you to run. And the less likely you are to run, the less likely your man here will have to put a bullet in you."

Lafferty's knees gave a lurch, his stomach a roll. "Can I sit?"

"Can he sit says he," said the fat man.

They regarded the sofa beside them, deep and plush and beige, five oversized sections arranged in the shape of an L. "That's one L of a sofa," Lafferty said.

It took a moment or two till the skinny man sniggered. Didn't the fat one chortle as well. "One L of a sofa," exclaims he, and they both gave in to the laughter. "One L of a sofa!" said the skinny man. They laughed for a minute or more, Lafferty standing bewildered behind his smile. The fat man wiped his eye. "Good one."

"I like this fucking guy," said the skinny man, jabbing his pistol toward Lafferty.

"Sit," said the fat man, waving his daffodils toward the sofa.

"What are the flowers for?" Lafferty said.

"Ladies love the flowers, sure they do," the fat man said. "And we deliver."

"Special delivery," said the skinny man.

"Here," said the fat man, "you can hold 'em over your oul hoo-ha there."

Thankful for little kindnesses, Lafferty took the flowers, holding them over his oul hoo-ha. He sat on the sofa, the fabric prickling his naked arse. The two men made no move to do likewise, hovering above him, feet planted apart. Only now, the shock of it sinking in, was Lafferty beginning to wonder where the hell Katherine Flanagan had got to, how indeed she'd managed to get away at all. Had she spotted them coming up the road and made off through the back? Was she hiding somewhere in the house? And of course, the deeper mystery, why two desperate specimens such as these had come calling in the first place. When the fat man put his hands on his hips, Lafferty saw the holster peeping out from under his stained brown jacket, the wee wink of a pistol. Across the room, the curtain was parted on the wide front window, and outside the gloaming was going deeper, the rusty leaves of the rowan tree in front giving a shiver to a white panel truck passing down the road toward Kilduff.

Lafferty, with little to lose, pushed at his luck. "Can you put down the gun?"

"I can, of course," the skinny man said, "but I won't. Mrs. Dunleavy didn't raise a fool."

"Good job," said the fat man. "Why don't you give him your bloody address too?"

"And why would I do that?"

"You just give him your bloody name."

"He wouldn't have known it was my fucking name if you hadn't just fucking said so."

"And who was your bloody Mrs. Dunleavy then? Your bloody nanny?"

The skinny man shrugged. "For fuck's sake, let's just get on with it."

They looked down again at Lafferty sitting on the sofa, daffodils over his oul hoo-ha. "One L of a sofa," the fat man said. "Good one." He wasn't smiling. "One more time, then. Where's the woman?"

One more time, then Lafferty told them. All he knew was she was in her bed when he went in for his tub. "What are you doing here in the first fucking place?" the skinny man wanted to know. "How do you bloody well know her at all?" asked the fat man. "How much do you know about her fucking business?" the skinny man said, and the fat man said, "How bloody long have you been dipping your toe in her tub?" Lafferty talked till his mouth was dry. His missus, he told them, contemplating throwing him out of her house for no good reason at all, had bullied him into marriage counseling in the person of Katherine Flanagan, LPC, IACP, a newcomer to the area, chosen because the missus, noticing the spanking new sign by the road every day on her way to work—a nurse over at St. Christopher's she was—judged it to be of the finest professional quality. And hadn't Lafferty merely chanced upon Katherine Flanagan at Connor's News Agent, just across the street from his turf accountant, Mickey G's, and hadn't one thing led to another. In his desire to come clean, to make a clean breast of it, to throw himself on the mercy of the court as it were, didn't the words come gushing out of Lafferty in a rush. How he attributed his extraordinary compatibility with members of the opposite gender not to the dimple in his chin, nor to the playful unruliness of his light brown hair—though those qualities certainly couldn't hurt—but rather to his innate ability to detect the tiniest, most subtle signal, such as when Katherine Flanagan, immersed in a session with himself and Mrs. Lafferty, had slowly drawn her eyes away from his and laid her bright red fingernail on the tip of her lip. So not at all surprised was he then, when following their chance encounter, he merely wondered if she might be willing to show him what he was doing wrong in his marriage, and she proceeded to do so, in a manner quite eager.

"Let me get this straight," the fat man said. "You're shagging your bloody marriage counselor."

Lafferty shrugged. "Not habitually."

The skinny man jabbed his pistol toward Lafferty. "I like this fucking guy."

The fat man's thick lips curled into a reasonable facsimile of a grin. "Me too. But then again, some of my best friends are stone-cold liars."

"What do you mean by that?" the skinny man said.

"What's your name?" said the fat man.

"Lafferty. Terrance Lafferty."

"You sound like a Dub," the skinny man said. "Any relative to Denis Lafferty from Summerhill?"

Lafferty seized the moment. He lied. "He's my brother."

"Small world," said the skinny man.

"Small indeed," said the fat.

"Do you know him well?" Lafferty said.

"Do we know him well says he," said the fat man.

The skinny one's black eyes finally settled, latching onto Lafferty's. "Well enough to know he's one of the grandest fucking liars ever to breathe Dublin air."

"A trait known to run in the family," the fat man said. "Tell us where the woman is. Tell us now. My manners are wearing thin."

"Did you look under the bed?" Lafferty said, his mouth as dry as a camel's arse.

"Did we look under the bed says he," said the fat man. The skinny man didn't answer. The fat man looked at him. "*Did* we look under the bloody bed?"

"Did *you* look under the bed?"

"How am I to look under the bed with my bloody knees? *You* didn't look under the bed?"

"For fuck's sake," said the skinny man, sulking toward the bedroom door.

The fat man never budged, the tips of his ears turning red. Hovering over your man, staring down at him, he drew his pistol out from beneath his stained brown jacket, two sizes too tight. Lafferty, his stomach in full riot, puckered up his arse, fearful of soiling the sofa. The flowers over his oul hoo-ha wilted and trembled from the heat and shaking of his hand, and his heart clambering in his chest like a hamster in a heated cage. He wished he was anyplace else. He felt the color fleeing his face like rats from a sinking ship. He wished he'd never been there.

Never there. Wasn't that the reason he was here in the first place. The first words out of Peggy's mouth at the first session the first time he ever laid his eyes on Katherine Flanagan, LPC, IACP: "He's never been there for me. Even when he's there, he isn't really there."

Through the wide window behind his wife that afternoon, Lafferty saw the broad sweep of fields dotted with sheep grazing among the hedgerows and stone fences leading down to the village tucked in the hillside. He saw the steeple of the church in the mist, the blue façade of the Commodore Hotel, and in his mind, he calculated just where the Pig & Whistle would be, down the street, beyond the green. How he wished he was there with his fistful of jar. Of course, it wasn't the first time he'd heard the words out of Peggy, not at all, but he'd realized, seated in upholstered splendor in the office out front, gazing down at Kilduff, that he'd grown immune to them. Hearing them again, Lafferty disagreed, and disagreed emphatically. He never thought of himself as never there. Wasn't he someplace all of the time?

The time they'd been evicted from their Dublin flat, hadn't he been at the Curragh, trying to win back the price of the rent. The time of the miscarriage, lamentable, tragic to be sure, but hadn't he been at the Pig & Whistle celebrating his impending paternity, and him with no earthly way of knowing. Any number of other times she'd complained he was never there, hadn't the cause of it been that she'd told him to get the hell out of her sight. Though Peggy's ears were deaf to his persuasions—her brown eyes indeed feigning pain and disbelief as they stared at him across the broad and pricey teak tabletop—Lafferty thought he detected a glimmer of understanding in the eyes of Katherine Flanagan, LPC, IACP.

Didn't it run in the family after all. Lafferty's oul man had never been there either.

And, at the end of the day, didn't absence make the heart grow fonder. Hadn't Lafferty himself witnessed as a youth the grand reunions, his oul man and his oul wain on any number of occasions, him waltzing her across the narrow kitchen floor between the table and the stove, and her with her head back to let out the laugh. Hadn't he seen with his own eyes the pair of them, arm in arm, making their way up Drumcondra Road in a zigzag stagger, half blind with the song and the drink and the joy.

Didn't never being there have its sweet side as well.

No sooner did the skinny man walk into the bedroom till a ruckus of noises broke out. The fat man over Lafferty bounced back a step, raising the gun toward the door of the bedroom, Lafferty shrinking on the sofa, hunkered over his daffodils. There was a shout, a thump or two or three, the sound of a scuffle, another shout, and a gasp and a curse, the fat man starting for the bedroom door just before the explosion, the bang of the gun.

Then the silence holding nothing.

"Eamon!" called the fat man. "Eamon!"

More of the quiet. The ears of the fat man the color of raw beef.

Katie by the door. Standing there suddenly, the gun in her hands in front of her face, looking down the length of her arms over the pistol, pointing straight at the fat man, like a right proper soldier, if not for the hot pink housecoat hanging down, gaping open. "Drop it!"

The fat man in the same proper stance, feet wide, staring down both his arms over the pistol, pointing at Katie, the sleeves of his brown jacket up to his elbows. "You drop it!"

Lafferty, slippery with sweat, caught a sweet scent of daffodil.

That was how they stood, squirming closer, squinting down their barrels. It seemed a long time passing. Lafferty off to the side, out of the line of fire, out of the line of vision, out of the picture altogether, might as well have never been there. A chill caught the sweat, and his back ached at how he was hunkered over, and he sat up a bit, fearful of making himself too big. But nobody noticed.

"Drop it!" Katie said.

"You drop it!" said the fat man.

Katie creeping closer, her housecoat peeping open another inch, Lafferty staring at the glimpse of her nakedness, the shadows of the woman's body, the navel, the hair down below it, astounded at how it left him cold, at how utterly irrelevant was the clothing and the nakedness and the flesh at the end of the day. Invisible, didn't he keep growing bigger. The daffodils spread out flat and dead over his oul hoo-ha, the one part of him getting smaller.

"Drop it!" said Katie. "Drop it now!"

"You drop it! Now!"

It occurred to your man he could rise slow and easy and creep away, leaving them to their own devices, to settle it however they may, leaving them pointing their pistols at one another ad infinitum, or at least till tomorrow morning when Katie's first clients arrived to find the pair still standing there pointing their pistols, yelling drop it. The skinny man he supposed was dead or mortally wounded, and he wondered where this warrior woman called Katherine the Great had come from, though he wanted nothing at all to do with it, whatever it was that it was. He wanted only to never be there. What he wanted, the only thing, was to be someplace else altogether where he could shake himself like a dog climbing out of the water and make it all fly away. He wasn't quite ready yet to stand up naked and tiptoe off, not yet, but the idea having planted itself in his mind was rooting around, searching for purchase, and was this close to finding it when the guns went off, *bang, bang*, one after the other within the span of the blink of an eye. The sound like a wind that boxed his ears, blowing his hair back, causing the sweat on his back to chill and dry in the instant.

Lafferty looked up, blinking. Katie and the fat man were gone.

The scent of gunpowder bitter in his nose, the wind of the blast had sucked away all sound, leaving nothing but pure silence in which Lafferty sat for a while. When, finally, he heard a gurgle and a distant chirp of bird, he stood. Wobbly he was, his muscles like pudding. He dropped the flowers on the table. Katie and the fat man both lay on their backs, the fat man just off the L of the sofa, Katie's head in the doorway of the bedroom. The fat man, his stained brown jacket up past his elbows and squeezing the tips of his shoulders, was lying with his arms and legs flung out, looking at the ceiling with wide open eyes, a patch of blood in the middle of the untidy white mound of shirt on his belly. Lafferty like a ghost in the quiet. Katie was lying the same, staring up at the top of the doorway, hot pink housecoat spread open across the carpet, her naked body splayed, the scar, her emergency smile, smiling out from her bottom rib, the hole between her breasts still oozing. In the bedroom lay the skinny man humped up on his stomach, the eye on the side of his face wide open as well, staring under the bed.

Does nobody ever die with their eyes closed anymore?

In the bathroom, he put on his clothes. Without an ounce of consideration, with no premeditation at all, as though it were instinct, he took a small bath towel from the polished brass rail and wiped down the tub and the faucet, then all about the toilet. Taking the towel with him to the bedroom, he wiped off the doorknobs, the nightstand, the headboard, the shade of the lamp he'd admired. Then, in the lounge, the coffee table where he'd braced himself standing up. The back of the chair he'd grasped, passing by. Any place he might have touched. Then he folded the bath towel, hanging it back proper on its polished brass rail.

Outside, it was nearly dark, the air clean and sweet. Lafferty shook his face into it, washing off the scent of the gunpowder, the smell of the blood, the odor of fear. Making it all fly away. He made his way down the road toward Kilduff, scarcely aware of his legs as they marched, nor his arms as they swung, exchanging nods with the odd sheep at the side of the road. Into Kilduff, he walked past the green where the Kilduff Cross stood, its once intricate Celtic design having been washed away by decades of Kilduff rain. It had been erected in loving memory of someone, but the inscription having long since vanished, no one remembered the identity of the dearly departed, a sad anonymity. Lafferty strolled into the dark and friendly confines of the Pig & Whistle.

There sat Pat Gallagher in the heat of battle, the complexion of him like that of a boiled lobster, arguing with Francie Byrnes, a bald and bitter barber, and a clutch of others. Pint in hand, arse on stool, Lafferty entered the fray. His opinion was as strong as the next man's when it came to how realistic the mechanical contraption that portrayed the great shark in the film *Jaws* had been, and when the argument escalated to the question of whether or not Elvis had ever been in the employ of the CIA, and then on to the British conspiracy responsible for the disappearance of Amelia Earhart, Lafferty was able to hold his own there as well. They argued well into the night.

He was there next morning with Peggy in the kitchen, her roof yet over his head, a fine splash of sun coming in through the green of the curtain. Wasn't he there. Her hands were shaking. He made her her tea, rattling the spoon in the cup. Listened to her tall tale. She bit into her muffin, and he watched the buttery crumb on the edge of her lip in a mesmerizing state of flux as the words flowed out of her. She was still excited, still in shock, still incredulous over the goings-on at St. Christopher's.

We sat there, in the same room with her, Terrance, you and me.

Sure, the IACP never heard of the woman. It was all a bloody hoax.

Nobody knows who she is. They're saying all kinds of things. They're saying she was a supergrass and the IRA clipped her. They're saying she was IRA, and it was MI-5 took her out. They're saying she was Columbian cartel, and it was a Mexican hit squad done her in.

There's no record of her at all. Nothing, nowhere.

Can you imagine if we'd been there? Can you just imagine?

A Very Good Cure

Maybe it was a sign when the phone rang and he was actually there to pick it up, for seldom was he there and even seldomer did he pick the bloody thing up. When a voice said, "Terrance?" the skin on his back clutched up in a chill, for he knew the voice, familiar as the sound of his own, though he hadn't heard it in years. "Terrance," the voice said, "it's me, Blackie—it's your da."

To be sure, the voice was feebler, shot through with something decrepit, not the strong vibrato he remembered as a lad, a drowsy head on the oul man's chest. "Blackie," said Lafferty.

"The Black is back," his da said, and Lafferty heard him hold the phone away to cough. "Listen, Terrance, son—I'd like to see you."

"You'd like to see me. *You'd* like to see *me*."

"I know I haven't always been there for you, boyo, but I did bring you into the world, and now, by God, I'm leaving it," Blackie said. "That must count for something."

"It must, must it?" So silly a thing to say, Lafferty knew, but he said it nevertheless.

He heard his sigh on the phone. Blackie's voice, far away, fading fast. "Here. See. I told you it'd be no use." Another voice came on, a woman's voice this time, warm and soft as a wool blanket, full of throat. "Terrance," she said, "my name is Kitty. I'm a friend of your da's. Now you listen to me. For if you don't, you'll be regretting it the rest of your life."

"I doubt that," Lafferty said. But he listened.

When the listening was done, he stood for a long time at the window, looking down Blue Bucket Lane. The sky over Kilduff was gray, a chill in the air of the early spring afternoon, yet the leaves of the hedges out front managed to capture light enough to glitter a bit in the breeze. He stood for a long time, soaking up the quiet of the house, letting it seep into his bones, turned into a statue by a voice on the phone.

The thing of it was, it was an odd bit of happenstance—he might have used the word ironic, had he ever used that word at all—that his own da should reach out to him after so many years just as Lafferty had learned he himself was going to be a father, for the very first time. They'd only just learned that Peggy, his wife, the would-be mother of his children, was pregnant at last. They'd been trying. Sure, there'd been a time or two when she'd been up the pole before—Lafferty couldn't be sure of the particulars, as he'd had to take Peggy's word for it, and they'd not always been on the most trusting of terms. But that time or two was by accident, despite Lafferty and his randy ways, not because of them, and that time or two had resulted in miscarriage, as though God had looked down upon Lafferty's dread and regret, and said, very well then, if you didn't really mean it, neither did I. This time was intentional, and this time they were taking every precaution ordered by the doctor and the book, and this time God would be smiling down (this time they were sure). Lafferty was ready, anxious. It was time after all he grew up. For time, this time, had just seen your man turn forty.

A flash of fur caught his eye, a squirrel, a rat maybe, a rodent of some kind or other scurrying into the hedgerow across the way. Just as he was becoming accustomed to the idea of fatherhood, here he was, having to reacquaint himself again with the idea of sonhood. A car came up the lane—the little brown Ford of Peggy, home from work. She pulled in, climbed out carefully; she was scarcely showing, but she did everything gingerly, as though she were ten months pregnant, not two. Lafferty watched her walking toward the house, the wee thing tucked up inside her there, growing, lining up to take the place of his grandda in the world. Spotting Lafferty in the window, a look of surprise crossed her face, which she caught and tried to smile away. She waved, her heart not wholly in it. She'd yet to grow accustomed to the shiny, new, domesticated Terrance.

From the kitchen, the kettle began to whistle. Time. Timing.

When he kissed her cheek, her eyebrow went up in suspicion, an old habit, and he took her sweater and hung it up, went to fetch her cup of tea. She followed him into the kitchen. Of course. She'd be wanting to know how his job hunt was going, and it wasn't going well, but your man changed the subject before she could raise it. "You'll never guess who's after calling," he said.

"Calling? On the telephone?"

"Yes. Of course. On the phone."

"The phone rang and you were here? And you picked it up and answered it?"

He sighed. He supposed he had it coming. Though the spoon as he stirred did clink a bit harsh and loud on her cup. "Yes. And begod if it wasn't my da."

He turned when she said nothing and saw her frozen in the doorway, a look of distrust holding her face entirely, the narrow black eyes in a squint. "Come," he said, a bit more impatiently than he'd intended, "sit."

"It was your da. Your father."

"Aye. The oul man. Imagine. After all these years."

"I can't," said she.

He allowed her to let it sink in. He sat across from her at the wee table as the fridge began to hum. A gray wren fluttered by in the gray air beyond the window. Taking a sip, she looked at him over the rim and through the steam, her eyes saying *what are you up to now*.

"He wants to see me. He says he's dying."

"I thought he was already dead," said Peggy.

"He's not bloody well dead . . . not yet." Even as the words were coming out of him, his brain was scrambling madly to remember: Had he ever used the funeral of the oul man as an excuse to escape on one of his escapades? He thought not; a granny or two, yes, but never his da. Lafferty went on: Blackie was in a hospital on the north side of Dublin, dying said he, bereaved and regretful at having lost track of his son, and—according to his woman friend with whom Lafferty spoke at length—longing to see his boy one last time on the proper side of the dirt. When Lafferty got to the part about the woman friend, Kitty, Peggy's eyes went even narrower. *What are you up to now, Terrance?* A handsome woman was Peggy, even in her distrust, dark hair clenched and curled, and fine fistfuls of flesh—Lafferty imagining the milk teeming up in her breasts.

"She gave me the bloody number," he said. "You can call him yourself if you like."

"Okey-dokey then."

Okey-dokey? "Okey-dokey then I can go?"

"Okey-dokey then you can give me the bloody number," Peggy said.

His da hadn't always not been there. For the first ten years of his life, in fact, he'd been there nearly always, at least when Terrance had needed him most, for weren't they in essence fellow travelers, comrades-in-arms, coconspirators in the face of the common threat, the fiercest, most desperate of dangers: the one named Flossie Doyle. The wife and the mam. Many's the bike ride they took by way of absconding, Terrance perched on the wee metal seat of the crossbar between Blackie's strong arms, up through the city and out through the countryside to the airport—for the place was in the country then—where they'd watch the airplanes lumber implausibly through the air, and pick blackberries from the hedgerows to sustain them on the long journey home. Or up through Clontarf to the Dollymount strand, a beach where the wooden bridge across the inlet had the planks laid long-ways instead of cross-ways, the glimpses through the cracks to the water down below striking terror into his young, quavering heart. There was a derelict hull in the bay at the time, a rusty old hulk that his da pointed to as proof positive of the folly of setting to sea. Solid terra firma was your only man, he said. The Wisdom of Blackie. More was, *When you think you haven't a care in the world, son, look long and hard till you find one*, a warning against complacency that held Lafferty in good stead through his first forty years, and sure enough, before the day was out, wouldn't Flossie be on another tear which, like as not, would find the lad and his da crouching in the corner behind the wardrobe, a finger to the oul man's lips, adventure gleaming in his eye, and they'd creep out, on hands and knees and tiptoes, the lad halfway between giggling and crying. Down the hollow stairwell to the freedom of the bike and another excursion, this time to the Daisy Market maybe, down near the quays, where, hunkered under the medieval stone walls, the cluster of stalls and lean-tos offered up piles of furniture, clothes, what-nots and bric-a-brac, all class and manner of antique junk, to bicker over, never to buy. Buying was not an option, as the shillings were sparse, and seldom a ha'penny for the lad. And when the haughty neighbors and relations frowned down their noses at his da for taking the dole, didn't his da always respond with another bit of his wisdom, and with the clear-eyed, open-faced disbelief that this particular bit hadn't already climbed into the vocabulary of every oul soul on the earth: *When someone wants to give you free money, begod you take it!*

   His mam in the early years a more distant memory, the red tangle of hair, the fury, and the tears on the face of her. Maybe it was the closeness to his da in those days that kept his mam so distant, for Terrance began to understand, after his da was gone, gone for good following a memorable dust-up in his tenth year or thereabouts, that the hardness of her was the only thing that saved her. It was the only thing between Flossie Lafferty, nee Doyle, and the devil in hell. Lafferty still saw Blackie on the odd occasion after that, and he remembered the pubs and the mates, the laughter and smoke, and the clusters of women on corners—for his da was the handsomest of men, the curls of his black hair glinting like a crown in the sun—and how they oohed and fussed over the bright-eyed little lad and the dimple in his chin. But didn't his mam trip one day, having been worn to a nub, her hair long since gone to gray, and tumble down the hollow stairwell, killed by her heart or by the fall, they never knew which to be sure. And after the oul man didn't show up at her wake, Lafferty never saw him again. Never looked him up. Of course, the oul man never looked him up, neither. There were rumors of jail, Mountjoy, Portlaoise even, but Lafferty never reached out, his da never reached out, and at the end of the day was it pride, or was it laziness? Or was it simply something best left untouched?

Lafferty decided to touch it again. His da had reached out. What was this thing, fatherhood, after all? At the end of the day, it might be a ramble, decent craic, and Lafferty was never a man to turn down a chance for a well-deserved spree.

Nearly noon of the next day, he made his way through the narrow streets of Clontarf after an hour's drive in from Kilduff, and the closer he got to the hospital, the more madly his heart was scrambling. Some of the streets were familiar, streets he'd ridden on the crossbar with his da, and fierce was his grip on the wheel, to stay the course and keep from veering back toward North Circular Road and his old haunts, to look up an old mate or two, Jimmy or Finny or Alfie, to spend some quality time at the black, polished mahogany of O'Faolain's bar, and all the lovely layers of smoke and talk. Wasn't it time to grow up after all. Not to mention Peggy and her nose would be sure to sniff it out. She'd relented after talking to Kitty, a long talk full of knowing sighs and affirmations, a good, womanly talk that Lafferty didn't hear the half of, and he parked the little brown Ford in the hospital lot and made his way inside under a gray, spitting sky, his head bowed under the drizzle.

He asked Sister at the desk the whereabouts of Donal Lafferty, and he rode the lift up to the wards, sticking his hands in his pockets to dry off his palms, trying to keep his breathing from bucking out of control.

The name was on a handwritten post by the door. A private room for recuperating. Blackie was on his side in the bed, facing the wall where the window opened out at the bottom, talking to a freckle-faced woman he took to be Kitty. Her eyebrows jumped up when she spotted him. "Terrance?" Blackie rolled over to see for himself, and Lafferty was gobsmacked: The hero was mortal. A skull covered with bluish skin, black hair stiff and sparse and edged in gray, large, lively eyes, the only thing left living on his face.

"Boyo," said Blackie.

By the bedside, Lafferty reached out, for what he didn't know. A handshake was out of the question. He touched the oul man's shoulder, then said the worst possible thing he could say: "How're you feeling?"

Blackie rose up to the task. "'I've a pain in my belly, says Doctor Kelly.'"

A childhood rhyme. Lafferty responded, "'Rub it with oil, says Doctor Boyle.'"

"'A very good cure, says Doctor Moore.'" Blackie smiled, a gray-toothed travesty of the original, his famous old smile. "By God, son, it's good to see you."

Lafferty, smiling stupidly, couldn't bring himself to say the same, and it was Kitty who saved him the need to. "He'd say the same to you, Black man, but he'd be lying through his face," she said in her throaty voice, coming up from the chair and around the bed to give your man a hug. She was a full-sized woman who moved with deliberation, not a doubt in her direction, her face wide, freckled, and calmly smiling, dark red hair swept back away from it as if windblown. "I'm Kitty," says she. "We're glad you came."

We. Lafferty said, wasn't he glad as well, and more unmemorable pleasantries passed between them, and Lafferty asked how long they'd known one another, how did they meet, and Blackie said sure, it was love at first sight, to which Kitty only gritted her jaw, acknowledging the unfortunate truth of it. Blackie pulled open his dressing gown to show his son the wounds. "See," he said, still smiling, "see how they're after carving me up?"

"And down," said Kitty. "For God's sake, cover it up."

"Some fancy stitch-work, that," said Lafferty, eyeing the lengthy, red-puckered scar down the oul man's chest. "What's that there?" he said, pointing at the dark red shadows on his ribs.

"Now they're after zapping me," he said. "That's from your radiation."

"He glows in the dark now," Kitty said. "He can't hide from me anymore."

Lafferty nodded. "They must think you've a good fighting chance then, with all this bloody treatment."

"Waste of the taxpayers' money," said Kitty.

Blackie nodded in resignation. "A little time, maybe, not much," he said, tucking his dressing gown back around him.

"He's dying," said Kitty. "Better off living with that."

"Living with dying," said Lafferty.

"All the more cause for a hooley," Blackie said. "There'll be no time for it after I've turned up my toes."

Lafferty, for a while wondering what bloody wonderland he'd stepped into, the pair of them nearly giddy over the oul man's dying, but he felt it too, relief of a sort, a happiness to be sure, reunion, something—maybe just good, easy, family craic. He sat at the end of the bed and he had to go first, had to tell them everything transpired in his life for the past twenty years, his rocky marriage to Peggy, her dragging him out to God-forsaken Kilduff in the heart of County Nowhere hoping for a fresh start, the fresh start long since gone stale, her work as a nurse, him eking out a living at his turf accountant's expense, though now he was turning over a new leaf, turning forty, looking at long last for steady work (not too diligently he failed to add), for wasn't herself pregnant at last.

"Ah, Jaysus, boyo, you're codding me," says Blackie. "Congratulations!"

"How wonderful," said Kitty. "How old is she?"

"Mind your manners," Blackie said. "None of your concern how old the woman is."

"Well, it ought to be yours," Kitty said. "Look at Brian."

"Ah, Jaysus," said Blackie, "does every thought that passes through your skull have to come out of your bloody gob?"

Kitty's freckles reddened. She turned to Lafferty. "My oul wan was forty-five when she had my brother, Brian, and he turned out to be a desperate specimen."

"He'd have been desperate if she'd had him at twenty."
"That's not what I've read," Kitty said. "After forty…"
Lafferty said, "Peggy's young enough yet, sure she is. I think."
Neither seemed to hear him. Blackie, still gazing at Kitty, said, "Damn fine thing she had him at forty-five then, isn't it? The way things turned out."

A dreamy smile came over Kitty. "Don't you say the sweetest things, Black man." Then she looked at Lafferty: "That's how we met—Brian was your da's cellmate."

"Cellmate?" said Lafferty.

"Ach, I'll tell you the whole story, son," Blackie said. "But let's take some air."

Kitty asked him to go down the hall and fetch a wheelchair, and Lafferty did. The nurse, her face solemn and gray above a name tag reading *A. Reardon,* looked at him suspiciously, and Lafferty wondered what exactly a Reardon was, and he wondered if every single person in any position of real or imagined authority anywhere in the land considered it part of their duty to look at him suspiciously. When he returned, Blackie was wearing a tattered pea coat over his dressing gown, standing diminished on his own two feet, waiting next to Kitty, and as they got him into the chair, Lafferty asked if they had any idea what a Reardon was, and it took a few seconds for the joke to sink in, and they chuckled obligatorily. Kitty said it was a sour old bitch, but Blackie defended the woman, saying she wasn't so bad, had performed his bedpan duties admirably. When they came outside to the hospital grounds, the rain had ended, but the benches and chairs held puddles of water, which he and Kitty wiped away as best they could. Blackie sitting snug and dry and portable. Kitty lit a fag, and Lafferty watched in disbelief as the oul man reached for a pull. Blackie only shrugged. "The breakfast of champions," says he.

At the first drag, the smoke exploded back out of him in a fit of coughing. Kitty reached for the fag, patted his back, took a drag of her own. When the coughing simmered down, the oul man tried to catch his breath, his blue face red and drained.

"I'm after cutting back," says he, with a notion of a smile. "Sure I'm down to one a day now."

They sat for a while in the garden by a golden chain tree, yellow blossoms damp and dull in the gloom. Here and there about the grounds other patients had made their way outside, wandering and smoking, some being wheeled in their chairs by a wife, a nurse, a husband. Lafferty listened to Blackie's story: How he'd done ten years in Portlaoise for a crime he was unaware at the time of committing, having fallen in with bad company on a spree, believing your man when he said wait here a sec with the motor running while I run in and pick up my meds. You couldn't rise up to the badness of some men, Blackie said, though his own optimistic and trusting nature had no doubt led him astray as well. Lesson learned the hard way, he smiled. Kitty was not so smiling, nor accepting, nor forgiving. It was a well-practiced rant, Lafferty perceived, Kitty enumerating her—and Blackie's, for she purported to speak for them both—grievances against the judicial system, the penal system, the social system, and one wig-headed judge in particular by the name of Frobisher. Lafferty also perceived that Blackie was laboring hard to maintain an air of interest in Kitty's tirade, that he was actually too weary to care, too far removed beyond it. And Lafferty found himself wondering again, the state where he'd found himself much of this day: Picturing his oul man, diminished state or not, dying or not, as an innocent, victimized dupe was not at all fitting with the image he'd lived with the past forty years of a quick-witted, confident man in control. Which was it? Was he a criminal, a man without morals, capable of armed robbery, capable of sitting on his deathbed, looking his only son in the eye and lying at him through his gray-colored teeth? And if he was, what did that say about Lafferty's own blood, the blood of his own son to be? But in the end, Kitty was earnest and convincing, and the oul man seemed genuinely abashed and sincere. There was not a doubt in Kitty's mind as to the truth of it, and Lafferty let his own mind go there as well, let himself believe that the drink and the age had caught up to his da, that he had indeed been duped, and that, at the end of the day, he was the man he claimed to be.

A thirsty man was what he next claimed to be. There was a pub with an off-license attached, an attachment any pub across the street from a hospital garden would have, and Lafferty trooped over like a good lad and fetched a bagful of stout. They sat and they drank, concealing the bottles a bit, and they talked and relaxed as the sun came around for a peep, yellow blossoms glistening and the air warming up all around them. Lafferty noticed the odd, white-coated person now and then glancing his way with the suspicion he expected and no doubt deserved. Kitty mostly listened to the men reminiscing, laughing at the antics of Flossie Doyle and Blackie's evasive maneuvers. How he'd taken the lad to mass on a Sunday morning to appease the missus, down to the Procathedral in Marlborough Street, where there was a commanding altar in the center and several lesser altars around the perimeter, masses taking place at each at varying intervals. In through the side door they'd go, walking along the outer ring, stopping at each altar to genuflect and cross themselves, and by the time they made it around, mass was ending at the last altar and they left through the opposite door, fifteen minutes in and out, religious obligation fulfilled, free to go to their desired destination, the quays, or the Daisy Market, the airport. Blackie caught his breath with a sigh and a shake of his head, jumbling up all the memories. Lafferty spied a Reardon approaching over the green, and they shuffled the bottles from sight. Blackie was due back in the ward, she said, sternly, for wasn't the doctor making his rounds. They'd be in straightaway, said Kitty. A Reardon walked away, spine straight and haughty, a desperate little waddle to her rear. Blackie sighed, contented, stood, pulled his pajama bottoms high beneath his old pea coat. Turned away from the building. Says, "Let's go for a ramble. Let's head up toward Donegal, let's leave this fucking place behind."

Lafferty and Kitty gave him the eye. Was it the stout talking? "Have you never been up to the Bloody Foreland?" Blackie said. "The most beautiful place you ever seen. When the sun goes down up there on the foreland, the crimson color soaks clean through the ocean, and the shore, and the rocks, and you never seen the likes of it. I seen but it once myself. And by God, I mean to see it one more time before I'm planted."

Lafferty was no less puzzled. "So... What? You think I can just pull up the car, we can all hop in and toddle off to Donegal as easy as kiss hands?"

Blackie smiled, took Kitty's hand and he kissed it.

Why not? Turnabout was fair play. Like the rambles of old, only Blackie was side-saddle in the old brown Ford instead of driving the bike, Lafferty behind the wheel instead of perched atop the crossbar. No less an adventure, more in fact, much more. Lafferty took a cotton to the idea, the explanation due Peggy notwithstanding. In the back seat next to the collapsible wheelchair sat Kitty, admiring the view up M1, smoking her fags, Blackie inhaling the second-hand smoke like sniffing the fragrance of orchids, though the coughing fits struck nonetheless. Tucked in beside her too was the oxygen tank and a bag full of pills for the pain, leftovers from life before the Black man's surgery—they'd gone into her place on Talbot Street to retrieve them, Blackie too, moving slowly, changing his pajamas for a proper pair of trousers, then savoring every room in the little flat, rifling through this drawer and that, this closet and that, as if he might never see the place again. Lafferty'd been touched when he'd told them to go outside to the car and wait for him, wondering if the oul man had said a prayer, shed a tear, before he'd made his way slowly back out for the ramble.

The stout took its toll, and they never made it to Newry before the oul man had to stop for a pee. Lafferty started to pull into a McDonald's when Blackie, aghast, grabbed at the wheel; he'd sooner stop in the lowest, most desperate Irish public house, thank you very much, than set foot in a bastardized, plastic American shrine of some sort. Of course, a man couldn't walk into a pub only to use the facilities; decorum and propriety demanded a round be ordered, and another out of courtesy, and so the next stage of the journey was even shorter, not even to Armagh before they had to find another pub near

Killylea, and the lovely, vicious cycle was joined. And didn't Blackie have his hooley after all.

On the road this time, Blackie swapped seats with Kitty so he could recline in the back, napping as best he could till the call of nature came around once again. The twin calls of nature: "By God, my back teeth are floating," says he, "and I'm gasping for another jar." Just past Ballygawley, Lafferty pulled into the carpark of a place called the Six Step Inn.

Blackie refused use of the wheelchair—he hadn't wanted to pack the bloody thing along in the first place—and he made his way slowly across the gravel carpark and in through the door of the inn, his arm over Kitty's shoulder, his vigilant son just behind. "Lovely," he said, then again, "Lovely." Off to the right, the light shone in through the window like a light through a tunnel, glinting off the ancient, polished splinters of the bar. Behind it a grand mirror, *Guinness* in gold letters, and a fat publican under a bogtrotter's cap, like all the caps on all the heads of all the curious old farmers eyeing them from the bar.

Blackie led them to a low, round table in the lounge, where he sat smiling, his chest heaving for want of air. His face was alive, Lafferty noticed, every muscle in it alive and well, even though the color was never worse, a deepening blue shot through with red, going to the color of a bruise. "Shall I go out and fetch your oxygen?" says Kitty.

"Fuck my oxygen," Blackie gasped.

When Lafferty fetched the jars of stout, Blackie called for a whisky as well. Lafferty looked at Kitty, her face a resigned plea that he couldn't really read, and he went for the whisky while Blackie found the loo, and when he returned and was seated again, his breath caught up to him, he raised the whisky glass and saluted. "Here's to the next little Lafferty," he said, "and not the last of a long, living line."

"Sláinte," said Kitty, and they drank.

Blackie wiped his lips on the sleeve of his old pea coat. "Begod, boyo," he said, "I can't get over it, a little Lafferty coming into the world, just as another's taking his leave of it."

"Isn't that the way of it," Lafferty said. "Though sure you'll probably be around to dance at the little gaffer's wedding."

"Ach, I wouldn't want to be," Blackie said, "not like this," and the sentiment was true, there was nothing they could say, so they drank again. A farmer at the bar pulled a penny whistle from his sock and played a familiar air, and they listened for a while before Blackie dredged up another memory to name, another favorite ramble of old when they'd go up in the Dublin Mountains to the Hell Fire Club, a ruin of an ancient hunting lodge near the summit where the occult had reputedly been practiced, and the stories were legend of the drinking and black masses and ritual sacrifices of black cats—of them at the very least, for wasn't the skeleton of a dwarf found buried there one time, along with a brass statue of a demon. Or so the story went. Lafferty wondered what would they talk about after the last memory had been trotted out and the past was exhausted and the future being ever so nil. But Blackie seized on the future, the immediate future, his latest grand ramble, and he looked at the long shadows slanting in through the window and reckoned they'd arrive at the Bloody Foreland too bloody late for sunset. But he knew a place where they could stay the night, an old friend of his who lived in the area, on a poor excuse of a sheep farm, on an isolated, barren hillside. He named the fellow: Tom Hogan.

"Tom Hogan," Kitty said. "Sure I don't remember the name."

"No, no," Blackie said. "He was long gone by the time I met up with you."

Lafferty frowned. He'd never heard of the man either. "Yet you're close enough mates we can pop in and stay, unannounced? You been in touch?"

"Ach, he'll be surprised, he will," said Blackie. "I can't wait to see the look on his gob." And he smiled the shadow of his famous old smile, his eyes glinting in the gloom of the pub, and he'd say no more on it, and the old farmer at the bar commenced another tune, a livelier tune this time, a reel of some sort, and every toe in the place was tapping, hands clapping as well, and didn't your man Blackie get up to show off a step or two (he'd been a fine one for the dance in his day), pulling

Kitty up along. But a turn or two and he was done, falling back down in his chair, exhausted, reaching for his jar, chest heaving, smiling broadly.

And a sense of well-being came over your man. It was easy. He hadn't suspected it would be so easy. Of all the times he'd seen him happy, Lafferty had never seen his da any happier, and it was then, on cue, the oul man's warning came into his mind: When you think you haven't a care in the world, look long and hard till you find one.

Up through the north toward Letterkenny they drove, the lowering sun in Lafferty's eye, long shadows stretching over the road. In some places, the hedgerows running alongside made it seem they were driving in a tunnel, at others the stone fences on the green hillsides seemed to meander on forever. Kitty turned in her seat beside Lafferty and stared for while at the oul man asleep in the back. "I can't help worry what the drink's doing to him," she said. "He's not used to it anymore—it's been months since he's been up to a proper spree of any sort."

"What's the worst that can happen?" Lafferty said.

"Maybe you're right," said Kitty. "Begod, he's sleeping like a babe now."

"I'm glad I come up. I nearly didn't, you know."

"A fine thing you did. You'd be kicking yourself forever if you'd missed the chance to catch up with old Tom Hogan, now wouldn't you?"

"Tom Hogan," said Lafferty, shaking his head. "What the hell's a Tom Hogan?"

Kitty's head shaking the same. "He's full of surprises, the Black man is."

"Is he now. I suspect he is."

Kitty looked over, put her hand on Lafferty's arm. "It's a grand thing, the change in him. He's over the moon you're having a child of your own, you know."

"Aye," Lafferty said. "What about you? Have you any kids?"

"Oh, I had a squall of 'em." She sighed, staring out the window on her side.

"How many?"

"Eight," she said.

Old habits die hard, and the first thing Lafferty did was glance at her, still staring out her window in a dreamy state, to assess the damage the bearing of eight children might have had on her body: very little in his estimation, a fine example of womanhood sitting here beside him in her plain blue dress and roomy wool sweater. The next thing he did was to try to comprehend the magnitude of bringing eight squalling new lives into this world, a monumental feat considering the mark the having of a single one was leaving on your man. Lafferty's eyes quickly found the road again when Kitty turned. He asked her about her kids, about her own life; he realized he knew next to nothing about her, this woman so close to his da, this woman who knew everything about him.

The road rambled on, the countryside in the gloaming growing hillier and more barren. Her kids were doing well, the girls all married and the lads too, except for Frankie, the youngest, only twenty-two, and fallen in with unsavory companions—including his Uncle Brian, Kitty's criminal brother, about whom she had little good to say. Frankie had himself been arrested once or twice, a cause of constant worry. She blamed herself, as the lad had been left practically on his own after his da, a lorry driver, had been killed on the road by a drunken American tourist sightseeing at high speed down the wrong side of the road. Kitty'd had to go to work then, in a bookshop down on Grafton Street where she remained to this day. Frankie'd been only ten and had grown up with a chip on his shoulder. It came to Lafferty that he'd been the same age when his own da had left him behind. But then his own da hadn't died, at least not yet; sure, wasn't his own da in the back at this very minute, sleeping off a snout full, anxious to get on to the next. Kitty said the thing of it was it was mostly the Americans who came into the bookshop now, and it was all she could do to smile and be civil, one of their kind having slaughtered her husband.

"How did you meet the oul man?" Lafferty said.

Kitty smiled and beamed his way through her freckles. "Through the grace of God," said she.

Lafferty remembers where they were: The road climbing a long hillside toward the silhouette of an old stone house standing lonely on the horizon, a streak of light dying just over the ridge to the west. They both smelled it at the same time: bitter, ammonia-like, piss, it turned out to be, and when Kitty leaned around to look, she could tell right away. But it was not until he'd pulled over, and scrambled to the back, and patted the oul man's cheek, felt for a pulse, put an ear to his chest, and then pounded on the roof of the car that Lafferty knew it as well. He sat on the verge of the gully by the side of the road in the weeds. Kitty came and sat beside him and wrapped him in her arms, patting his head to her chest. He had the sensation of air leaking out of him like a punctured tire.

After a while, Kitty murmured. "Shh, shh…it's like he's just sleeping."

"Aye," Lafferty said. "Sleeping it off. Sleeping it off a long, long time."

It was still. Desperately still. A slight buzz in his ear. Lafferty couldn't detect another sound, not a bird in the air, not a car on the road, nothing but a dark, quiet house at the top of the hill, this woman beside him, breathing, holding on to him for dear life, and the little brown Ford sitting idle, the back door open, the dark form spread across the seat like so much inanimate cargo. The night coming down in silence. Finally, Kitty spoke again. "Is there anybody else in the world who'll miss him? Is it only me and you?"

Lafferty thought about it. "Tom Hogan?"

At that, the spell was broke. And they had to giggle, the two of them, like a couple of kids in church, the two of them lying back, rolling in the weeds, laughing in the dark.

They brought him home again to Kitty's place on Talbot Street, stepping out into the wee hours, a distant clamor of downtown noise, the lamplights gleaming on the face of the rowhouse bricks. Above, the clouds were dirty gray with the underglow of the city. Your man was able to carry his da inside like a baby, he was that light, with only a grunt or two and them as dignified as he could make them, and they put him into his bed and rang the hospital up and sat down at the kitchen table to wait. They left him dressed, Lafferty, without the heart to strip his oul man down. Kitty put on water for tea, Lafferty opened a stout from the bottles lined up on the shelf, Kitty took one for herself, and they watched as the water boiled away to nothing, the steaming from the spout the only living sound in the air. When they spoke, it was whispers. On the back of the door hung the oul man's yellow dressing gown, and on top of a bookcase was a picture of him standing beside Kitty, his da in his healthier days, smiling his old smile, wearing sunglasses where a sharp spot of light glinted like a star. Handsome man. After a while, they came and they took him away without much of a fuss at all. Kitty signed the papers.

    Afterwards, it was empty. Kitty made her tea then. It was the middle of the night and far away they heard a horn sound somewhere down a Dublin street. She made him tea as well and they sat at the table a while sipping, himself surprised at how good it tasted after the ocean of stout. But his head was clear. He was incredibly sober. They talked quietly about arrangements, his da having made them all in advance, he'd insisted on being cremated, for wasn't he always cold, since the radiation after the surgery—the first radiation, the first surgery, when there'd still been a thimble of hope. Then the whispers ended and they sat in the quiet again. It was over. So over and empty. After a while, Lafferty looked outside through the one little window just when the night was at its blackest, and he said he'd better be leaving. He'd better be heading on home. Kitty reached and held his wrist to the table with her hand, saying, no, stay.

    "The missus'll be worried," said he. "She'll be expecting me."

    "Not until tomorrow. She wouldn't expect you till tomorrow. No woman would."

    "You don't know Peggy."

    "I do. I know that after twenty years, she'll be there. Tomorrow. And I know you mustn't leave me alone, not tonight, not now. There's a good boy." Her face was new with quiet fear, as if he'd never seen it before, all the freckles and wide green eyes glowing new.

The air was coming in and out of him like a low-voltage current. It hadn't occurred to him till then, till the thought of rest had entered his head, just how weary he was. And wasn't she right, he couldn't leave her alone in the night, not in the dark. There would be daylight soon. And so they went into the bed, there was only the one bed, the one she and his oul man had slept in for years, the one his oul man had reposed upon so recently dead, and they shared it, and Kitty turned out the lights. She needed to feel him there, so she rested her hand on his arm, and he dozed soon enough, but it was a fitful sleep, and he was wide awake again after what might have been a minute or an hour. He couldn't say if she was sleeping. He put his arm over her, and she squirmed easily, asleep or awake, nestling into him, and then he went asleep.

After some time, when the window was the color of mustard from the early morning light, she said, "What's that poking at me?" though she knew very well what it was.

"It's a circulation thing. Or maybe I was dreaming of someone else. Maybe Peggy."

"Well point it the other way, Terrance, there's a good boy."

And he did, somewhat triumphantly, the new Terrance.

And that might have been the end of it. He was proud of himself, how he'd grown. He'd learned something, he'd begun to figure this thing out, this father-son thing—bollocks, this life-and-death thing, for all that. He'd begun finally to get a handle on it, and he fell asleep again, deep and dreamless, the sort of sleep he imagined a baby slept, or the dead, and that should have been the end of it, but then along came the Gardaí banging loudly on the door.

Two of them. And when Kitty let them in, her eyes still heavy with the sleep, the big guard with the red cheeks said what do you know about the gun. "What gun," says Lafferty.

"The handgun," says the big man, "the Ruger .38 found in the pocket of the pea coat worn by Donal Lafferty, deceased."

There was nothing your man could say, being gobsmacked again as he was. Kitty's face went crimson, as crimson as the Bloody Foreland, and she murmured that there must be some kind of mistake, but Lafferty knew right away that there wasn't. And he pictured his mam there in Kitty's place, Flossie, pictured the nodding, affirmative, I-told-you-so look on her face, and he remembered then and wondered why, and he remembered it was not the first time he'd wondered why, his da had not so much as shown his face at her wake. And he wondered, most of all, who was this man, this Black man, Blackie, his da?

Over the Garden Wall

Two days after Christmas, two weeks after his son, Harry, had barged squalling into the world, the house was teeming with guests, drinks in their hands, teeth shining out of their gobs, there to welcome the wain and celebrate the season. One, a woman, a pretty woman clutching her bag, kept staring, and Lafferty, staring back, noticed her eyes weren't of a set, one eye staring him down, the other gazing out over his shoulder. There was something about her. Not only the staring, he was accustomed to that, to women gawking at him, what with the endearing dimple in his chin, his unruly good looks. What with his reputation. They were all guests of his wife, Peggy, her family and friends, coworkers from the hospital, and there was nothing out of the ordinary in them wanting to look him over, assess the goods, examine Peggy's ne'er-do-well pig of a husband, and wonder why she kept him around at all.

Having turned forty, having at last brought a child into the world, he was trying to mend his ways, to mature, to grow the bloody hell up. But reputations stay stuck on you like mange on a mutt, and Lafferty, at the end of the day, couldn't blame the lot of them for staring, for judging. And the one who kept gawking, the pretty one with the tangled black hair and lopsided green eyes, she might well be the one who took his reputation, chewed it over, liked the taste of it, and took it as an invitation. The one he would have to avoid, if his new leaf was to remain turned over.

What's wrong with this picture? When he was a lad, Lafferty would stare at the picture in the puzzle book till he found it, the wheel on the bike with no spokes, the clown with the missing ear, the square button in the row of round. A flirting friend of Peggy's, though, did not a square button make. Sure, there was something else. Something more.

He stepped outside for a wee bit of cogitation. Peggy'd barred the smoking from the premises, considering the babby's newborn lungs, and the little stoop and sodden yard about was crowded with chattering, undaunted smokers. Sodden butts ground into the dirt like a crop of potatoes. All up and down Blue Bucket Lane was parked a motley row of cars, and Lafferty noticed, again, the little blue Fiat down at the end of the row, a man still sitting inside it. He'd thought nothing of it at first, just a man and a cigarette, an anti-social sort, the stubborn sod who'd not wanted to come in the first place, who'd quarreled with his wife. But there he sat, still. Too far away to make out clearly. The clown with the missing ear? No. He'd not be the first pouting man who'd wanted to stay home and watch his game on the telly.

It was something else that didn't quite fit. Then again, maybe it was only himself. His new son, his new leaf, his new life, making him wonder did he fit in at all. Back inside, carols spilt from the kitchen, laughter from the hallway, lively craic, and he found himself watching the circle of women kneeling by the Christmas tree, cooing over the baby boy wrapped in blue beneath it. Peggy'd stuck him there, like a necktie or pair of gloves or box of chocolates—the most priceless gift of all, she said. Lafferty, with a contemplative gulp of stout, was assessing the degree to which he should agree with the sentiment, knowing full well there was a time he'd have scoffed at such fluff, when doesn't he feel a nudge at his arm. And the woman with the green, lopsided eyes says, "Isn't he just precious?"

"You bet," said Lafferty. "Precious indeed."

"Which one's his mother?" said the woman, and the bell rang. On his second try, he found the proper eye to stare into. "Do you not remember me at all?" said she.

Lafferty blinked. "Mrs. Hogan?"

"Call me Enya?" says she. Says the square button.

He remembered. The B&B in Donegal, scarcely three months before. Glancing at the gathering round the tree, the cooing women, Peggy in the forefront, gawking in adoration at the babby. Nudging Mrs. Hogan toward the corner for a bit of privacy. "What brings you to Kilduff?" seemed a nicer, gentler question than what the hell are you doing here.

"I was hoping to have a wee word with you."

Peggy looked up from the child toward the pair in the corner, other ladies following one by one, a dawning of suspicion. Lafferty looked at his wrist, where his watch would be had he a watch to wear, as though Mrs. Hogan's inquiry was simply about the time of day, and he pointed toward the loo, as if Mrs. Hogan's inquiry was simply about its whereabouts, mumbling meet me out back in the garden with scarcely a movement of lip. Ambled away with a nod toward the tree ladies. Through the kitchen, a great sloppy man named Browne clasped him about the shoulders in a rude plea for Lafferty to lend his voice to the roaring chorus of *Good King Wenceslas*, but Lafferty gracefully demurred, making his way out to the garden. There he waited. A chill in the damp, sunless air. He could make out down the road the little blue Fiat still there. The lump of a man still within it.

Mrs. Hogan coming at him, her fingers working imaginary beads.

"How the devil are you after finding me?" says he.

"You put your name and address down in the guest book," says Mrs. Hogan. "Do you not remember? Do you not remember me at all?"

He did. He'd forgotten even signing the bloody book, so taken was he at the time by the stunning apparition of Mrs. Hogan, the ambush of sudden loveliness in God-forsaken Donegal, like finding a gem in the muck.

Peggy'd insisted on a getaway, an overnight holiday before the baby arrived, just the pair of them—the first time they'd been away together in donkey's years. He suspected she was putting him to the test, to judge if he might make a proper husband and father for all that. They spent the night at the Gorse Hill B&B, the Hogans' establishment, and truth be known—please God, Peggy never would—he hadn't truly passed the test. For hadn't Mrs. Hogan that night had a need and a hunger and other ideas.

"I do. I remember you."

"Don't hate me," says she.

"Hate you? Why would I hate you?"

"After I've told you the news."

"What news?" Though by now he knew what news.

"I—I'm in the family way."

The knowing of the news did nothing to soften it. Your man may have cringed.

"I was out of my mind, for God's sake," she said, "I'm sorry!" Sudden wetness in the good green eye. "Himself pissed out of his senses, again, bloody blind and roaring and filthy, again, and—" This time the full sob escaped her. "Do you hate me?"

"No, of course not, it's only—"

She was in his arms before he could finish the sentence, having leapt there like a fairy, where Lafferty held her as though she'd been dipped in paint.

"Now, to be sure," he said with a modest grunt, for she was not as light as she looked, "you're saying it couldn't be his then, Mr. Hogan's, for sure?"

She unwound herself, dropping, backing off, presto, chango, mortally indignant. "No, Mr. Lafferty," says she, "it could not be. Why, I can't remember the last time him and me…"

He gathered in a great trembling chestful of air. "And does he know?"

She sniffled and frowned and maybe a nod. A raucous rendition of *Silent Night* came tumbling out of the kitchen. Her eyes, each on its own, fell to the ground, the grays and browns of dirty old December, the opposite direction of your man's eyes, that were looking toward the gloomy sky over the cars parked down the road.

"Mrs. Hogan," he said, "Enya—what kind of car does your mister drive?"

Presto, chango. She smiled, smearing the tears with the back of her hand, suddenly bright as a snowflake. "Why, a wee Fiat. He can barely squeeze into the thing."

"And the color," he said. "Is there any chance the thing could be blue?"

"Aye. Blue as a button. Why do you ask?"

Though he was not as given to rash impulse as he'd been in his younger days, the difference between Lafferty at forty and Lafferty at twenty would not be readily apparent to a blind man on a fast horse. Within minutes, he was hightailing it. Whatever consequence he might have to face from Peggy, whose old brown Ford he hijacked for the hightailing, whom he was abandoning to the mercies of a gossipy mob, however he might have to fend off her fuming and fury, it seemed nothing in comparison to the fury of a large and hostile man whose wife he'd left up the pole. On the night in question, he'd heard the drunken roar of him beyond the guest room door at the Gorse Hill B&B, a roar fierce, desperate, and mortally frightful.

And now, hadn't he seen in the rearview the little blue Fiat nosing out onto the road behind him as he sped away down Blue Bucket Lane.

"Himself is behind us, following," said Lafferty.

"Holy mother of God," says Enya, "I don't understand how..."

"You're after saying he suspected. Could he not have looked in the guest book too?"

Enya cocked her head to stare quizzically. Crowded by her feet was the bulky canvas bag she carried, large and worn and stained, an odd sprinkling of multicolored plastic gemstones glued on the side in a design such as a child might craft, a crooked yellow sun with rays spraying out, flowers or weeds or trees or some such underneath. She turned to show him her face full of alarm. "Begod—shouldn't we go back for the child?"

"For Harry?"

"Yes! For the boy, the boy, for the precious baby boy!"

Such was her state of excitement, so red her face, he was at a loss to place the pieces properly. "He's fine—he's fine. Well looked after, believe me. In good hands."

The words quit coming out of her then, but the look of panic remained, until, just as quickly, an emptiness took its place, as though she were trying to remember something beyond recall, something she never really knew.

"Where should we go?" he said. He wanted to know—for he hadn't planned beyond making good the escape—though at the same time, he wanted to rein in the suddenly bucking bronco beside him.

"I haven't a baldy notion," she said.

"We'll find a place, have a pint, make a plan," said he, calm as a clam in command. Though already he knew. Even now, he already knew where he was taking her.

She turned to look, but the little blue car had fallen from view. Sinking back, she reached over and took his hand. Her own hand hot and damp.

It sank into him that she was a stranger, this woman who, before this day, he'd been in the presence of for maybe fifteen minutes of a lifetime, the intimacy of those minutes notwithstanding. That night had been a dream—the scent of the ocean in the breeze over a hillside in wild Donegal when he'd stepped outside, unable to sleep—Peggy, pregnant, had been snoring for two. Still shaken, he was by the drunken roar of Mr. Hogan coming home late and thoroughly langered before he'd passed out, his own raging snore from somewhere in the house. And Mrs. Hogan accosting him there in the wee moonlit garden, pulling him down atop her in the damp, dewy grass. No choice but to meet her demand for love, so fierce was her hunger.

Now, holding the hand of this person he didn't know, this person who purportedly carried another child of his own, he felt out of sorts. Nevertheless, he clasped her hand in return, squeezed it reassuringly. For he was not the sort to wound the feelings of another if he could help it, particularly one so like a frightened kitten.

This was his own turf, far from the boglands of Donegal where Daniel Hogan, Proprietor, Gorse Hill B&B (so said the sign in the front), had marked his own territory, and it was Lafferty who knew the shortcuts and cut-offs, the lay of the land in general. And soon found himself following a leisurely lane northward up the island, across the rolling midland plains, sheep country, stone walls and hedgerows of hawthorn and holly, the occasional grand vista of fields and farms, varying degrees of green trying to stay brave in the gray December day. And no sign of the Fiat behind them.

When her hand fell limp in his, he looked at her sleeping. On the run and fast asleep. And oddity, to be sure.

Or not? The great relief of having delivered herself to him, of having placed herself and her worry into his hands, had no doubt scrubbed her mind clean, freeing it to easeful sleep. *Delivered herself to his protection.* This sleeping woman, this frightened creature, placing herself in his hands—didn't the very thought of it puff him up for a moment.

Just as quickly, it left him, like air squealing out of the balloon.

The role didn't fit. He'd tried it on before. All the people in his life—all the women—he'd loved and failed, back down all the years, back to Flossie, his own mother. And now a son, Harry, Harry in the world. The thought of holding the well-being of the wee babby in his hands filled him with doubt and dread, though the more he thought it over, the more it came to him what a waste of perfectly good dread it was. There was no doubt in his mind that Peggy—one of the first of his failures—in no way believed him to be capable of any degree of protection whatsoever. Of Harry or of anyone else on God's green earth.

As Enya slept, the notion of protection leaking out of him entirely, he plotted his way back to the north, to Donegal, to deliver the woman back to wherever and whatever she'd come from—to do quite the opposite of protect her. Allowing any inklings of guilt and betrayal to crawl back into the dark recesses of his blameless mind, where they rightly belonged. Above, a bird of prey sailed high, disappearing into the overcast of clouds. When Enya finally stirred, she looked about bewildered, with a desperate frown that, before his very eyes, melted into a beguiling smile.

"Tell me about him," said Lafferty. "Your oul one. Is he savage and fierce as he sounded that night?"

She nearly leapt from the seat looking back, but the road behind them was clear. "Yes," she said. "No."

"Yes? No?"

"You wouldn't want to be near him when he's into the gargle, which is nearly always. He's a beast, fierce and mean and loud, though at times when he's not pissed out of his mind, he can be gentle as a lamb."

"A lamb? That one?"

"He loves his poems. He's forever reciting me poems."

"*Poems*? You don't say. A man of surprises. What sort of poetry? Yeats? Moore?"

"Sure, I don't know one from the other. Such as this: I eat my peas with honey. / I've done it all my life. / They do taste kind of funny, / but it keeps them on the knife."

"I see. Lovely. And what does your poet do for a living?"

"Why, the B&B."

"You couldn't make a living off that, sure you couldn't."

"It's not so bad in summer. There's the dole as well. And of course, he's forever trying to get his hands on my fortune."

"Your fortune? You have a fortune? What sort of a fortune?"

"Why are you asking me all these questions?" came out too harsh for its own good.

Lafferty raised an eyebrow. "A wee bit of chit-chat is all. Shouldn't we be getting to know one another better, what with the news you're after telling me."

Enya's cross frown retreating.

"The news of the child," says he.

"Aye," she said. "The child."

Lafferty said nothing more. Her mention of a fortune snagged in his mind as such mentions were naturally wont to do. Her imaginary fortune, he imagined. He was beginning to suspect much of Enya Hogan's world was imaginary.

"Where are we going?" says she, stiffening and bristling.
"North." He looked over, fearful of her reaction. "The last place he'd think to look—the place where you're just after leaving."

She looked at him softly, her pretty face cocked to see him all the better with her good, true eye, and the chest of her heaved, and she reached over past his hand this time, to touch his pocket. She said, "Aren't you the sweetest man? Then, just as quickly, she turned to see a thing passing by. "Oh look, there's Jesus," said she, and by the time he was able to peep in the rearview, whatever it was was gone. Whether it had been a Christmas artifact bedecking a cottage by the side of the road, or the genuine article Himself, he would never know for sure. With Enya Hogan, it seemed, you could never know for sure.

Up into Donegal, the hillsides and boglands growing more barren and brown, he spied a pub by the side of the road, a place called Gilligan's Island. He liked the whimsy in the name and hadn't he after all promised to find a place, have a pint, make a plan. And didn't his legs need a grand stretching after two hours on the road. And not a whiff of a notion of where to go to now that he was nearing the edge of the island, of what to do with this one beside him, this creature of ups and downs and highs and lows and little in between.

When he pulled into the carpark and shut off the motor, she didn't stir, asleep again. He looked at the handsome face of her, the chin tucked down toward her chest, her feet crowded in by her big canvas bag. Her chest. Bosom gently heaving with her breathing, her oversized tan jacket fallen open, her hands laying easy in her lap, where the soft dress gathered up in bunches. Her lap. He thought of the night in the moonlit garden, the mortal pleasure of the instant, and didn't the stirring commence in his own nether regions. It had been ages since he'd had a dalliance with his own missus, what with wee Harry having invaded, an occupying army, both before and after his birth. And wasn't the lust the last thing he needed just now.

He resolved to not give in. Another intimate episode would represent another degree of commitment, and wasn't commitment another last thing he needed now. He resolved to maintain a courteous manner, helpful, sympathetic, dispensing only as much charm as he dared, and that as distant as he could disguise it.

At that moment, she came awake and saw him watching, her good green eye homing in, coming nearer, almost without him realizing the approach, coming nearer as though by instinct alone, and wasn't her hand up his leg and onto his own lap before he knew it.

He felt out of sorts, again, the same odd discomfort, the hand of this stranger having reached into his trousers, yet didn't he nevertheless clasp the neck of her, squeeze it reassuringly. For he still was not the sort to wound the feelings of another if he could help it, particularly one so like this frightened kitten.

Walking into the place called Gilligan's Island afterwards, she threw back her head to laugh at the sky, and didn't your man laugh along. For the promise of a pint in a newfound pub, the mellow afterglow of the antics in the little brown Ford, the sense of freedom—however fleeting he knew it had to be—from the routines of the everyday, dreary domesticities, all conspired to send him high as the sky that they laughed at. The pub was a ramshackle establishment with a tin roof and, inside beside a turf fire, a juke box playing: *I shot a man in Reno, just to watch him die.* He took her into the empty snug at the end of the bar for the privacy, for it occurred to him, somewhere within the transitory joy, that Gilligan's Island was, after all, on the main motorway from the midlands up through Donegal.

A handsome snug it was, polished wood and frosted glass, two comfortable stools trimmed with something akin to leather, and, most important in Lafferty's mind, a solicitous barman who was hearing their orders before they were firmly settled into their seats. He ordered a pint of plain, she a lemonade.

"My condition," she said, patting her middle. "They say the drink is bad for the wain."

The wain. He felt the slippage begin. "So they say," says he. "It's a wonder then we're not a nation of imbeciles and lunatics, if there's any truth to it at all."

"Are we not?" says she, and Lafferty had to squint to see the joke. She said, "Have you thought about how close our baby and little Harry—Harry's the name of your other, is it not—how close in age they'll be? Won't it be grand? Won't it be the grandest thing? They'll be best mates—like brother and sister they'll be, or brother and brother, I don't know which yet, but then of course they will be. Half-brothers they'll be."

Lafferty nearing full free-fall by now. "We'd best figure this thing out."

Her one green eye smiling, the other one over the moon. "Sure, I've been figuring all the while. We can buy a pub someplace, a pub like this one—maybe even buy *this* pub."

"Buy a *pub*? With what? My good looks?"

She smiled and touched his thigh. Again. "Handsome you may be, but maybe not quite *that* handsome."

Wasn't your man at a loss. The blood in him beginning to run for cover. "We'd do well to think of a realistic plan, something a little more—realistic."

"What's not real? Sure, you love the drink after all, you can be a real publican, make real, honest money, all your mates'll come in to have a jar with you. I can cook in the kitchen, at least now and again, when I'm not busy with the wains. Harry and our child—we must think of a name—Harry and our child, they can play in the carpark. We can build a play contraption there—a jungle-gym."

"And where will the bloody cars park?"

She frowned. "*Dream* with me, Mr. Lafferty."

"Terrance," says he.

"*Dream* with me, Terrance Lafferty, then."

"I can't bloody dream. I'm not bloody sleeping."

"You can dream if you try. If you want."

"We've no money. We can't buy a bloody pub."

"There's always money."

"Where?"

An odd crinkle to her brow. "There's always money."

"And what about my wife? What about Peggy?"

This was what caused the shadow to cross her wounded face, her eyes to soften and moisten in differing directions, though there was something else there as well. Something in the eyes of her shifted, hardened, something like resolve taking shape in the shadows.

But Lafferty was in with both feet. "I can't just bloody walk out of my life."

She said nothing, pointing her chin out bravely over her untouched lemonade.

He downed his pint, motioned for another, but the only taste of it was brooding and sour. Of all the escapes he'd pulled off in his lifetime—his specialty, escape—none before had ever been in slow-motion. Finally, when it was evident she was sulking, intent on sitting silent, the part of him that was not the sort to wound the feelings of another, particularly one so like a frightened kitten, began to rise up again. "We'll think of something," he said at last. "Some way I can help. Some way we can manage."

She came out of her sulk. "Here's another then," she said. "Over the garden wall, I let the baby fall. / My ma came out and she give me a clout, / over the garden wall."

Coming out of Gilligan's Island, Enya clutching the bag she'd been swinging so gaily going in, clutching it to her chest now like a wounded teddy bear, they saw Peggy's little brown Ford had been parked in. A big man emerging from the little blue Fiat that had parked it in.

All his life, Lafferty'd heard talk of this thing called the Fight or Flight Instinct. All his life he'd never truly believed in it, like Santa Claus and the tooth fairy, for the only thing he'd ever been possessed of was the Flight Instinct.

He turned on his heel and ran.

Enya behind him just as quick. Daniel Hogan's roar, "Stop! Wait!"

Back inside the pub were lounges, alcoves, a barroom, a dining room, any number of snugs to choose from in the ramshackle establishment, and there was the door to the kitchen where a back door would be, and there was the loo with maybe a window. Lafferty's choice. Enya had darted her own separate way, Hogan no doubt still lumbering across the carpark. Inside the jacks, he saw the window too small for egress. Two stalls. He went into the one, closed the door, latched it, stood panting and sweating like a stevedore. If Hogan came in, the jig would be up. *When* Hogan came in. Nowhere to hide. His feet could be seen under the door. Up he stepped onto the toilet. His head could be seen over the top. He crouched. Squatting on the seat of the toilet—there was no lid, only a seat, he had to take care not to slip in—didn't he feel the complete bloody eejit.

Albeit a *hidden*, complete bloody eejit. Some measure of consolation.

Probably a minute that seemed like ten, and his thighs began to ache, his ankles to tremble, his knees to threaten to pop. It occurred to him he could make himself comfortable until he heard the bloody door, and he started to make himself comfortable when he heard the bloody door.

Followed by footsteps. That stopped at the door of the stall. The door was pressed with a wee squeak, one, two, three wee squeaks, then the voice. "Fee, fi, fo, fum, I smell the blood of an Offaly man," was, while not a roar, nonetheless familiar.

Lafferty held his breath.

The door to the stall beside him squeaked open, followed by a grunt, the groaning of floor and fixture, a shadow, and Lafferty looked up into the face of the big man staring down. Not an angry face. An anguished face. A tear dropped from it onto the floor by the toilet, where many an unmentionable fluid had fallen before.

"Can you help me, Mr. Lafferty?" said he. "Can you help me bring her home?"

They walked outside together, Lafferty and Daniel Hogan, the former's left foot soaked through and through, having splashed it into the toilet bowl as he'd tried to stand on wobbly legs. Hadn't your man Daniel Hogan laughed then, hadn't his tears of laughter commingled with those of his sorrow, the misfortune of another man seldom failing in that regard, at least not in Lafferty's memory. Outside, in the carpark, they stood staring together like old mates at Peggy's little brown Ford. Lafferty took advantage of the occasion to inquire of your man, Hogan, as to whether or not he had neglected to take the keys from the little blue Fiat when he'd exited so hastily giving chase. Hogan didn't reply. Together they stared at the vacant spot where the little blue Fiat had been, wondering where, oh where, could she be.

Hogan thought he might know. Less than an hour to the north were the ruins of a place called Carrickbarren Castle. Hogan had found her there before. They'd stopped one grand day after an outing when their lad was only toddling, and the child had been so delighted, exploring the open stone steps and ramparts and walls with such joy that Enya had never forgotten. Since the boy died, she'd returned several times, as if in hopes of finding him there.

"You'd a child who died?" Lafferty said.

"Aye," said Hogan. "Billy."

"Billy." Lafferty remembered it then, in the foyer at the Gorse Hill B&B three months before, a picture on the wall on an equal footing with that of the Savior and His bleeding heart, a photograph, enlarged, behind glass, of a yellow-haired boy with the ears of an imp and a dirty face. Blurry, a snapshot not intended to be the lasting memory. Lafferty'd thought nothing of it at the time, room in his mind for only the stunning vision of Enya Hogan.

Billy. How did the lad die?

Too delicate a question to ask. He didn't ask it. Hogan was well into his cups—Lafferty suspected that to be his normal state—though all the roaring was over, a fated and restless calm having settled over him. He rambled on in his voice like low thunder. Stuffed into the passenger seat where his wife before him had been transported like a canary in a cage up from Kilduff, and didn't Lafferty wonder if Hogan could imagine the shenanigans that had taken place, could maybe even sniff the lingering scent of them. And the more he went on about her, about Enya Hogan, nee Bannon, his wife, his pet, unknowable, untamable, both wild and needy, the more Lafferty began to worry that the scent would surely come through, reveal itself, and he remained alert to the possibility of eruption from the volcano sitting dormant beside him.

Not an easy life for Enya Bannon, as her husband would have it: abused by a drunken mother who died young, the daddy she adored deserting her—a thief, truth be known, who scored big and vanished off into parts unknown—leaving her all on her own, wild as a wren, before the nuns had taken her in and suffocated her. As a wee lass, she would pin the prickly sowthistle in her hair and run naked through the heather on the hillsides, imagining herself to be a Celtic goddess, how she'd paint up her face with the juices of berries, till the nuns, stern in all their horror, had beaten that nonsense out of her.

It was with the losing of Billy that the glue had finally come undone—though Hogan conceded that his own miserable indulgence in the drink hadn't helped—the losing of Billy, knowing all the while that he'd been her last and only, that she was incapable of bearing another.

"She can't have another child?" Lafferty said.

Hogan shook his head, glancing over, sly blue eye over fat red cheek. "But she's after telling you otherwise?"

Lafferty didn't reply, staring instead out through the windscreen up the lonely little road they were travelling, allowing the topic to scurry away.

After a proper pause, he said, "She's after telling me you like the poetry."

"Ach," said Hogan with a rumble of a chuckle and a dismissive wave. "She loves her silly rhymes, she does. I use 'em to lull her down, soothe the savage breast—a useful tool in that regard. Her and Billy used to laugh—the one feeding off the other—till the tears would be streaming out of their faces, the pair of them."

"She recited me a couple. One about peas and honey."

"One of her favorites, that one is." He recited the thing. "Didn't Billy have to try it himself, eating his peas off his knife. Honey and all—such a face he made."

"And another about a garden wall. About a baby falling over the garden wall."

Hogan let his chuckle slip away, wiping at his cheek with the back of a fat hand. "Garden wall? I never told her any such about a baby and a garden wall."

"Something about her ma giving her a clout?"

"Oh, that part I can believe. But it's not one of my own."

"Maybe she made it up."

"We'll bloody well ask her. After we bloody well find her."

Less than an hour later, when the evening was beginning to come down over the rolling bogland up the coast of Donegal, and the storm clouds thicken out over the Atlantic, they found the little blue Fiat parked in the gorse where the lane ended at the ruins of Carrickbarren Castle. The gray light held a pale luminescence, the day suspended halfway to night. The ancient stone tower looked to have been lopped off halfway up, a ragged cut, while a stone wall with only a parapet or two remaining trailed off, guarding nothing, a few more odd, meandering walls and piles of rubble nearby, all of it overgrown with the brambles, all of it roofless. Ivy clinging up the stones. Out toward the north and the west, the sky was black, storm winds stirring, carrying with them the scent of the ocean.

Hogan unfurled himself from the little brown Ford. Lafferty followed. "Where the devil's she off to?" mumbled the big man. Then he sang out, another roar, "Enya—Enya, darling!" and listened, but there was only the whisper of a breeze in response.

Lafferty called out, "Mrs. Hogan—Enya!"

They stood for a moment by the car, listening. Hogan said, "You go that way, Mr. Lafferty, I'll poke about over there," and off they went their separate ways.

He heard the rumble of Hogan calling for his wife, even after they'd lost sight of one another. Lafferty made his way through the rubble down the wall, eyes scanning the high grasses and sedges and heather of the boglands surrounding, calling, loud as he could, though his call was dwarfed by that of Hogan up beyond the tower. Was she hiding? Was she hurt? Had she wandered off? The light was failing.

A sense of urgency quickened in him, then, just as quickly, the sense of urgency brought all the other urgencies to his mind, urgencies such as the missus, Peggy, at home, all alone with wee Harry, waiting, wondering where he'd got off to. The hell there'd be to pay.

There came Hogan's call again, softer, different in tone, "Enya," the tone of discovery, of revelation, then again from up beyond the tower, barely heard, "Enya? Love?" Then a hollow knock of some sort, a quiet commotion, and nothing again, only the quiet of the restless breeze from out over the ocean.

He hurried toward the sound, like swimming upstream, the dread was that thick.

He found Hogan, on his back, on the ground, blood glistening on the dead, ruined face of him. A flash of motion, a soft rushing sound, and a glimpse of what he took to be a woman, naked, running off through the heather, vanishing up into the bog.

He found her clothes among the stones and brambles. The tan jacket sprawled like a victim, limp rag of a dress a few feet off, a pair of knickers, a dreary brassiere, and the bag, the oversized canvas bag with the crooked yellow sun tipped over, not far from the tower. Something peeped out of it. He dipped in his hand and pulled out a bundle of cash.

A tidy stack, rubber-banded, old Irish money, punts, not Euros. Pulled out another. There were five bundles altogether, inches high, soft to the touch, lovely and supple with age.

He climbed the open stairway in the tower, stood looking out over the highest stone still standing, scanning the darkening bog, searching for a sign of the woman. The breeze in his face, the primal smell of ocean, his hands gripping a stone placed there by a man five hundred years before.

His left foot had an oddness about it that set it apart from the other, from the rest of his body altogether, the foot that he'd dunked in the toilet. Still damp it was. Lafferty lifted it, shook it. *You put your left foot in, you put your left foot out*—didn't he curse himself then, mayhem and tragedy all about, a fine fellow (for all it would seem) lying dead in the ruins of an ancient castle, an injured, damaged creature rushing headlong into the storm, and him with a silly song rampaging through his brain, *—you put your left foot in and then you shake it all about.*

Should he not report the whole desperate affair to the Gardaí? Of course he should. Hogan lying there dead, his head bashed in. His face. Not the back of his head. He'd been facing her then, looking at her, looking into the eyes of her as she raised up the stone. Into which eye had he stared, into the one that bore down on him, or into the one that wandered out over the bog? Should he not report it all to the Gardaí? Should he not report the money, the thousands of punts? Of course he should.

He should. But then again too, after more than a bloody hour, shouldn't his bloody foot be bloody well dry?

The hell there'd be to pay. In the wee hours when he finally arrived back at his home on Blue Bucket Lane, the missus was still awake. Your man braced himself going in through the door.

And didn't she call out softly from the bedroom.

"Terrance? Terrance? Is it you?"

"Aye. I'm back."

"Where were you?"

"I had to run out. An errand for a friend."

"Brilliant, love. You'll have to be quiet, there's a good man. I'm only just after getting him down. He wouldn't go down for me at all, at all—too much excitement in the day."

Savage December

The first time Lafferty saw her, she was standing by the side of the road in Kilduff, a dead dog on the end of her leash. Molly Scanlon was her name. The dog was brown and furry and twisted and dead (Lafferty couldn't name the breed, being neither a dog man nor a cat man, nor even a guppy man), and Molly's mouth fallen open at the sight of the van speeding away, the van that had just destroyed her dog. A dastardly hit and run. Duffy, he learned later, was its name. When the van had vanished round the bend by Connor's News Agent and was gone from sight, her head turned back toward him, a face so homely it was pretty, buckteeth, pointy chin and eyes like saucers, especially now, so wide in shock and beginning to tear, and the next place they fell was on your man. Nothing was said, and she was in his arms, an embrace transcending the want of words. She needed comfort. He gave it. And himself needing it as well, it seemed, for whatever reason God only knew, but it felt like a comfort he both needed and deserved. They stood hugging, swaying, for some time, dead Duffy on a leash in the gutter at their feet.

The comforting continued in her wee room above the Pig & Whistle, the box of milk he'd been sent to fetch for his wife, Peggy, growing ever more tardy and forgotten into that long, long evening.

At the time, his son, Harry, was five. Since the day he'd learned of his impending paternity, around the time he'd turned the corner at forty years of age, your man had tried to kick the habit, the habit of being, as Peggy and her lot would have it, a habitual womanizer, a faithless bastard. A lover of life and women and all mankind was the phraseology he much preferred. He'd not always been successful, but he was getting better; he'd not been able to quit cold turkey, but he was cutting down. Molly was the first time he'd fallen off the wagon in a while.

In her bed, the light failing through the plain yellow curtains, the noise from the Pig & Whistle filling up the gloaming, she asked him hadn't he better be on his way, wouldn't his wife be looking for him. He said she would.

He said, "What about Duffy? Should we not bury him then?"

"I suppose," said she. "We can't leave the poor thing to rot."

"Should we mark his grave somehow?"

"Sure, he's only a fecking dog, Terrance."

Lafferty considered the wisdom in her words. In the dim light, she drew close to him under the covers. In the dimness, she was no longer so wretched, no longer a cleaning woman in their nibs's estates, she was not living in this hovel of a room—she was a proud and lovely woman, the scent of talcum on her skin, a scent that made him long for something from a time before he could remember. She'd told him early on she was pregnant, and after they'd decided where to bury the dog—too soon after, he realized in hindsight—he asked what were her plans for the future. Had she a friend, a family, was there anyone there to help out? There was no one, she said, not really. She sat up in the failing light, a squawk from the bed, and her untamed hair, trying to flee her head, resembled a halo from the glow through the window beyond. She intended to do the best she could, she told him, and Lafferty, realizing the best she could was scarcely a pot to piss in, imagined her standing bewildered, her baby dead in the gutter at the end of the leash.

How could he not comfort her? She was thirty and homely and brave and no prospects and up the pole, the would-be father, a man with no honor, and—so far as poor Molly was aware—no last name either. He'd left her with a pup named Duffy and no hope at all. Only a heartless bastard would not comfort the wee girl, and of the many things Lafferty was reputed to be, a heartless bastard was never among them.

The comforting continued for months. She had the child and named him Owen. Lafferty prevailed upon the unknowing generosity of his wife, Peggy, a nurse with a fine income and a bit in the bank, who, he figured, would not notice a few bobs missing here and there from her tidy stash, and he provided Molly with the means to procure a crib for the child and a Jolly Jumper, and other wee comforts. A pot to piss in.

When the weather was fine, they went to a spot he knew, the tumbled-down ruins of a cottage up a lonely boreen overlooking a sweep of fields where the yellow gorse and the purple heather waved and bobbed in the breezes. A perfect place to bring a lover, a fine place to pack a basket and the boys, and go to spread a blanket for a picnic and watch them run amuck. By the time Owen was able to toddle about, Harry, Lafferty's own, was six and had assumed the mantle of big brother, taking command over the baby, showing him the finer points of making his way in the world, not always to Owen's delight. On a spring afternoon in May, the sun had finally broken through after days of sodden weather, and there was no holding back the boyos, Harry and Owen, who ran and splashed and jumped by the old stone wall near the ruined cottage as if it was the first day of sunshine on earth. Down the sweep of fields, stone walls crisscrossed, the grand tapestry of a mad weaver.

"Ach, they're going to be filthy and drenched," said Molly, though she made no move to retrieve her child, who was bending near the stones, as toddlers do, nearly tumbling onto his oversized head. Harry leaped in a nearby puddle.

"Where there's muck, there's luck," said Lafferty.

"What does that mean?"

He shrugged. "My oul man used to say it all the time."

As soon as the old saw had left his lips, didn't Owen commence screaming bloody murder. They looked, and there he was, flat on his bottom in the mud by the wall, face twisted in fury and mortal anguish, Harry standing over him examining the thing in his hand, a calm and expert appraiser at six years of age, looking over the misshapen metal ring he'd just yanked from the hand of the babe.

Harry. Lafferty studied his first and only son. He'd been just as taken as the next man by the miracle of birth—though Peggy hadn't allowed him to set foot in the delivery room, much to his great, unadmitted relief—by the creation of life out of sperm and egg, by the wee creature emerging from his wife, and didn't he expend as many ooh's and aah's as the next man at all the miniature parts and the way they fit together. And little was he concerned by the lack of regard in which the infant seemed to hold him, for not much could occupy his attention at that point except for the breast and the milk, a sparkly item here and there, and whatever displeasing article might suddenly inhabit his nappy. But still, even later, even after the little fellow's eyes and mind became capable of focus, Lafferty seldom was the object of that focus. He and the fruit of his loins seemed to be little more than fellow travelers, indifferent companions at best. After the first years of marriage, Peggy had become utterly immune to Lafferty's charms, a trait the little fellow seemed to have inherited. His hair, when it arrived, was red. Neither Terrance's nor Peggy's showed any trace of such a color. The little fellow, as he grew older, seemed to have a confrontational nature, opposed to that of Lafferty, and he seemed a rough-and-tumble chap, unlike his da as well. Watching him standing over the screaming Owen, holding the ring—an old, discarded bull ring, or so they supposed at the time—in casual gloat and taunt, didn't your man wonder where such traits had come from, for they were absent his blood entirely.

He distinctly remembered thinking those words that day, even before Peggy had sprung her trap.

The next day it was, or the day after that, he returned to his home—Peggy's home—on Blue Bucket Lane from a visit to Molly, a visit where comforts indeed were again exchanged. There, he found tacked to the blue front door snaps of him and Molly dancing the horizontal hornpipe as well as copies of withdrawal slips with her name that he'd forged. Standing in the window staring out, over Peggy's shoulder, was Clive, the dairy lorry driver. Red-headed, rough-and-tumble Clive, and his nose in Peggy's hair.

And all the locks were changed. And all the damage done.

Five years on, hard and lonely years. December had just turned savage, baring its ugly teeth, and Lafferty woke to the grumbling of the window, the cold fingers of the draft fondling him in his little cot. It took a minute to get his bearings, not the first time he'd awoken in the morning, wondering where the hell he was—in how many different places had he come awake in all his years on the planet? Surely hundreds. Thousands perhaps. Only nobody nowadays at his side. His eyes took in the shabby little digs in the gloaming, the threadbare sofa, the rag of a rug, the spindly, mismatched chairs, a dilapidated table beneath a clock on the wall, a cuckoo clock of all things, one that Jimmy fancied—of course, Jimmy's! Jimmy's digs was where he was—the cuckoo expired, clock frozen at seven-thirteen. A smell of cat piss. Clacko, fat and furry, walking like a prince away from his box that hadn't been cleaned for a week. Having pissed on the floor out of peevishness.

Lafferty got up and peeked in the bedroom. Clacko was climbing back up for the warmth of Jimmy and his comforter, Jimmy, his mouth open, snoring, one sock on, one sock off, his high-topped sneakers in a tumble on the floor. So innocent when they're sleeping, thought Lafferty. Not so innocent last night at Maximillian's.

A city lad, born and bred in Dublin, Lafferty'd been away many years, an exile necessitated by his want of keeping Peggy's roof over his head when she moved to the little country village, Kilduff, to further her nursing career. Until the crashing end five years before, when she'd finally tossed him out on his ear. It was true, he was learning, what he'd heard about the passing years, their viciousness. Once upon a time, he'd plenty of mates, though now, in his fiftieth year, the number was dwindling. And now wasn't he reduced to the borrowing of a few bobs from this old mate and that, twenty from the next, and himself entirely without the means to repay them. Gainful days at his turf accountant's had grown inexplicably rarer and rarer, odd jobs that suited his temperament and talents rarer still. In his fiftieth year, he seemed to have lost his touch with the horses, as well as with the girleens, and found himself evading his erstwhile mates and all their red and demanding faces.

All but Jimmy. One of the few still good for a bob and a pint was Jimmy, good not only for a bob and a pint, but for a cot and a corner as well. He supposed Jimmy was that hard-pressed for mates, being a goofy case, goose-necked, Adam's apple big as a fist, and a scar on the top of his head from where the bar stool did its damage years ago, knocking him even goofier than he had been before.

Maximillian's was a local a few blocks from the canal, a hole in the wall far less grand than the sound of its name. Jimmy fancied the barmaid there, a girl called Oona. During the years of Lafferty's exile, Jimmy'd been barred for bad behavior from O'Faolain's, a favorite watering hole of their youths, and from the Thorn and Thistle, McGarrity's, and any other number of long-ago locals. And wasn't it touch and go last night at Maximillian's as well. Jimmy'd always been a hard case down the years, a wild man with drink taken, meek as a sheep without it, and after the thump on the head that broke his skull, there was no telling which way the wild in him might go charging. Last night, three lovely old gents, well into the gargle, had been singing at the bar, and Jimmy, who fancied himself a crooner, joined in. It was fine then for a while, the four of them, arms about one another's' shoulders, *Will ye go, lassie, go,* till Jimmy wanted to do *Boys of the Old Brigade*, and the old gents being leery of rebel songs demurred, and Jimmy insisted, and the more the demurring and insisting went on, the more fierce the look on the face of Jimmy, the more fearful the look on those of the old gents, till finally intervention was in order. Oona, small but wiry, and Lafferty broke up the quartet, but Jimmy, miffed, kept singing by himself at the far end of the bar, while the old gents tried to croon on, Jimmy singing *Kevin Barry*, *The Rising of the Moon*, any rebel song he could conjure up, loud enough to wake the dead and no regard to tune, and finally Oona said to put a lid on it or he'd have to go, and didn't Jimmy lock himself in the jacks and keep singing at the top of his lungs.

Jimmy needed a mate, not so much as a minder.

When Jimmy showed no signs of joining the waking world, Lafferty headed downtown to pick up a pair of gloves, a wool muffler if one was to be had, maybe an overcoat as well if he could find one that suited. Leaving Jimmy snug in his bed where he'd tucked him.

Passing down a narrow lane of cobblestones and old shops, something caught his eye in amongst the musty volumes, foreboding busts, old globes, and assorted ancient clutter in the window of a shop called *Tinley's Antiquities*. Encased in polished wood and glass, it bore a brass plate with the inscription *Viking Arm Ring circa 950 AD*. Not really a ring at all, it was a misshapen oval, ornate, darkly gleaming silver, intricately twisted. *Inquire Within* says the note on the door. He stood for a moment taking it in through the iron bars in the dim window, for didn't the thing look familiar, something about the shape of it he was sure he'd seen before, déjà vu had him by the knees, but then along came another gust down the street, pushing flurries of snow in a worried swirl, biting through your man's threadbare tweeds to the very bones of him.

On to Clerys then—the Viking arm ring had hung around since 950 AD, sure it could wait a wee bit longer—narrow lanes blossoming into proper streets, and no matter which corner he turned was the teeth of an icy wind. *Jesus*, he muttered, *Holy Mother of God*, in the face of an especially fierce gust, onto O'Connell Street, broad thoroughfare, the wind even more brutal, and he headed face down, heedless of traffic, light for a Sunday afternoon, toward Clerys, sparkling with your Christmas lights.

He stood thawing for a moment inside the door, feeling sensation return to his skin, watching people bustling in bright lights, smelling the fragrances, eyes alighting out of habit on the girls, city girls, colder and meaner too, like the streets. Up the escalator, the Viking arm ring came back to his mind: he'd seen it before—perhaps in a different life, perhaps he'd been a Viking warrior, maybe the ring was one that had graced his own biceps, which back in the Viking times was no doubt a less scrawny specimen. Looking through the men's gloves, the salesgirl came up to him, lovely, flawless white skin, lavish black hair, a shock of white teeth. But, gazing into the bottomless green eyes, wasn't your man banjaxed to see nothing there. A robot at his service. All his life, the electric shock of contact, the chemistry, had been two-way, but now the girl on the other end showed not a spark of recognition, could she help him, was there anything she could show him. Was there ever. A modicum of decency to start with, an acknowledgement that a human being of tender sensibilities was at the other end of her gaze, the milk of human kindness. Perhaps even the milky skin of your breasts. If he were a Viking warrior by God, she'd take notice.

"I was here yesterday," says he, "and I seem to have lost my mittens."

"There's a Lost and Found," said the girl around a rigid smile. "In Customer Service. Down in the basement."

He knew where the bloody Lost and Found was. Had his inquiry been so devoid of charm as to deserve a mechanical response the likes of that? He probed quickly again for a spark in her eyes, and, finding none, nodded her away and headed down. Quite possibly a lesbian, he decided. The lady in Customer Service was, praise be to God, one he'd never before encountered, a Christmas hire perhaps, and she was older and fleshier, and, despite a tremble to her chin, eager to engage in a meaningful exchange of eye contact and promise. "I lost my gloves," he said. "The nice girl in Men's sent me here."

"Ah, yes," said the lady. "What did they look like?"

"They were leather. Rather new."

"What color?"

"It would depend on the light. At times they look brownish, blackish at others."

"I see. Well. We have a box of gloves here—"

"I'll have a look, thank you."

He picked out a fine pair, the third pair he tried on, and was sorting through the mufflers as well, all the while reassuring with his smile and the dimple in his chin the lady whose own smile was faltering by the minute, when the squall of a nearby toddler stopped him short. He glanced over toward the cluster of fake Christmas trees where the tyke—boy or girl, he couldn't tell, dressed all in yellow—had flung itself to the floor, screaming in mortal anguish. Anguish of a familiar class. Another toddler, another time and place, Molly's toddler, Owen, sitting in the mud and muck by the stone wall, squalling because Lafferty's own boy, Harry, the older of the two, had just yanked from his hand the ring that moments before Owen had yanked from the mud of that ancient field. The self-same battered oval, Lafferty suspected, now grandly proclaiming itself to be a Viking Arm Ring, circa 950 AD.

He headed back into the Dublin streets, still cold despite his fine new gloves and muffler. He decided again to forego the bus fare, better invested in a pint, and retraced his steps among the steeples and tall buildings rising up to the little lane housing *Tinley's Antiquities*. The *Viking Arm Ring circa 950 AD* there on display. He eyed it as close as he could, his nose pressed to the window like a child's at a sweets shop, and he studied the intricate silver twisting of the thing, ornately etched, which, he admitted, he hadn't seen before—it had been black and tarnished then, caked in mud. It was the unmistakable cockeyed shape of it, unusual and unique, the same wee gap where the ends didn't quite meet up that made him certain it was the same.

In the upheaval after its discovery, Lafferty hadn't given it a second thought. At the time, he'd believed it to be merely an old nose ring for a bull, the class of item used far and wide by farmers to keep the beasts under control. He'd said so to Molly then, telling her to throw the dirty old thing in the bin. She mustn't have. What had she done then?

What must be the worth of such an artifact?

Jimmy was up and gone. He found him at Maximillian's, head full of aches and contrition, eyes timid and bloodshot and shying away from Lafferty's. "I'm after telling Oona I was sorry," says he.

"I had to remind him what he was sorry for," said Oona, polishing a glass. "He can't remember, or so he says. Bloody whiskey amnesia."

"Bloody whiskey oblivion," said Lafferty.

"I remember the beginning," Jimmy said, "we sounded pretty good. Didn't we? Some fine harmony." The question was for Oona, his eyes for Oona only.

"Finny got a summons for pissing in the street while Pavarotti here had himself locked in the jacks," said Oona. "You're paying it for him."

"Oona, boona, can o' tuna," Jimmy said.

"Jimmy, Jimmy, Jimmy," she said. "What am I going to do with you?" Oona was a pip, a tomboy, blond hair pulled back straight, hair you might suspect of being dirty, eyes you might suspect of having seen it all. Any thoughts of Oona and sex were afterthoughts in Lafferty's mind, she in her plain jeans and baggy men's shirts. She'd come from nowhere like she owned the place, so Lafferty suspected Seamus, the owner, was riding her. Either that or she was playing for the other side entirely. Jimmy, in his oblivion, was undeterred.

Another gent came in and Oona went away, Jimmy's eyes trailing like a puppy's.

Lafferty said hadn't the damnedest thing happened on his way down street. He told Jimmy about *Tinley's Antiquities*. He told him about Molly and her wain and the bull ring, and the Viking arm ring circa 950 AD and all. "How do you like my new gloves?" he added.

Jimmy acknowledged a fine pair they were indeed and wondered could he prove the bull ring he'd found and the arm ring in the window were one and the same item. Maybe, Lafferty said. If he could learn from Molly what she'd done with the bloody thing afterward, then maybe he could trace the connection. And so far as that was concerned, now that he thought of it, maybe Molly'd sold the bloody thing to this Tinley fellow herself, and maybe Lafferty was due a share of the booty.

"Why the villainous bitch," said Jimmy, watching Oona labor over a fresh pint.

"I can't believe she'd have it in her," said Lafferty. "I need to talk to her."

"Where is she now then?"

"I haven't a foggy notion," said Lafferty. "She'd vacated her room above the Pig & Whistle last I heard."

"Fecking Riviera, probably," muttered Jimmy.

Lafferty wondered would the publican not have to know. Bobby Devine, who owned the Pig & Whistle, or had anyhow at the time, would he not have to know where she moved to in order to forward her post? Jimmy agreed it was logical, and they figured they could ring him up, but they didn't have a number, but they figured they could look it up, but Lafferty said would it not be just as easy to drive down and find out in person, thinking of Jimmy's ancient Peugeot. It was only an hour away, said he, maybe a wee bit longer. "As easy to drive as to ring?" Jimmy said, looking at last at Lafferty, who said, "We could look him in the face, find out what he knows. And, sure, maybe Molly's still there—still in Kilduff somewhere, or nearby."

"So," says Jimmy. "You're wanting to spy on Peggy, is that the thing?"

Lafferty was surprised. Just when you think he's thick as an onion, Jimmy sees through you like an empty glass. "I suppose we might take a detour down Blue Bucket Lane if we're in the neighborhood," he said.

"Begod," said Jimmy. "You're still carrying the bloody torch. You still got a soft spot for her, don't you? You brought it all on yourself, you know."

Now it was Lafferty's eyes shying away. Did he still have a soft spot? Or was it only the mean passing years? "Only wondering—do you suppose that Clive fellow is still about?"

From down the bar, Oona looked up. Jimmy blew her a kiss.

They sat shivering and drinking in the ancient Peugeot on Blue Bucket Lane, a squalid stretch of bland cottages that had taken on the aura of a mystical nesting ground to the eyes of

Lafferty. The dairy lorry was parked in front of the cottage all right, and the blue door from which all the snaps and clippings had been removed. Nothing stirring within. The hedge in the front was frosted with snow, the gray of the sky getting darker, and more filled with foreboding, and Jimmy asked how long they were just going to bloody well sit there. He asked should he turn on the car for some heat. "What bloody heat?" said Lafferty. "The bloody heater doesn't work."

"It works a little," Jimmy said.

"I felt more heat from a bloody turnip than from that heater."

"More than you felt from the likes of that one, too, I'd wager," muttered Jimmy, with a nod toward the cottage. To that your man said nothing, and it wasn't long till a car pulled up in front of the lorry and out climbed Peggy and Harry and Clive. A new yellow car. Her little brown Ford a thing of the past. Harry skipped through the blue front door followed by Peggy and Clive, the arm of him on the shoulder of her. "He looks like a fit one, he does," said Jimmy. "You came to grips with him, did you?"

Lafferty allowed as to how maybe he had.

"And he got the better of it?"

Lafferty said nothing for some time. Then, "I was trying to reason with the man."

"Let's go in and sort him out," said Jimmy with a squirm.

"No. Not now." Nor any time, he failed to add.

"Let's go in and skull the bastard." His knuckles were white-gripping the wheel. He took another rude swallow from the flask.

"No," said Lafferty. "That's not what we're here for." He stared at the cottage, Jimmy fidgeting beside him.

"What the fuck *are* we here for?" Jimmy said, in a curious, desperate tone, as if he needed to know why they were there, but it was utterly beyond him, out of his grasp, like a lifeline to a drowning man.

Lafferty didn't answer. Looking again, he saw Peggy's shadow at the window. Had she noticed the odd car in front? Was she watching him watch her?

A curious numbness came over him, and he let it carry him away. Could she even see him, or was he as invisible as he felt? An odd thing, he suddenly longed to hold her warm body against his—hers, Molly's, anybody he'd ever loved. He needed to be held, anchored, warmed. He was blowing away. Watching through the frost of his own breath, he felt oddly hollow, light, dizzy, a single flake of snow flurrying away on the wind, all the years that had been his being blown away.

He heard a snuffle and saw Jimmy wipe at his cheeks and glanced over to see your man look away. "What?" he said.

Jimmy said, "Do you think Oona fancies me? At all?"

A slap in the face of a floundering man. Lafferty said, "Let's get the bloody hell out of here," and Jimmy faltered, blinked, snuffled again, and started the car. Lafferty reached over and pressed the horn that wheezed like a leaky bellows, and Jimmy raised a one-fingered salute toward the cottage, which Lafferty affirmed, and they headed toward the Pig & Whistle. A bloody reunion at the pub was what it was, Bobby Devine still there all right and some of the old boyos to boot, and there were drinks and good craic all around, and Jimmy and Lafferty couldn't reach into their pocket, and sure, Bobby remembered Molly from the room upstairs, pathetic thing, and sure, she'd left a forwarding address, long since lost, but he recalled she'd moved into the corporation housing in Dublin, Ballybough House, it was. And never a single, solitary, bloody letter had ever come for him to forward.

She was there. *Molly Scanlon, #424*, on one of the mailboxes clustered at Ballybough House. He waved away Jimmy waiting in the Peugeot in the street, the Peugeot staggering off, Lafferty heading up the outdoors stairs to the fourth floor, looking out over a sea of misbegotten flats and terraced cottages. When Molly answered the door, her brow dipped, the opposite of the direction he'd expected, though it hardly registered at the time. How long had it had been, after all, four years? "Terrance Lafferty, as I live and breathe."

"As do I," he said.

"What brings you here?"

"Ah, Molly," he said, reaching to touch her cheek.

She winced, glancing over her shoulder. Owen was sitting beneath a blanket on a barren sofa, staring at the telly. He scarcely recognized the lad, how he'd grown, to an age now where he could, of course, understand the meaning of the spoken word. Lafferty stepped into the shabby digs, patchy paint and threadbare rug, a draft through the ill-fitting window he could feel from across the room. On the screen, an old movie, a leading man with plastic hair jabbing his finger in the chest of a gangster in a striped vest. The look on the face of Molly was entirely not one of delight, contrary again to his expectations, and he was a bit confused, though the confusion hardly had time to settle before Molly said to the boy, "Do you remember your Uncle Terrance then?" to which Owen looked up blankly and said, "When's da coming home?" which was when your man noticed the boots in the corner, the coats on the back of the door, all of a distinctly masculine class.

All the air and the hope leaking out of him. "Is it a bad time then?"

She glanced at the clock on the counter. "Sure he won't be home yet for a while."

"Is he the one who gave you the…"—glancing toward the boy—"the dog, Duffy was it?"

"Oh, no. Liam's a builder. I met him building at the house where I worked."

"Oh. I see then."

She glanced again at the clock. "Will you have a cuppa?"

"No, thank you," he said, "I mustn't be keeping you."

"It's not that…Terrance, I wish I'd known…" she said. "Liam isn't as…he isn't as *friendly* as you."

"I understand. I did have a question, though."

"Oh?"

"Do you recall," he said, "the last picnic we had out by the MacGregor estate, the time Owen found the ring?"

"The last picnic…"

"When Owen found the ring. The old bull ring. And Harry snatched it away from him. And Owen started screaming bloody murder." Owen looked up from the telly with a frown.

"Oh, yes, of course. It was so pretty out there."

"What become of the bull ring? I said it was a worthless old piece of rubbish, you should toss it in the bin."

"Let me think," said she, and after she did, she told him she hadn't tossed it after all, there'd been something about it, the heft and the shape of it. She'd put it in her bag and forgotten it till a month or so later she noticed it when she looked in her bag for an aspirin for the migraine that struck her at Mrs. Royce's as she was cleaning the jacks. Mrs. Royce saw the thing when she pulled it out. She thought it unusual as well, asked what it was, where it was found, and Molly told her, and Mrs. Royce said her husband's cousin dealt in antiques and perhaps he could give her a better idea, whether or not it was indeed only an old bull ring, and so Molly handed it over. And when she thought to ask Mrs. Royce later—a week or two later—whatever become of it, Mrs. Royce said her husband's cousin had told him it was nothing. A worthless old bull ring all right, nothing more.

Lafferty wanted to know the name of the cousin.

"I've no idea, Terrance. Mrs. R never said."

"Could you find out?"

"Why?"

He started to tell her about Tinley's Antiquities and the Viking arm ring, but hesitated. A lie felt better suited. "I saw something in the markets down by the quays amongst a pile of clutter. It had the same shape, and I was just wondering could it be the same one, and how it could have got there. My mate, Jimmy, he fancies old bull rings."

She thought for a moment, a shadow crossing her eye. Maybe she believed him, maybe she didn't. But wasn't Liam due home any minute. "I could ring Mrs. R, I suppose."

"Could you then? Could you ring her now?"

She went to the phone. Owen was nodding on the sofa, drifting off in front of the telly where an old-time car chase had commenced, running boards and all. Mist hovered up against the window, lights from the flats and cottages down below shining through the fog like ghostly buoys on an ocean. As Molly called, he thought of her eyes then, all the hope and love and mortal desperation, and when she hung up the phone and looked at him, it was gone, all of it. "She said his name was Tinley. Francis Tinley. Does that help?"

Lafferty shrugged a little shrug, smiled a little smile. "Where there's muck, there's luck," he said. And then he said goodbye.

Through the foggy lanes to Grafton Street. The wind had quit, and his new gloves and muffler and his bellyful of booze were enough to keep the fires smoldering. The Starbucks had Wi-Fi, and it was there that your man headed to look up antiquities and see what he could learn about this Tinley fellow and this Viking Arm Ring circa 950 AD and the trade in general. No sooner was the search underway than a stylish young woman in tight jeans, high boots, and a bulging sweater came to tap him on the shoulder.

"Excuse me," she said rather sharply.

Lafferty looked up with his dimple and smile. "Yes?"

"What are you doing?"

"Something I needed to look up. Antiquities, to be exact."

"That's my laptop," said she.

"Oh? It was sitting here all on its own. I thought it was for house use."

"I was only getting my latté."

"I'll be finished in a jiffy."

"You've some cheek."

"Thank you. Yours are quite lovely as well."

He learned plenty, though he'd have liked to have learned more. After less than five minutes, the stylish young woman hovering about his shoulder, threatening to call the Gardaí, he finally gave in. He was dismayed and nonplused that no amount of smiling repartee on his part could win her over, and he remembered he was fifty now, an invisible man now (the dimple in his chin notwithstanding), and he was, or so the evidence would suggest, no longer an object of appeal to the opposite gender—though it was a tough sale, trying to convince himself it was entirely true. At any rate he was too preoccupied at the moment with the bits he'd been able to glean in that brief five minutes' time. Tinley's Antiquities, as it turned out, had a grand online auction site, and he'd pinpointed the very artifact for sale, the Viking Arm Ring circa 950 AD, a rare specimen indeed, 95% silver, certified by the National Museum, craftsmanship of unprecedented quality, unique among all the artifacts from all the hoards unearthed heretofore, bidding now up to nine thousand, two hundred Euros.

Muck and luck indeed.

He made it to Maximillian's just before Oona called time. She brought him his pint of stout. Jimmy was drinking porter and whiskey, well in his cups, a glassy shallowness in his eyes that Lafferty had come to regard with apprehension. He told him what he'd learned about the ring. "You're codding me," says Jimmy.

"Not a'tall, a'tall. Over nine thousand quid."

"What are you going to do?"

"The question of the hour."

"We could do a smash-and-grab. Quick and simple. Easy-peasy."

"We could. The old quick-and-simple-easy-peasy-smash-and-grab."

Jimmy slapping the bar with a smack, wobbled up to his feet. "No time like the present."

Lafferty said, "What if it's the shatter-proof glass then?"

Jimmy slumped back to his barstool in a heap. "You don't suppose. The bastard."

"I do. And the bars. What about the bloody iron bars in the window?"

"You didn't mention the bloody iron bars in the window."

"Ach, you didn't ask."

"Time, gentlemen, time," called Oona. She began to gather up glasses.

"Oona, boona, can o' tuna," called Jimmy.

"Jimmy, shove your can o' tuna up your bloody arse," Oona said. "Drink up."

Jimmy ignored the cold rejoinder, drunk beyond despair. Said to Lafferty, "We could smash his bloody face and grab it then," drunk beyond delicacy.

Lafferty thought reason might work better. When he explained in person to Mr. Tinley—he described the man in the photo on his website, gray-haired, bespectacled, shoulders as broad as a kitten's, entirely unformidable—that he was fully aware of the provenance of the piece and of the dishonest and devious means by which Mr. Tinley had come into possession of it, and that he was willing to share that information not only with the authorities but with the public, where Mr. Tinley's good reputation resided, then he thought an accommodation might be forthcoming from your man. Jimmy was following Lafferty's every word intently, studying his moving chin as it spoke as if watching a mouse in a cage. When he turned back to his glass, it was gone. He lifted an empty crisps packet as if the glass might have ducked beneath it.

"Where's my fucking porter?"

"It was empty, Jimmy," Oona said. "It's past time now."

"I had a swallow left."

"There was nothing in it, Jimmy, it was empty. There's a good lad now."

"There was a fucking swallow left!" He jumped red-faced to his feet, sweeping his arm down the bar, littering the floor and stools and laps of stragglers with ashtrays, butts and ashes, wrappers and assorted trash, shouting all the while for his swallow, and when he went to lift up a barstool to do further havoc, Lafferty and another man and Oona leaped in to nip the conniption, but Jimmy would have none of it, growing ever more fierce in his efforts to remove himself from their grasps. Finally, they managed to bulldog him through the door, thinking a good savage dose of December air might be your only man.

After a bit more flailing and swaying and wobbling, another curse or two, Jimmy began to shiver, the blood all gone from his face, and the other man, a stout fellow, stepped back inside muttering *bloody hell* as Oona went to fetch Jimmy's coat. Lafferty took your man by the shoulders to hold him back or hold him up or both. Spoke to his mate with soothing words. Asked him where was the Peugeot, but Jimmy had no earthly clue. Lafferty said okay. It's okay. He stood holding his shoulders, the white breath of them heaving out in the air, till he was sure he was steady, then he said wait here, will you wait, and Jimmy nodded. Lafferty said I'll fetch the coats and get us home.

Back inside, the stout man was pulling on his coat, the other stragglers as well, heading for the door, mean glances at Lafferty and his association with disorder. Oona had taken Jimmy's coat from the stool, and when Lafferty came to get it, doesn't she stick her hand between his legs, helping herself to a heaping handful. Standing there, at the end of the bar, all the patrons heading for the door, backs turned to them. A scent of sweat in her straight blond hair, and her eyes, an inch from his, seeing it all. "Terrance," says she, "I could use a bloody good shagging."

He answered contrary to his nature. "Jimmy—you know he's crazy about you."

"He's a mentaller, Terrance, a weird bloody duck. Get him home."

It was a short, quick sigh he gave, a fast, rational decision. "If I must."

"Can you bloody well hurry then?"

"It's only three blocks down."

When he went outside, though, wasn't Jimmy gone. Had he watched through the window? Streetlamps in the fog, great glowing globes. Lafferty stood, wondering should he follow, deciding against it. Your man had staggered home blind any number of occasions, the fresh air would serve him well. And wouldn't Clacko be glad of it. The old cat was hungry. The old cat in fact was famished. The old cat had his needs, and sometimes the needs wouldn't wait.

The tomboy's room was shockingly white and frilly, china dolls on a shelf, light through a lace curtain from the street keeping away the darkness the whole night through. Oona got her bloody good shagging, as did your man, but wasn't it all only gasping and moaning and a moment or two of devout religiosity. Nothing more. When he wanted to chat her up afterward, wasn't she too tired. Hadn't she been on her feet the whole bloody day. All she wanted now was her sleep. And when your man wanted to hold her then, to cuddle in the normal, customary, post-coital manner, didn't she tell him she couldn't be comfortable, sure she couldn't sleep at all with another person clinging to her skin. She curled up on her side of the bed, leaving him to his, and she fell into deep and easy sleep, but his own was only the quickest of winks, and when he came awake, wide awake, the sky outside the window was bright and gray, the light from the streetlamp only a memory. Oona beyond his touch. And he wondered again. In how many different beds had he awoken in all his years on the earth, in how many different places?

The shabby little digs in the gloaming, the wind at the window again. Bitter cold. Jimmy'd made it home all right, Lafferty could tell by the high-topped sneaker tipped over near the door. The expired cuckoo, covered in dust, drooped out of its little door, the clock still at seven-thirteen. Was it right? Twice a day, every day, maybe now was its moment. Knackered, needing sleep, he eyed his little rumpled cot. And then peeked in at Jimmy.

One sneaker on, one off, snoring, his mouth open, Clacko curled up close by his chin. So innocent when they're sleeping. Lafferty saw his shirt then, Jimmy's. There was red on it. He stepped in for a closer peep. It looked for all the world to be blood, dried blood, a rusty color, and a bit on his knuckles and smeared on his hands as well. Then, moving closer still, he saw by the pillow, just above Clacko's purring fur, not far from your man's open, leaking mouth, what appeared for all the world to be a ring.

A Viking arm ring, circa 950 AD.

And he thought of the first time he'd seen the bloody thing.

When Harry'd snatched it from the hands of the babe.

The Worthless Turtle

Stepping out of the raw evening onto the sodden floorboards of Slattery's Public House, Lafferty immediately spotted the girl all alone at the bar, a marooned sailor spying a speck that might be a ship, blinking his eyes in the gloom. The bar was sparsely populated, vacant barstools abounding; nevertheless, he chose the one at her elbow upon which to perch.

"Do ye mind? You look as though you could use the company." A hand through his ill-mannered brown hair, speckled with gray, and with droplets from the spitting rain, he smiled his most charming smile, displaying the dimple in his chin.

"Not at all," she said. "Have ye come to keep me warm?" She was bundled in a yellow cardigan, brown hair willy-nilly on her head, cheeks sunken, eyes sleepy and skittish all at once.

Just the man for the job. All his life he'd lived to keep warm those of the gentler gender who needed the warming, and though his services had not been so much in demand since the dawn of the day of the smartphone, he prided himself on his readiness. And he marveled at the instant connection with this one, the easy compatibility, like slipping into an old shoe.

"Aye," he said, "Terrance Lafferty, man-oven, at your service."

"Man-oven," she said, and a chuckle. Or was it a shiver? Her hand moved on the bar an inch and a half toward his own. "Call me Daisy."

"Daisy. Is it your name, or are you just in a flowery mood?"

"It is my name, today. Yesterday I was Rose. Tomorrow maybe I'll be a Lily."

The barman came over, red splashes for cheeks. It was a pub unfamiliar to him, his own locals having barred him for his unfortunate, and unfortunately recurring, insolvency.

He said to Daisy, "Fancy another?" hoping against hope she'd decline.

She turned to him, a hard shiver coming over her. He noticed then the wee dimple in her own chin, not unlike his own, and it was then that something clicked, that everything—his outlook, his expectations, his mood—began to change. She clasped the cardigan closer, grasping the brooch that he spied on the scarf at her neck. "No," said she, reaching for her bag. "Let's go to where it's warm," and Lafferty sighed with relief.

Nevertheless, it was with an odd, sinking feeling that he followed her out into the street. Dublin born and reared, he considered himself street-wise as the next man despite a respite of nearly twenty years in the midlands, in the heart of County Nowhere, where he'd followed his erstwhile wife, Peggy, in an ultimately futile attempt at keeping her roof over his head. A decade had passed since his return.

And though he'd every confidence in his charm, that only needed the rust knocked off it now and again, the charm he'd practiced in his younger years when love was there for the plucking, ripe peaches on low branches, the truth was that the ease with which he'd won young Daisy over was nothing to do with it. His suspicion that she might be a lady of the evening was losing traction as well. Something else was at play.

Through the soft cold rain, they walked down the dirty lanes of Finglas, past storefronts shuttered and shamed, past rude tenements, a wary eye out for unsavory sorts in the streets. Not the kindest of neighborhoods, rougher even than his own. Her place was not far, a five-minute scurry, above a boarded-up shop—*Bridal Bliss Boutique*—where murals of bygone brides in princess gowns were fading from the face of the weathered bricks. Up creaking steps, down the hallway past a door where the melodic sounds of a tender ballad leaked out—*Yummy,*

yummy, yummy, I got love in my tummy—past another where a bed was squeaking sounds of love.

Daisy's room was hot as an oven, a little gas stove in the corner gasping and yawning wee blue and orange flames. There, he saw her in bright light for the first time. The red-rimmed, hollow eyes, the shivering, twig-sized cut of her.

He saw a wilted Daisy, sickly, lovely—and somehow familiar.

Everything had changed. Lafferty would be hard-pressed to say exactly where or when the change took place, but somewhere between the barroom and the bedroom, any inkling of randiness that might have inhabited his blood had leached away entirely, like color from a stricken face. Nor could he say exactly why. He'd come to the realization that this girl, this Daisy, was clearly not a lady of the evening (not that a lady's vocation had ever stood between him and love before). She was a sorry young thing, masquerading, without success, as a lady of the evening.

She felt the change as well. Her masquerade over, her mask off, she stood beside the rumpled bed, exposed, caught in her lie. She clutched at her yellow cardigan, in anger, despair, pulling at the scarf about her neck, the sound of a tear stopping her short.

"Shit," she muttered.

"What?" he said.

"It's my brooch," she said. "The pin's already bent." She removed it from the folds of the scarf, a gaudy piece big as a walnut, encrusted with tiny, multi-colored gemstones. She examined it closely.

"Is it worth something?" he said.

She tried to latch it. "To who?" she said, not looking up. "It's only costume jewelry, worthless. My fella paid two quid for it at a shop down on Ballyboggan. But I love it."

"You've a fella?" He glanced toward the door.

"He's long gone—this is all that's left of him." She held the brooch up, caressing it with her gaze. "It's a turtle, you see. They say turtles are supposed to bring you good luck—to me, sure it's priceless."

"And how's that luck thing working out?"

She looked at him crossly. Her face turned white. She gave a violent shiver, clamped her hand on her mouth and scrambled through the door, into the loo across the hall. He heard the muffled sounds of regurgitation. When she returned, it was with a sway and a wobble, her brown hair damp and frazzled, her eyes darker, more hollow than before, her nose runny, a wee trickle of snot gleaming in the light of the lamp by the bed. Her face a cold sheen of sweat. Tears leaked from her eyes.

Withdrawal, he thought.

She wiped her nose, smearing snot. "Mister, I need some money."

"Money?"

"Please? I need it."

He pulled coins from his pocket, shuffled them about in his palm. "I've got, let's see, just over three quid—would that help, yeah?"

She laughed, not a little, but a hefty rumble too big for her britches, and she crumbled beneath the weight of it, falling to the floor, and by the time she got there, an untidy heap on the threadbare rug, the laughter had given over to tears. She shivered, making her way on hands and knees over the dirty rug where she leaned against the bed and the rickety wee stand, hugging her skinny knees, her eyes shut tight. "I sure can pick 'em, can't I?" she mumbled to no one in particular. Her eyes came open, big and raw. "Why you?" she said.

"I get that a lot," Lafferty said.

She flicked her hand like shooing a fly. "Leave," she said. "Go. Please. Oh, leave the three quid—it might help."

He dropped the coins on the bed. "Isn't there anything…"

"Just *go*," she said. And again, when he hesitated, "*GO!*"

Your man could take a hint as well as the next. What could he do?

He left her there, reluctantly. He left her there, leaning against the bed, her turtle peeping over her shoulder, bringing her no luck, no luck at all, as complicit as was he.

Next morning sitting over his cuppa at the table of Mrs. Hannigan, his landlady, the image of Daisy weeping in a pitiful heap refused to scram from his head.

He had worries of his own. His own rent was overdue. Mrs. Hannigan came into the kitchen and spied him there, as he knew she would. The wizened oul face of her lit up bright as the rouge on her painted oul cheeks.

"Mr. Lafferty," she said, "there you are. Good. Have you your rent ready? I'm ready to take your rent. I've been ready in fact since Friday."

"I do, Mrs. Hannigan," said he. "And I've a wee favor to ask as well."

Suspicion deepened the wrinkles of her brow. She'd been a looker years ago, and her hand moved up past the painted lips to the curly gray hair for a primp. "A favor?"

"A loan. Something's come up. I'm in need of a wee loan."

"Don't think for a minute I'm going to start paying you to pay me your rent."

"Not at all, at all. A loan is all. I'll pay it back. With interest."

"Very well then," said she, huffy, not happy. She led him through the kitchen, glancing about to ensure the coast was clear, down the soft, silent carpet of the hallway to her bedroom. Lafferty was soon at work paying his rent, mindful he was paying it well, with interest, to satisfy the oul creature. His mind was elsewhere.

The image of Daisy, the snot and the tears on her haggard young face, the uncanny familiarity, the sense of déjà vu, would not let him be.

Fifty quid in his pocket, he set out for the boarded-up bridal boutique in Finglas. It was a fairer day altogether, patches of blue through the clouds overhead, hope in the air. He'd a box of chocolates under his arm, having heard that sugar served to calm the breast of savage addiction. If he could put her on an even keel, perhaps then he could help. In his pocket was a scrap of paper upon which he'd scribbled the numbers and addresses of Ana Liffey, St. Vincent de Paul, and the Samaritans, outreach programs he'd looked up in Mrs. Hannigan's parlor after his rent was well and fully paid.

Up the stairway of creaks and groans, past the doors, silent now, no love in the tummy, no squeaks of bed, to the door of Daisy's room, a tap, tap, tap, but nothing stirred. The door was ajar. A nudge, a peek, and he saw her there. All the strength spilled out of him and he slid slowly down the doorjamb to the floor, clutching her chocolates.

She was sprawled on the dirty rug, a black band about her arm still, the needle still in her hand, the dimple still in her chin. Still. On her face a look of savage, hard-won peace.

He waited there with her. Contrary to his nature. Ordinarily, he'd quietly quickly vamoose. But he couldn't leave her alone, not again, not for a second time.

All his life, he'd avoided red tape, any manner of entanglement, but he made the sacrifice, the least he could do, and when he thought of himself as thinking he was making a sacrifice, and poor Daisy lifeless on the floor, didn't he, for an instant, despise himself. Only for an instant.

He'd called 999 from the neighboring room, the neighbor being a worn-out, bruised woman, drunk as a lord before noon. A motley congregation assembled in the hallway, a woman in curlers, a man in pajamas and tattoos, a wee fella in decrepit old tweeds, a bog-trotter's cap on his skull, and a red-cheeked woman indignant that someone would have the gall to die down the hall on her only day off.

The coroner arrived. Lafferty watched from a neighboring planet. A crew arrived and a gurney. He told them he was her lover in order to stay, and the one cheeky lad says, *lover or father?* and didn't your man take offense.

He would remember the offense he took as the height of irony.

He rode in the back of the ambulance to the hospital. Tried holding her hand for a bit, till the dead chill of it made him pull back. Something about her, the pitiful thing beneath the gray blanket, so lately alive, so forever stilled, would not let him turn her loose.

This was how he came to be there when her next-of-kin turned up.

Her mother's name was Moira Bell. The name alone sparked no recognition, but when he got a closer gander, old memories began surfacing, gasping for air.

She was an attractive woman, though the years were beginning to have their way, lovely black hair losing its luster, infiltrated by gray, the complexion of her pretty face growing slack and rough about the edges. Wrinkles sprouting like weeds. She was a tough woman, cheekbones like clenched fists, a hard life there on her face for the world to see. When she saw him, learned who he was, came to touch his arm and look into his eyes to see how her daughter had died, didn't her eyes stay poking about in his till they found something to latch onto. Her brow fretting in wonder.

"Do I know ye?" she said.

"I'm after wondering the same," said he. "Do ye now?"

She put her finger to his chin, remembering the dimple, then stepped close, putting her arms about him, squeezes like heartbeats. "My baby," she said, and Lafferty was keen enough to realize she meant her daughter, the girl dead on the gurney in the room she'd just come out of, not himself. He was fairly certain of it.

Didn't Moira confirm it for him, backing away, patting his chest. "Not you, love," she said. She turned, gesturing limply toward the room. "Your wee little girl."

He was not a thick man. The meaning, the world of implication of the four words came crashing over him like a tsunami, his little girl, his own flesh and blood, lying dead, her mother at his elbow.

His first instinct, true to himself, was to turn on his heel and hightail it, as fast and as far as he could.

But she held fast to his elbow. "My God," said she. "Did ye know?"

"No," he said. "Yes." For didn't the heart of him know before the head.

The name of the pub was O'Faolain's, just off Drumcondra, where now stood terrace housing. He remembered the black Guinness awning of O'Faolain's, the flowerpots brimming with the pretty posies of summer, the place elbow-to-elbow in the lovely smoke and the racket at the long black bar, the utter bliss of not yet having spent thirty years in the world. Nearly thirty years ago, not long after he married Peggy, not long before he followed her to Kilduff, forsaking his Dublin altogether. It was the night he and the girl found each other through the thick smoke and the throng, homing in on each other as though they were the only two people in the place, the only two people in the world, he and the girl with hair like midnight and skin like cream. An attraction so true and deep he could think of it only as a state of grace. And, like all states of grace, wasn't it fragile and fleeting, and shattered by morning.

And the girl's name was Moira.

Not until late that night could they finally find quiet time together. It was at Moira's place in Drumcondra, one of the brick terrace houses built in the '20's in the shadow of Croke Park. Her neighbor beyond the wall had twenty cats and the smell of cat piss crept into her parlor, as did the occasional cat itself, but the burning of candles kept the smell at bay. Word had quickly spread among family, friends, neighbors, who'd congregated in shock and mourning. When all but a few were gone, Lafferty and Moira were left in a quiet corner by the piano, by the burning candles, remembering O'Faolain's.

"I tried to look you up after," she said. "I found out you'd left the city."

"Aye. Green acres was the place for me." Across the room, a lingering, tipsy mourner spilled his drink with a yelp of regret. They scarcely noticed.

"Scared you knocked me up, so you skedaddled—was that it?"

"Not at all. I'd never have guessed. You could have found me—there were plenty that knew where I was."

"And why would I want a no-account git such as yourself around me or my babby?"

"Of course you wouldn't. And as I recall, you had a fella—what was his name, the madman, the mentaller?"

"Fergus," she said.

Fergus. How could he forget? Savage, vicious, hopped up on steroids and speed, stalking Moira to the ends of the bloody city, rampaging, wreaking havoc. It was him put an end to the state of grace, the lovely state of grace after O'Faolain's. "You'd not recognize him now," she said. "He quit the pills long ago, put down the hod, took a job selling widgets or some such. He's done well for himself. He's still about."

"Aye, Fergus. I can imagine how he took it when he found out you were up the pole."

"He wanted to marry me, is how he took it, give the lass a father."

"You're codding me. He thought it was his own then?"

"He did. I set him straight though—it couldn't have been. The pills had seen to that."

"Maybe you should've. Married him. Sure, Daisy might have been better off. Yourself as well." He waited for her to poo-poo the very notion, but when she didn't, when she showed no inclination whatsoever to poo-poo, he quickly moved on. "God's sense of humor," he said, "of all the bloody pubs in Dublin." He'd told her how he and Daisy met at Slattery's. He told her how he'd sussed out her troubles, the drugs, the withdrawal, looked up the outreach, tried to help, too little, too late.

"Join the club," Moira said. "I tried, we all tried, everyone tried. But I botched the job. Didn't we all."

"She mentioned a fella, the one that gave her a brooch—"

"That ugly turtle yoke, yeah. She always wore it, she loved it so—kept it about for good luck. So much for turtle luck."

"And the fella? He's out of the picture?"

"They're all out of the picture, Terrance, every bloody one of them. Of course, you wouldn't want 'em in the picture, would ye, not that shower of maggots. If they weren't using her for a punching bag or pumping her full of dope, they were going about overdosing themselves."

"Jesus," he said. "That fecking turtle ought to be sacked."
"If I come across it in her things, I'll bin it. Or shall I give it to you? How's your luck these days, Terrance?"

"Me? I feel like the luckiest man in Dublin."

"Lucky? Meet your daughter one day, find her dead the next? Lucky?"

He felt a right bloody eejit. "I found you again was all I meant."

"You're right. Of course. There's that. Always a bright side, yeah?"

"Did you never think of me at all?"

"Every day. Every time I looked at the dimple in Daisy-girl's chin." She touched the dimple in his own.

"The last thing she said to me was *why you?*" He skipped the *just leave, go* part. "And the way she looked at me. I wonder. I can't help but wonder if she knew. That I was her da."

She patted his cheek. "I wonder if she knew what year it was."

Uncle something-or-other came out of the kitchen, a woman peeping over his shoulder. A stout man, white shirt bulging out between the buttons of his black waistcoat, drying his hands on a tea towel. Lafferty'd met him earlier—Moira'd introduced Lafferty around as the villain who took her virginity, an outrageous lie not meant to be believed, he believed. The uncle nodded solemnly, took Moira's hand. "We're on our way, love," he said. "We're after tidying up the kitchen a bit for you."

"Oh, you needn't have," she said. "Terrance was looking forward to it. He's a madman in the kitchen as well as the bedroom."

Uncle something-or-other cast a skeptical frown at your man. "No bother at all, at all. Take care, love. We're so sorry for your loss."

"Oh, aye. Me too."

The door shut behind him. Now they were alone, him and Moira and the candles burning low. She plunked a note on the derelict old piano, harsh and discordant and entirely misplaced.

"Do you fancy a ragtime tune?" she said.

"No. Do you fancy a hug?"

A brave facsimile of a smile. "You're a sweet man, Terrance. That I remember."

"And non-fattening," he added.

His quip was met with silence. She stared at the floor, the tarnished brass pedals of the piano. "Who'll remember her?" When she looked up again, her eyes glistened. "Who'll ever even know she was here? She wasn't here long enough, she never made a dent, like a bloody ant on a bloody rock."

She looked to your man as if he might have the answer. He did not.

"*Daisy Bell, 1991 – 2017*," she said. "That's all that's left of her. Two bloody words, two bloody years, carved in wee letters on a bloody wee stone you wouldn't pick out from a thousand like it. That's all. Nothing more."

She plunked the keys, one at a time, each note deeper than the one before it, going down, till she came to the one that wouldn't plunk.

Over and over, she pressed it, a chain of dull, hollow thunks.

Moira's need for comfort was great as his own, and didn't he need it plenty. And indeed, weren't there moments of magic, they were that natural together, echoes of the first and only other time—the dream, the long-ago night after O'Faolain's. To his mind, it recalled that night in many ways, the stray light through the open window a sheen and a shimmer on the soft skin of her, the sounds of Dublin far off in the night, and all the rest of the dream, all the moistness and deepness and softness and warmth.

But this night, he was awakened from the deep sleep afterwards by his shoulder being rudely jostled. "Terrance, are you awake? Are you awake, Terrance?"

He blinked his eyes open, wondering for a moment if he was. "Aye," he said. "Who can sleep at a time like this?"

"She was here," Moira said, "Daisy. In my dream. She came to visit me."

"Aye. She would, now."

"She was a wee girl again, her hair in pigtails, jumping up and down, the eyes of her big as balloons—begging me, 'Mummy, please Mummy, please Mummy!' Just like when she was my wee girl, Terrance—it might have been a memory, not a dream."

"What's she after begging for?"

"When she was little, if I so much as whispered the word 'zoo' she'd start in, 'Can we go, Mummy, please can we go,' just like in the dream, hopping up and down like a terrier."

"A happy time, then, grand. Dreaming of happy times with her."

"Not at all. I'd have to tell her no, we can't go to the zoo, I've no money to go to the fecking zoo, and wouldn't she end up in tears."

"So take her to the fecking zoo in your bloody dream."

"It isn't what she's begging for, Terrance."

"What then?"

"She wants to be remembered. She's begging for a grand marker on her grave. That's what she wants— 'Please Mummy, please, put something to remember me by. Don't forget me, Mummy!' A proper memorial, Terrance. The very least I can do. One that everyone will see, one that says something about her, what she was, *who* she was—maybe with a picture of her on it as well. They have those, you know, I've seen 'em. She must have something grand."

"By God, do it then. Put up a grand oul marker for her."

"You don't think it's bollocks?"

"Not at all, at all. It's a grand idea."

She went up on one elbow. "There's a problem."

"Of course." There was always a problem. He remembered how the state of grace was ended the night after O'Faolain's, shattered so soon after waking.

"I can no more afford a bloody grand headstone now than I could afford the bloody zoo back then."

"Aye." He frowned in the dark and sweated a little.

"She's your daughter, Terrance. You wouldn't—"

"If only. But I find myself a bit embarrassed."

"Of course you do." She sank back. "I'm up to my eyeballs myself. Still paying for her first rehab, never mind the others. Never mind the funeral."

Between them, they hadn't credit enough to buy a packet of crisps. There were the horses, he'd struck it big on a nag more than once, if only he could get a decent inside tip, if only he could get back to his local where tips such as those first saw the light of day, if only he wasn't barred for stretching out his credit beyond redemption. If only. On the pillow, he felt the shaking of her head. She said her boss down at Dunnes had a sympathetic ear—many's the time she troubled him about Daisy—and a good head on his shoulders that might hold a good idea, or maybe, though it was a long-shot, an offer of a loan himself. She was sure he fancied her.

He thought of Mrs. Hannigan. He could try his landlady, he said, who'd indeed sprung for a loan before, albeit a more modest one.

Moira leaned in, a bit of the years showing through now in the nearness. She took his chin, squeezed it by the dimple and wagged it. "I won't ask why your landlady's after lending you money, Terrance. I'm sure it's on account of your spotless credit. What the devil else could it be?"

"Maybe she sees me as the son she never had."

"She never had a son?"

"Seven of 'em, actually, but who's counting?"

He felt more than heard the chuckle of her, her body leaning on him, warm and lovely. They stared at the ghost of a glow across the ceiling from the lamppost down on Russell Street. His head was swimming, the grace slipping away, he was trying to hang on, trying to suss out how to go about approaching Mrs. Hannigan when didn't Moira utter a word, an accursed word, the last word he wanted to hear: *Fergus.*

Fergus had money enough. He was crazy about her, always had been, always would be. Hadn't he offered to help before, with Daisy's rehab most recently, other times in the past as well, when she'd found herself in this precarious pickle or that. Hadn't she always refused. Her independence was too high a cost.

"You'd marry the scut for money?"

She reared up a wee bit. "I'll *have* a memorial for my little girl's grave."

"We can manage. You and me can, together. No Fergus need apply."

Again, she touched his chin, just at the dimple, lightly. "You're a sweet man. You do mean well." With that, she rolled away, taking with her what was left of the grace.

It was the smell of coffee finally rousted him from a tedious imitation of sleep. Down the squeaky staircase, he went into the kitchen where Moira sat, her wee laptop on the table before her, photos spread out all about. Photos of Daisy Bell. Their daughter. Moira gave him a weary smile, nodding toward the coffee on the counter. He found a mug in the third cupboard he tried, as Moira behind him kept clicking away. Filled his cup, stood staring for a moment through the window at the back garden, mostly weeds and rubble under a sullen sky, though a bushy green thing or two of a species unknown to your man sprouted here and there. On the brick wall by the rusty wrought iron table, a fat orange tomcat dozed.

He went and stood behind her, looked over her shoulder at the gravestone on the screen. A girl's name across the top in large, flowing script, delicate, curling flowers etched in opposite corners, a verse and a remembrance—*Always in our hearts where you'll live forever*—and a portrait of a pretty girl engraved into the black granite.

He put his hand on the curve at Moira's neck and shoulder. She glanced over her shoulder, though not quite far enough to find him.

"This one," she said.

As soon as he said, "How much?" he regretted it.

He felt, more than heard, the sigh. "€7,000, give or take."

A tap at the front door. She cocked her head like a spaniel, shoved her chair back, bang against his knees, hurried off down the hall. The rattle of the door, voices, Moira's and a man's. Lafferty staring at the tombstone.

She came back into the kitchen, the man in tow. "Terrance," she said. "I don't believe you ever met Fergus."

Not what Lafferty expected, even though Moira'd mentioned he'd changed. He was entirely unformidable in a sweater-vest and limp-collared shirt, every thinning hair neatly laid across his scalp. The last time Lafferty'd seen him, he was pumped as a football, a wild man wielding a barstool over his head with one hand as though it were a baton.

"Not officially," said Lafferty, offering a smile, sticking out a hand. Fergus made no effort to reach out a hand of his own, nor any to smile. Said Lafferty, "As I recall, Fergus here's the fella who tried to bludgeon me to death one night."

"Aye," said Fergus. "And Moira tells me you're Daisy's father, her very own father who left her to die in a puddle of puke."

Moira said, "I just knew you two would hit it off."

Mrs. Hannigan was in high spirits. One of her tenants had just died. Fair play, thought Lafferty, the cause of her high spirits notwithstanding, for now mightn't she be in a more generous mood. He intended to pop the question about a loan this morning after paying his rent.

The deceased tenant was Mrs. Sievers, a lady a bit older than Mrs. Hannigan, a lady whose two-fisted wielding of her twin canes had cleared many a passageway before her, gangway, denting many an innocent shin. Mrs. Hannigan patted the gaudy gold necklace on her bosom, a smile on her painted oul lips, a twinkle in her rheumy eye. She took it off, held it up. "Isn't it lovely? I admired it on the oul floozie for ages."

He recognized the thing, a gold chain with chunky links, clusters of what appeared to be pearls sprayed out at the bottom. Like clusters of daisies. Daisy's. He'd seen it often about Mrs. Sievers' wrinkled oul neck. "And she left it to you, did she? A generous soul."

"Generous? That one? Don't make me laugh. She'd squeeze a penny till it squealed, that one would." She patted his knee, shifted her weight on the edge of the bed, drawing squawks of protest. "She was in arrears, Mr. Lafferty. You know how that is. Let's just say her account is now fully settled." She winked, one scallywag to another.

"It must be worth something, yeah?"

A prideful smile on the painted oul face, a scoff. "You have to ask?"

He waited till after, when his own rent was paid, when the oul wan was flush and mellow, her accounts settled up, and she was entirely satisfied. He broached it then, his need of a loan.

To his mind, the need now was more urgent than ever, not only to memorialize the daughter he never knew, not only to keep her mother near—now the dream had happened twice, two states of grace—but also to keep this gouger Fergus at bay.

He wondered if he might trouble Mrs. Hannigan for another wee loan (he would negotiate the meaning of "wee" as they went along). She lent him a sympathetic ear. He embellished the story only modestly, as modest embellishment was all that was needed. He told her about finding the long-lost daughter he never knew, how there was no mistaking the immediate chemistry, and that just as he was getting to know her, just as he'd been reunited with her mother and the three of them planning a future, together again, as a family, his little girl took a tragic overdose, tragic and fatal. Oh, to be sure, her drug problem had been known for some time, she'd been in rehab, they were reaching out for help yet again when the tragedy struck. They were devasted. And, to make matters worse, weren't they strapped as well for the cost of the burial, for the cost of a decent stone to remember her by, one to do justice to her life and memory. Her mother was as out at the elbows as himself, temporary to be sure, but until they could manage to get their heads above water, was there any possibility Mrs. Hannigan might float them a wee bit of a loan for the headstone, only for a short period of time, only until they regained a smattering of solvency?

"Not on your nelly," said Mrs. Hannigan.

He found himself later that morning on his own squawky bed in his own dusty room, deep in the throes of self-pity. Wondering what Moira was doing now. And with whom?

It was not his custom to look in the mirror, but the dingy wee glass above his dresser was unavoidable, and what was there was not the clean, clear-eyed, fresh face, the handsome dimple, and charmingly unruly hair of yore.

Instead, he saw eyes the color of an old walrus tusk, a sad dimple in a shabby, unshaven face, hair lifeless and wilted and going to gray. He saw the failure Moira must see. The has-been that never was. He saw the same loser his daughter had seen in her only earthly glimpse of her da.

It was not his custom to reflect on his life, on his fifty-five years spent mostly looking for love, seldom for meaning beyond the meaning of love, and consider it an ill-spent waste. Nor was it his custom to dwell on his erstwhile wife, Peggy—who, if she'd had her way, would have convinced him long ago of the truth of what he saw in the mirror on this morning—nor on his own son, Harry, his and Peggy's son, fourteen years of age by now if memory served him right, and not a word from him the last ten of them. Peggy'd made certain of that.

A son, a daughter, and he'd yet to be a father.

He heard the front door clatter and looked down to see Mrs. Hannigan walking away downstreet toward the shops. It was not his custom to wallow in self-pity. It was his custom to do what had to be done.

Thus, he found himself later that afternoon beneath the three golden balls of Brereton's Pawn Shop on Capel Street, a gaudy gold necklace heavy in his pocket.

Your man never considered himself a thief, never before, nor even as he was jimmying the lock to Mrs. Hannigan's room. First off, he doubted Mrs. Sievers had actually been in arrears—the old lady was always prompt and fastidious and, by all appearances, well provided for. Second, he figured he'd been overpaying his own rent for some time now and was due a bit of a refund. If there was anything left over after the cost of the headstone, then he would certainly do the right thing. As to what the right thing might be, he'd negotiate that after the worth and costs were known.

No worries, as it turned out. The broker, a narrow-shouldered, balding chap in his green visor, puffy sleeves and tight waistcoat, told him the necklace was worthless. At a glance. Didn't design to examine the thing under his hand lens. What it was was gold-toned zinc, faux pearls made of glass. He'd not give him five quid for it.

The broker shoved the worthless piece back at him, and there it sat, untouched, like something shat by a Kerry bull.

Lafferty tapped the top of the glass case in a fret.

Back to the bloody drawing board. He took the thing and dropped it into his pocket. There was still time enough to spirit it back to Mrs. Hannigan's vanity.

On his way to the door though, didn't something catch his eye.

In a well-secured case under lock and key, a display of fine jewelry, rings, bracelets, earrings, necklaces—and brooches. None in the shape of a turtle, but there were some with likenesses to Daisy's, the colors of the stones, the set of them, the style maybe, something, likenesses he didn't know enough to put a finger to. He called the man over and inquired. The broker didn't bother fetching the key along, not for the likes of Lafferty. Yes, he said, fine jewelry from the first half of the last century, didn't your man have superior taste, pieces by outfits Lafferty'd never heard of, such as Cartier, Tiffany, Bertoia, and the like. The broker could show him some costume jewelry up in the front of the store—in fact, was he aware that most of the costume jewelry was inspired by designs such as these in the high-priced case? Your man was not. He thanked him kindly.

Hurried up to Moira's place on Russell. Moira was still gone. Now though, he didn't fret where. Or why. Or with whom. Your man was on a mission. It took him no time at all to locate Daisy's brooch among her things in a box—three boxes held all her things—that had been stashed under the bed in the back room, buried in shadows and dust. He took it over to the window, to the light. Examined the thing close. On the back, on the turtle's tummy, he could make out a name: *Van Cleef & Arpels*. The broker hadn't mentioned that name in particular so far as he could recall, but didn't it look impressive. Didn't it sound impressive.

Half an hour later, back at Brereton's, he showed it to the broker.

The broker took up his hand lens.

And wasn't the broker impressed.

The day turned warmer, the blanket of clouds overhead a delightful linen white instead of your normal scowling gray. Making his way back up to Russell Street, Lafferty couldn't wait to see the look on the gob of Moira when he told her the fella at Brereton's had offered him €10,000 on the spot. He'd demurred, Daisy's turtle still tucked away in his pocket. Who was to say the price mightn't be better at another shop where the broker wasn't so snooty? As well, it wasn't his to sell. There was that—your man was not a thief. He couldn't help but wonder though, how the grand oul difference between the cost of the gravestone and the worth of the turtle—€10,000 minus €7,000 or so—might be put toward the forgetting of Fergus.

He expected she'd still be gone. He intended a grand reveal. In the parlor, the smell of cat piss was more piquant than usual, so he decided to move the surprise party to the wee garden in back. He'd borrowed a ten euro note from Mrs. Hannigan's dresser drawer, enough for a bottle of cheap champagne and a large bag of the bacon-flavored crisps. Moira's favorite. He'd only just set about searching her cupboards for fancy glasses when a titter caught his ear. Looking out through the window, he saw them there in the garden, Moira and Fergus, laughing over fancy glasses, a bottle of expensive champagne on ice, and what looked to be posh hors d'oeuvres. On the wall the fat orange tomcat gazed down on them with naked disdain.

Moira looked up at the shadow in the window. "Terrance? Is it yourself?"

"Aye. In the flesh. So to speak."

"Come out," she called. "Come join us."

He went as far as the doorway. "What's the occasion?"

"Fergus is buying the gravestone!" Moira was tipsy. Fergus as well, beaming like the lighthouse at Howth. "Daisy will have her grand oul marker!"

It was not your man's custom to dwell on what-might-have-beens. Nevertheless, same as any mortal, he was not always able to keep the regrets at bay. Sometimes they came skulking in, often in disguise, rats burrowing in through the stoutest of cellar walls. He dreamed that night that he and Daisy were on a grassy pitch under a sky too blue to be true, a flock of lovely white clouds, and they were having a catch, tossing about a scuffed old ball, laughing and chasing, having a grand oul time. In the dream, she was spry and alive, happy, and a feeling of great relief swelled up inside him, realizing she was not really dead. Then came the waking.

He went to McGill's, the funeral parlor, to pay his own private respects, to grieve in his own private way, having decided to forego the wake at Moira's. He had a word with McGill, the undertaker, who'd done his best with Daisy. He kindly stepped aside to let Lafferty spend some moments alone with his daughter. He'd done the best he could, but Lafferty couldn't help but sadly compare the happy young face of the girl in his dream with the painted, plastic version on the coffin pillow.

He thanked McGill, a stout and solemn little man, had a final word with him, a final request, then took his leave.

Just down the street was The Rose, a pub that looked neither too shabby nor too posh. He had his regrets to keep at bay. He had his grief to navigate. When first he stepped inside from the gray and the gloom, he looked about the room for any possibility of comfort. And didn't he spot it there straightaway, a girl all alone at the bar.

Most of the people who were at Moira's before came back again for the wake, them and a few others besides. Daisy was laid out in the parlor, across the room from the piano, where fresh candles burned. McGill stood by the head of the coffin. His job was to be steadfast. To not leave the girl alone till he took her away to put her into the ground.

Precious few were the remembrances, not a lively wake at all, the life remembered being too tragic and short, too ill-spent.

What murmur there was from the mourners came to a hush when Moira stepped up for a moment with her daughter. She bowed her head. Fergus stood just off to the side, an expression on his face both grim and glad, full of grief for the loss of the girl, full of delight for the loss of Lafferty. Moira, staring down, frowned and blinked.

She said to McGill, "Where was that? That ugly turtle yoke?"

"Her father, ma'am," said McGill. "A Mr. Lafferty, I believe? The gentleman with the jersey worn through at the elbows? He's after telling me the young lady loved the worthless oul bauble and would very much want to be buried with it."

Moira turned, laying her hand on Fergus's arm, a warm flush overcoming her cheeks. "Isn't that just like him?" she said. "So sweet. Such a sweet man."

"Lafferty?" said Fergus.

Acknowledgments

Gratefully acknowledged are the following publications in which these stories first appeared:

"Stayin' Alive," *KAIROS Literary Magazine*

"The Ring of Kerry," *New England Review*; reprinted in *The Best American Mystery Stories 2013*

"Cannibals in Canoes," *The Antioch Review*

"The Purloined Pigs," *Ellery Queen Mystery Magazine*

"The Three-Sided Penny," *The Missouri Review*

"A Penny Saved," *The Saturday Evening Post*

"Lafferty's Ghost," *Fiction*; reprinted in *The Best American Mystery Stories 2016*; performed live on stage by *Stories on Stage*, September 2021

"A Very Good Cure," *Sewanee Review*

"Over the Garden Wall," *Potomac Review*

"Savage December," *The Missouri Review*

Thank you to Cornerstone Press, particularly publisher and director Dr. Ross Tangedal, senior managing editor Karlie Harpold, cover designer Abby Paulsen, and assistant editor Jazmyne Johnson, for their work on bringing this book together.

DENNIS MCFADDEN was the celebrated author of the story collections *Hart's Grove* (2010) and *Jimtown Road* (2016) and the novel *Old Grimes Is Dead* (2022). Over 100 of his stories appeared in publications such as *The Missouri Review, New England Review, Ellery Queen Mystery Magazine, Alfred Hitchcock Mystery Magazine, Coolest American Stories 2024*, and *The Best American Mystery Stories*. He passed away in August 2025.

www.ingramcontent.com/pod-product-compliance
Lightning Source LLC
LaVergne TN
LVHW041804060526
838201LV00046B/1127